THE WOMAN

Richard's laughter ended abruptly, leaving a strained emptiness that sent a shiver down Jill's spine.

"Is something the matter?" she asked.

Richard didn't answer. He had paused stock still on the pavement, three paces behind where Jill stood, a look of curiosity on her face.

Everything in Richard's field of vision fell away except the sombre lines of the hearse-like limousine. His eyes focused on the automobile's side-view mirror which reflected a chrome framed cameo of terrifying loveliness.

The Woman had made her lips blood red just for him.

Her eyes seemed to drill directly into Richard's soul, laying bare his most primitive emotions. She licked her lips, running her tongue suggestively along their delicate outline, intimating a promise of savage passion that Richard had only allowed himself to dream about in his most private moments.

As he stood there like a sleepwalker, Richard sensed the extraordinary power that The Woman was exerting.

"Richard, is something wrong?"

Jill's voice seemed to come from a vacuum traveling down an endless corridor of deadening silence.

Richard continued to stare at The Woman. She smiled and nodded a wordless agreement. Richard trembled with desire . . .

Ed Kelleher and Harriette Vidal

And the Word was made flesh and dwelt amongst us.

—John 1:14

LEISURE BOOKS NEW YORK CITY

To Diana—for telling.

A LEISURE BOOK

Published by

Dorchester Publishing Co., Inc.
6 East 39th Street
New York, New York 10016

Printed in the United States of America

PROLOGUE

Bad Hoffberg, Germany, 1820

THE RHINE was always present. Rushing mightily past the tiny village, it provided a constant surge of sound that enlivened the otherwise tranquil surroundings. To the sturdy wine-making inhabitants, the sound of the river was a friendly hum that had long since entered their consciousness.

Dusk gave the village a dreamlike charm. Long shadows reached across the vineyard slopes as if Nature herself were laying a comforting hand on the sleepy hamlet.

As church bells finished ringing out the evening prayer, the townspeople, weary from a day's work, made their way slowly down the hillside to the village square.

A scream silenced the river and cut through the twilight air.

Blond and smiling, Franz, the innkeeper's oldest son, swung the axe with all the force of his young, muscular frame. The old woman's head, cleanly severed from her torso, thumped to the ground and rolled its bloody way across the square's cobblestones, its mouth still open in frozen fear.

Villagers ran for cover as Franz waved the axe high above his head. Crippled and confused, nine year old Werner was incapable of reaching his mother's outstretched arms. Franz buried the axe deep between the boy's shoulder blades.

The mother stood transfixed in horror, as she watched the last spasms of her son's mutilated body. Reason told her to run but her dying child's agony left her paralyzed. She was an easy victim as Franz, spittle running from his mouth, hacked at her repeatedly. Blood gushed out of her body, bathing the crazed Franz who began to dance merrily.

Inside the small crowded room, the screams from the square were barely audible. The worshippers' chants, coupled with their sensual moans, formed an undercurrent of sound that was all pervasive.

"*Ave, Mater! Hosanna in excelsis! Ave, Mater!*"

At the center of the room stood The Woman.

The rays of the setting sun highlighted her olive-skinned beauty and danced in her shimmering raven hair. Attired like the others in a long black robe, she remained apart, an ethereal presence demanding adulation.

"Ave Mater."

Suddenly helping hands were propelling her upward to an altar-like structure, from which she could survey the writhing forms of her subjects. Her robe slipped from her shoulders as eager hands reached up to fondle her naked, voluptuous body.

"Hosanna in excelsis!"

The room began to pulsate. Joyfully, The Woman threw her head back, opening herself to her legion of lovers. Her cries of pleasure heightened their mounting passion. Her admirers, men and women alike, engulfed her, forming a throbbing blanket of human flesh.

The door opened quietly.

Six men in the doorway took in the erotic tableau. With expressions of disgust, they crouched at the entrance. Pulling their black robes tighter, they watched as The Woman neared the peak of sexual excitement.

Their elder, gray haired and imposing, rose to his feet. He signalled the others to follow. It was the moment they had waited for.

The Woman never saw them approach. Buried under a swarm of lovers, she never heard the cries of pleasure turn to shouts of warning.

The elder rushed forward as his colleagues cleared a path, hurling bodies left and right.

Reaching the altar, the five men wrenched The Woman's lovers from her, leaving her vulnerable. The elder stepped forward as The Woman moaned in orgasm.

From his robe, the leader removed a metal instrument, more than a foot in length, tapered to a razor precision—a sharpened crucifix.

Grasping it firmly, he took aim and plunged it deep into her chest, piercing her heart.

The Woman let out an unearthly shriek. A hush fell over the room.

The Woman's eyes snapped open as she glared at her assassin. The elder motioned to his companions. The six men fell to their knees. The Lord's Prayer filled the room:

"Pater noster, qui est in coelis . . ."

Sprawled on the altar, blood running from her breast, The Woman cried out for help.

"Oh, Lucifer . . ."

She gasped for breath. Then, heaving a tormented sigh, she was still.

The six men, alone now in the room, stared down at her lifeless form. The leader made the sign of the cross and spoke in a whisper.

"Amen."

New Orleans, The Present

Monday morning was always hectic for Roger Stern. Two days worth of mail had to be attended to before the 10 a.m. executive staff meeting. When the meeting broke—usually about 11:30—there was barely an hour to handle all the overseas phone calls. And then it was time for lunch with Amalgamated Steel, the firm's oldest and most demanding client.

This Monday morning was no exception. Roger finished the mail with only minutes to spare before the meeting. His report to the board was crisp and concise as usual, displaying the ability and talent that had moved him up the corporate ladder so quickly, making him at thirty-four the youngest vice president in the company's long and venerable history.

The meeting ended on time and Roger breezed through the trans-Atlantic calls. Lunch was filled with Amalgamated Steel's litany of complaints, but Roger handled things with his customary charm and evasiveness.

Now it was 2:15. Roger handed his American Express card to the waitress and breathed a sigh of relief as Amalgamated Steel shook hands and hurried out the door to Bourbon Street. Roger walked to the hatcheck counter. The red-haired attendant smiled at him as he handed her the numbered ticket.

"The tan Burberry, right?"

"Yes," replied Roger. "And there was a package."

The hatcheck woman helped Roger into his coat and turned to retrieve his parcel from an overhead shelf. She handed it to him.

"What have you got in here, lead?"

Roger smiled playfully. "How did you know?"

Outside, on the street, the sun was blinding. Roger loosened his tie and felt the first beads of perspiration break out on his forehead. His stomach began to tighten. His pulse quickened.

The sidewalk was crowded. Roger felt himself being swept along by a tide of strangers. His eyes clouded over. He gripped the package underneath his arm.

Almost before he knew it, he was at the entrance of his building. He stared at the revolving door. Perspiration flowed freely down his face.

The elevator was packed and silent. Roger stood in a corner. His knuckles whitened as he grasped the handrail. The floor numbers flashed overhead as the car rose swiftly. Roger gulped for air. He glanced around nervously, but no one seemed aware of his condition.

At the 20th floor, Roger moved woodenly toward the door. Glazed and fevered, he stepped trance-like from the car. The doors closed behind him.

Roger's head began to pound as he made his way toward the pretty blonde at the reception desk.

"Did you have a nice lunch, Mr. Stern?" The girl offered Roger a pink message slip. "Your wife called. She's at the beauty parlor."

Her words reverberated in his head. He stared blankly at the message slip, took it from her hand, crumpled it and tossed it casually to the floor. He continued on, into the office.

The secretarial pool hummed with the sound of six electric typewriters. From a raised platform, the supervisor, a matronly woman of about 50, kept a fixed watch on her charges, making certain that the girls maintained a steady pace. Keys clicked and margin bells rang as Roger began unwrapping his parcel.

Two of the secretaries looked up and smiled a greeting at him as they continued typing. A third girl's smile turned to a look of slack-jawed horror as Roger discarded the wrapping paper, revealing a .357 Magnum revolver.

The first shot exploded, splattering the girl's head across the room. The other women turned startled toward the source of the noise. An eerie silence set in as the women struggled with the reality of what was happening. Roger squeezed off the second round.

The supervisor's body, blown clear off the platform, danced madly in death throes, before collapsing in a corner like a broken puppet.

A girl in the front row let out a terror-stricken scream. She sank to her knees and whimpered.

"Oh, God, I don't want to die, please don't, oh, please don't . . ."

Roger smiled tenderly as he aimed the gun at her face.

"Oh, God, no, please don't shoot . . ."

He pulled the trigger. The girl's face shattered into a thousand pieces.

Bits of flesh and bone clung to the desks, the walls, the typewriters and the neatly stacked white pages. The four remaining women dove for cover. One of them, a slender brunette, was almost to the door when Roger got her in his gunsight. He fired, driving her lifeless form halfway to the elevators.

Roger calmly surveyed his handiwork. Three girls cowered under their desks as he walked mechanically toward the floor to ceiling window. His fifth and last shot demolished the glass.

Standing in the open frame, he watched the shards of glass fall downward to the street. He took a deep breath, then threw back his head, letting out a blood-curdling whoop.

A wry smile on his face, he stepped through the opening and began his descent.

It was nearly 3:30 when The Woman's taxi arrived at New Orleans Airport. Flawlessly beautiful, even in the bright sunlight, she strode calmly toward the building. Once inside, she proceeded to the departure lounge, where several dozen passengers were already lined up. The public address system rang out.

"Flight 81 for New York City, now boarding."

A look of triumph on her face, The Woman walked through the gate, onto the aircraft.

Part I

THE WOMAN

CHAPTER ONE

The Evil was old. Of that there could never be a doubt. For all its wisdom, The Evil couldn't place just when it found itself free to roam. It knew it would gain strength because that was the Way it was ordained.

"Hurry up, Annie, it's after seven."

Richard Bloch stood outside the bathroom door, sipping a Scotch and water.

Annie Mulligan's reply was muffled. "I'll be ready in a minute, honey."

Richard walked over to the bedroom mirror. Admiring the lines of his neatly-tailored three piece suit, he ran a comb through his collar-length sandy colored hair. With his trim, muscular build and ruggedly handsome features, he exuded a healthy self-confidence, as he adjusted his tie for the tenth time.

It wasn't like Annie to be late. Even as he waited, Richard knew that they would arrive at the theatre seconds before curtain. Two years of living with Annie had given him an appreciation for her fine sense of timing.

The bathroom door opened and Annie bounced into the room. Her wheat-colored hair, still a little damp from the shower, framed her heart-shaped face. Her Victorian white silk blouse, a legacy of her grandmother's, was nicely complemented by her floor-length black velvet skirt.

Richard kissed her lovingly on the cheek. "You look like an antique Valentine card."

Annie beamed. "Your tie's crooked."

She reached up to straighten his navy blue tie, running her fingers along the silk fabric.

"Nice. I haven't seen this before. It is new?"

Richard grinned. "Of course. This is a special occasion."

Annie turned off the light and led him toward the front door. "Got the tickets?"

"Sure," he replied.

This was a special night, Richard thought to himself, on their way down in the elevator. How often does a guy's sister open in an off-Broadway show? Leslie had worked hard for her big break and might be just hours away from theatrical stardom.

Richard and Annie made a handsome couple as they emerged from their apartment building. Stone gargoyles peered down at them from the cornices of the fifteen story pre-war structure as they walked toward Riverside Drive.

Richard had waited patiently for over a year before a vacancy had come up, enabling him to move into the building, considered one of the better addresses on the Upper West Side for those in the 25-40 age bracket. Though his modest teacher's salary hardly put him on a par with the young executives who comprised the majority of tenants, he'd been just able to manage. When Annie had moved in with him, her salary gave them a financial leeway that bordered on luxury.

Annie was radiant as they strolled along the Drive. She stole a glance at Richard's finely chiseled profile, silhouetted against an early evening sky. Even after two years, she still felt a warm glow in his presence.

"I'll bet Leslie's biting her nails," said Richard as they neared the garage.

Annie laughed. "What about that Bloch self-assurance? I thought your family was famous for it."

"We are, with two exceptions. In front of a first night audience and before a herd of charging buffalo."

Richard guided Annie up the ramp to the parking level of the garage. Outside a light rain had begun to fall.

"Ten minutes, Miss Bloch."

Leslie looked up from her make-up mirror and turned to the stage manager, who stood in the doorway of her dressing room.

"Thanks, Al. That should give me enough time to faint."

Leslie's stomach turned over. Silently she congratulated herself for having ordered a light salad at lunchtime instead of the lasagna dish she had really wanted.

She finished applying her freckles and stood up. She reached for the blue-checked gingham dress and slipped it carefully over her head so as not to dislodge the blonde, pigtailed wig. Nerves gave way to giggles as she admired her farm girl image in the full-length mirror.

Five years ago, fresh from a New England junior college and enrolled in her first term at a Manhattan acting school, Leslie had envisioned her legitimate starring role debut in terms of a revolutionary Medea or a breakthrough Desdemona. Certainly a far cry from a homespun farm girl in "Straw Hat," a new farce by a totally unknown writer.

The exaggerated freckles and rosy, clownlike cheek makeup could not conceal the angular beauty of her face which, coupled with her slender five foot nine figure, had gotten her the best male roles in the all-girls boarding school she had attended. Now as she stood on the threshold of New York success, all of that seemed far behind her.

"I declare! You look cuter than a newborn hog in a mudhole," said Jill Martin, as she came into the dressing room.

Costumed identically, she struck a pose, hands on hips. With a short, compact figure, Jill appeared a diminutive though better proportioned version of Leslie.

"Look who's talking, Jill. You remind me of a reject from 'Hee-Haw.' "

Jill inspected herself in the mirror. "I'm so

nervous I've been to the bathroom eight times."

Leslie punched her playfully on the arm. "I know. That was me pounding on the door."

"I took a look outside, Leslie. It's a full house."

Leslie nodded. "I was afraid of that."

Jill examined a telegram that was pasted to Leslie's mirror. She read it aloud.

" 'Dear Leslie, I know you'll be wonderful tonight. This is the beginning of all your dreams come true. I love you, Richard.' "

Leslie smiled. "How do you like that soppy brother of mine?"

"I don't know," replied Jill. "The wire he sent me just said 'Break a leg, Kiddo.' "

Sitting in a third row aisle seat, Richard laughed, recrossed his legs and leaned over to Annie.

"It's clever," he whispered. "Little Sister just might have hit the big time."

Annie squeezed his hand. The audience laughter built to a crescendo and there were outbursts of applause.

On stage, the last minutes of "Straw Hat" were being enacted. In the setting of a barn, the five performers were approaching the play's final confrontation.

Burt Shulman, a fortyish character actor portraying a traveling salesman, rolled in a haystack with Jill who resembled the archetype farmer's daughter. Leslie stood beside two actors who were dressed in straw hats and overalls and who pointed shotguns at the frolicking couple. Burt and Jill looked up startled. One of the farmers stepped forward.

"Looking for needles?" he asked.

Jill jumped to her feet and ran over to the older farmer. "Daddy, it's not what you think."

As the audience laughed, Burt scrambled out of the haystack. He reached for a nearby pitchfork and took up a stance of self-defense.

"I was just trying to sell her some liniment," he explained.

Leslie folded her arms and glared at him knowingly. "Looks to me like you were giving her a free rubdown."

The farmer's tone was conciliatory as he nudged Burt in the chest with the shotgun. "Son, put down that pitchfork. We got us a wedding to discuss."

Burt inched toward the stage right exit. "I can't marry your daughter. I'm already married to her." He pointed to Leslie.

"Don't remind me," snapped Leslie. The audience roared.

Surprised, Jill glanced at Leslie. "You're married to her? You never told me that! Give me that shotgun, daddy, I'm gonna handle this myself."

Burt dropped the pitchfork. "Oh, oh, this is where I came in."

He made a frantic dash for the exit as the others followed in pursuit. The curtain came down. There was a wave of audience applause.

Richard and Annie rose to their feet.

"Oh, Richard," exclaimed Annie. "They did it! They really did it."

The curtain rose and the five actors stood hand in hand for their bows. The theatre resounded with cheers as the audience afforded them a standing ovation. A stagehand appeared from the wings and presented Leslie and Jill with bouquets of flowers.

Minutes later, the atmosphere backstage was high-spirited. Cast and crew joined in an excited babble of relief and congratulations.

Jill and Leslie hugged each other happily. "I think we got us a hit," cried Leslie, straining to be heard above the clamor.

"What am I gonna do?" laughed Jill, "I've never been in a hit before!"

A bottle of champagne began making the rounds. Leslie took a healthy swig and handed the bottle to Jill.

"Must be a hit," said Leslie. "It's imported."

Jill took a sip and nearly gagged as she was enveloped in an ardent bearhug. She turned in annoyance to face a leering Burt Shulman. Jill disengaged herself from his grip and pushed him away.

"Listen, lover boy, watch those hands."

Burt feigned a look of innocence. "I was just giving you a good luck hug."

Jill's tone was sharp. "I'm talking about that haystack scene. You know what I mean? Don't squeeze the merchandise."

Leslie took another gulp of champagne and giggled.

"I can't help it if I'm a method actor," protested Burt.

"Yeah, the grope method," muttered Jill.

Leslie laughed, then looked up to see Richard and Annie approaching. Burt wandered away.

As Richard embraced his sister, the years seemed to fall away and they were children again, sharing a secret excitement, tucked away in a special hiding place, in a treehouse in Southern Vermont.

He held her lovingly at arm's length. "Hey, I think your freckles are running."

Leslie grinned through tears. "It's called crying, Richard."

Richard kissed her on the forehead. "You were just sensational. It's going to run forever."

A spray of champagne doused them as a cork flew across the stage. Annie clasped Leslie's hands.

"You were just wonderful."

Jill put her arms around Richard and Annie and waved the champagne bottle.

"Ah," she said, "the sweet smell of success. The last four shows I did were posting a closing notice right about now."

"Well," said Annie, "there's no danger of that."

"Let's not be too hasty," said Leslie. "The reviews are yet to come."

Jill gave Leslie a conspiratorial wink. "The critics are gonna love us. I feel like our luck is changing."

* * *

It was raining heavily by the time they reached Sylvester's, the family-run restaurant that had been a second home to the "Straw Hat" company during weeks of rehearsal. Cheerful and noisy, dominated by a lengthy oak bar, Sylvester's had played host to more than a few theatre parties since its speakeasy days back in the Thirties.

Sal, the maitre d', had set aside several tables for the Straw Hatters, and the party was well underway as Leslie and her entourage checked their rain-drenched hats and coats. At the rear of the room was the cast table and Richard guided them toward it, as well-wishers pressed up against Jill and Leslie, offering congratulations. There was a spontaneous round of applause.

Jill and Leslie surveyed the room. There arrayed before them were men and women, many of whom had been strangers only weeks before, but who now formed a close-knit working unit. Rehearsal incidents, harsh exchanges, even a few shouting matches were forgotten now. The two actresses felt touched by the moment. It had all been worth it.

The television reviews were unanimous. Broadcast to the attentive throng via the tuned up TV set over the bar, they reflected the critics' enthusiasm for "Straw Hat." Channel 2 hailed the play as a "delightful spoof." Channel 4 praised Leslie's "marvelously subtle abandonment." And it remained for Channel 7 to sum it up, as the "Straw Hat" company sat in anxious silence, hanging on every word.

The critic's voice rang out across the room. "Leslie Bloch and Jill Martin are pure magic as a couple of farmer's daughters any traveling salesman would be pleased to climb into a joke with . . ."

Several of the cast members groaned. Leslie caught Jill's eye and laughed.

"Take it from the horse's mouth," the critic continued. 'Straw Hat' is a terrific new comedy that deserves to run until the cows come home."

Sylvester's resounded with cries of "Yeah! Alright!" Sal, the maitre d', approached the cast table, wheeling a cart containing a chilled magnum of champagne.

"Compliments of the house," he said as he expertly uncorked the bottle.

Glancing at the champagne label, Jill did a mock double take. "Isn't this great? When we had the cast party for my last show, they served red wine, vintage Wednesday."

Sal poured a round for the table and raised his glass in a toast. "Here's to a great bunch of kids. I hope the show runs a couple of years, 'cause, frankly, I need the business."

Richard touched glasses with Leslie. "I'm proud of you," he said softly.

"That means a lot to me, Richard. Thank you."

Leslie felt a hand on her shoulder. She turned to see Hal Weile, the playwright, a small trim man of about forty, neatly turned out in a dark tweed suit.

Hal's expression was deadpan. "Do those reviews mean I can quit my day job?"

Leslie laughed. "On the royalties from this, are you kidding? I would have quit at intermission."

Jill looked at Hal earnestly. "Hal, if you're writing a new play, I would like a larger part. In fact, how about a one woman show?"

"You got it," said Hal, sipping his martini.

Jill scrutinized his drink. "That looks pretty deadly, Hal. How many of those have you had?"

"Believe it or not, it's my first. Burt Shulman's already on his fifth."

He pointed toward the bar area, just as a crash was heard. An elderly customer glowered at Burt, who stood helplessly over the jagged remains of what had just been her highball glass. From the stage crew table came a derisive cheer.

"That's three glasses, Burt," shouted the stage electrician.

"Wanna go for four?" called out the light man.

"How did that happen?" asked Burt, slurring his words. "I wasn't anywhere near it." He stared stupidly at the broken glass.

Leslie frowned. "Hal, maybe you should do something."

Hal nodded. "I'll ask the bartender to start watering his drinks." He drifted away from the table but was soon surrounded by a crowd of new arrivals, shaking his hand excitedly.

Richard dipped a piece of shrimp into some tartar sauce. He leaned over to Leslie. "Are we still on for Monday?"

"Absolutely. I'm looking forward to it."

"The kids are going to be excited. Especially after those reviews."

Jill teasingly speared the shrimp from Richard's fork. "What's happening Monday?"

"Richard's directing 'Romeo And Juliet' with his students," Leslie replied. "And he's asked me to sit in on a rehearsal."

"Oh, that's really nice," said Jill. She took a bite of shrimp.

"You're invited too," said Richard. "Want to come along?"

Jill paused for a moment, then wrinkled up her nose. "Can't. I got classes. But I'll take a raincheck."

"Great," said Leslie. "Between the three of us, we can probably rewrite Shakespeare."

Richard poked her on the arm. "*Among* the three of us," he corrected.

"Be quiet, smartass, eat your shrimp," said Leslie, kicking him good-naturedly in the leg.

Annie smiled and toyed with her champagne glass. She didn't feel entirely comfortable. As she admired Richard's easy-going manner and his talent for mingling with cast and crew alike, she wondered what the others must think of her. A trifle shy in these surroundings, she'd barely said a word all night.

Annie drained her glass and poured herself a

refill. Across the room, she could see Burt Shulman beginning to stagger in their direction. She took another sip and felt a little lightheaded. When she spoke, the words came out as if by their own power.

"Don't look now, but methinks the shitfaced leading man is headed our way."

All eyes turned toward Annie, then followed her gaze as Burt came lurching over to the table, narrowly avoiding a collision with a head waiter carrying a tray of glasses. Burt wrapped his arms around Leslie and Jill.

"Okay, which one of you broads is gonna jump into a joke with me?"

Jill looked at him sharply and squirmed out of his embrace. "Burt, you already *are* a joke."

Leslie turned up her nose in an expression of distaste. "You smell like an explosion at the Smirnoff's plant."

Sliding down to table level, Burt found himself face to face with a bemused Annie. "Who's this marvelous creature?" he asked, his necktie brushing across her salad.

Jill grabbed him by the shoulders and pulled him away. "A woman who's fortunate enough *not* to have to work with you."

"She's cute anyway," slobbered Burt, "but she don't have tits like you, Jill."

Richard started to his feet. "I think that's enough."

Burt reached out clumsily for Jill's breasts but she neatly avoided his grasp.

"It's you that I'm nuts about, Jill," he said, stumbling against her shoulder.

"You're nuts, period."

Jill shoved him away roughly. Tripping over his own feet, Burt fell heavily to the floor. He lay there for a moment, dazed and uncomprehending.

There was an outburst of laughter, followed by amiable applause. Striking the pose of a boxing referee, Hal lifted Jill's arm triumphantly into the air.

"The winner and still champion . . ."

Jill grinned and took an elaborate bow. On the floor, Burt stirred. He struggled to bring his eyes into focus. Hal and two of the stagehands helped him to his feet.

"Come on, Burt," said Hal, "you've had enough. We'll get you some coffee."

As he was being led away, Burt glared accusingly at Jill. An unspoken threat hung in the air.

The rain had not let up. By midnight, the party was beginning to show signs of waning. Richard stood underneath the awning of Sylvester's watching the torrential downpour sweep across the avenue. Behind him in the vestibule of the restaurant, Annie, Leslie and Jill were waiting. Richard had volunteered to get the car, which was parked in a garage five blocks away. Now, realizing how drenched he was going to be, he wished he hadn't.

Richard pulled up his coat collar and thrust his hands into his pockets. Taking a deep breath, he went to meet the rain head on. He walked quickly along the deserted street as the wind blew sheets of water in his path. Umbrellas were useless in a storm like this, as was evident by the remains of several, which lay discarded on the sidewalk, like battered metal skeletons.

Even as he hurried along, Richard glanced about, taking in the storefronts, the deserted street and the light from the tower of the Empire State Building, just visible through the blanket of mist. Though he had lived in New York for ten of his thirty-two years, there were moments when he felt like a tourist seeing it for the first time. For a small town boy from Vermont, the city was a never-ending source of secrets and surprises.

Richard relished his time spent with Annie but had a special relationship with the city that he could only experience by himself. Over the years, he had found his private places—Tudor City Park, the walkway of the Brooklyn Bridge, and a quiet corner of the Cloisters. Richard's life was relatively free of pressures, but on those occasions when he felt troubled, he knew he could sort things out by secluding himself in one of these inviting havens.

Richard even had a phrase for all of this: "out of harm's way." Alone with his thoughts in the silence of a private hideaway, he felt strengthened, almost invulnerable. At such moments, it was hard for him to conceive of anything harmful ever coming his way. There were even times when Richard dared to believe he was living a charmed life.

But all of that was about to change.

The Woman was half a block away when Richard spied her. She stood outlined against the night, almost glowing in the eerie light of the streetlamp. Dressed in a trenchcoat, she held an umbrella which seemed strangely unshaken by the powerful gusts of wind. She turned slowly to catch Richard's eye. He halted and caught his breath. He had never seen a more beautiful woman in his life.

Her lips parted slightly and a smile played at the corners of her mouth. Richard stood transfixed. He found it impossible to avert his eyes from her penetrating gaze.

All sounds stopped, except for Richard's quickening heartbeat. He felt as though he were being drawn into a mysterious void dominated by The Woman's overwhelming presence. He stood riveted to the pavement as rain poured down his face, mingling with the cold sweat that had broken out on his forehead.

He felt the first stirring of sexual excitement. The Woman's smile broadened. Richard felt naked before her.

He had no idea how long he stood there before The Woman turned away. He only knew that by the time he tried to follow her, she had disappeared into the night.

He also knew she would be back.

CHAPTER TWO

"HONEY, DID you hear what I said?"

Annie stood beside the bed, looking down at Richard who was curled up on his side, his head barely visible above the covers.

"Huh?" he mumbled.

"Do you believe Leslie and Jill are going to split another bottle of champagne tonight?"

"Sure, why not?"

Annie began brushing her hair. "I guess they were pretty excited about the newspapers. Jill said she wanted to commit the *Times* review to memory."

The blankets stirred as Richard rolled over to his right side restlessly.

Engrossed in her brushing, Annie chattered away, oblivious to Richard's preoccupation.

The brush fell from Annie's hand. Giggling, she picked it up.

"Look at me," she said, "on two glasses of champagne. I'm in no shape to do inventory tomorrow morning."

There was no response from Richard. Annie resumed her brushing.

"Mr. Clark will be there at 7:30. He's the only man I know who watches 'Sunrise Semester.' "

Putting down the brush, Annie sat on the bed and began tickling Richard's earlobe. He smiled and leaned over to kiss her. Her arms encircled him lovingly.

Annie felt a warm tingle of excitement. Before she'd met Richard, sex had been fun but she hadn't had a relationship that was this comfortable. Richard was the most giving man she'd ever been with. He always tried to satisfy her and usually succeeded.

Richard pushed her away gently. "I really don't feel very well. My stomach."

"You've got it wrong. The line is: 'Not tonight, I've got a headache' and it's the girl who says it."

"I'm serious, Annie."

Concerned, she placed a hand on his forehead. "I warned you about the guacamole dip. It looked lethal. I'll get you an Alka-Seltzer."

Richard laid his head back on the pillow. "Thanks."

He closed his eyes. Annie studied him for a moment, then hurried into the bathroom.

When she returned with the medicine, Richard was asleep.

Sometimes Annie Mulligan thought she belonged in another century. Even as a child in Maryland, she'd had an inordinate attraction to objects from the past. She would sit in rapt attention as her grandmother unfolded tales of a time long ago when life seemed much less complicated. Annie felt at home in those tales —often more so than in the present.

Growing up, Annie's fondness for the old-fashioned led her naturally to country auctions, flea markets, tag sales and the like. By the time she graduated from college, she had accumulated a sizeable assortment of antiques, of which she was very proud.

Upon arriving in New York four years ago, Annie had found work as a librarian, then as an assistant manager in a small Madison Avenue gallery specializing in nineteenth century art. But neither of these jobs had provided much of a challenge and it was only when Howard Clark wandered into the gallery that things began to jell for her careerwise.

Mr. Clark was the proprietor of the Forgotten Lore Book Shop, a venerable establishment dealing in rare volumes, which had become practically a literary institution in Greenwich Village. Located in a landmark building near the river, it had served four generations of book collectors and numbered among its patrons prominent writers and poets, leading lights of society and even a few members of royalty.

Annie's first conversation with Mr. Clark centered, not surprisingly, on rare books. Her knowledge of the subject and her appreciation for the finer points of book collecting did not go unnoticed by the Forgotten Lore owner. Learning that Annie was less than satisfied with her present job, he offered her a position at his book shop. One visit to the store convinced Annie to accept the offer, though she confessed later to Richard that she had expected the place to be a bit more glamorous. After she'd worked there a few days, its quaintness had completely won her over.

The shop took up both floors of a two-story brick building on Grove Street. Its exterior was ornate and old-fashioned in appearance, with stained glass windows and an antique brass bell at the entranceway. Inside, the shop was a monument to dusty elegance. There were floor to ceiling mahogany shelves stacked with thousands of volumes, while a good portion of the available floor space was taken up with shipping crates, unopened cartons and stacks of still to be filed books.

When Annie had first arrived, there was barely room to walk around and she negotiated the aisles carefully, spending as much time as possible behind the antique marble desk that was like a fortress at the center of the room. By setting aside an extra hour each day, she was gradually able to unpack and file the incoming books and send the outgoing crates on their way. Within a month, the floor was relatively clear of obstruction, enough so for Annie to introduce several objets d'art from her personal collection. These ornamental tables, lamps and figurines went a long way toward brightening the shop's appearance, giving it a rustic charm. Not only did Annie now feel more at home, but Mr. Clark supported her improvements wholeheartedly.

Mr. Clark's approval was important to Annie. She had developed a respect and genuine fondness for her employer. His even-tempered personality made working conditions enjoyable and his precise understanding of the rare book world inspired her admiration. His patience and willingness to share his knowledge made her a ready listener and served to increase her already formidable appetite on this subject that was becoming such an important part of her life. Not only had Mr. Clark rescued her from a humdrum gallery job but Annie felt that he was training her as his protege.

Richard occasionally teased Annie about her pupil-teacher relationship with Mr. Clark. "If you're looking for a father figure," he would say, "couldn't you do better than that?" When Annie would pretend not to hear, Richard sometimes launched into an exaggerated impersonation of the older man's gaunt appearance and slightly stooped way of walking. Though she felt guilty, Annie couldn't resist laughing at Richard's antics.

On Saturday morning, Annie was groggy but

she managed to reach the book shop at 8:30. As she'd predicted, Mr. Clark had been there for an hour and was well into the inventory. A six crate shipment of children's books had arrived the previous afternoon. Mr. Clark was halfway through the first box when Annie settled down on the floor beside him. Gently opening one of the volumes, she found herself fascinated by the artistry of the pen and ink illustrations.

"Be careful, Annie," said Mr. Clark, with a knowing smile. "Once you start looking through them, you're hooked. I learned that about children's books a long time ago."

"My, God, they're so beautiful and delicate."

"Yes, and I doubt if a collector would let a child near any of them."

Annie laughed, rolled up her sleeves and began opening the next crate. She and Mr. Clark worked steadily through the morning hours and paused for only a brief lunch break. When the shop opened its doors at 12:30, Annie had become so engrossed in the inventory, that she almost thought of the occasional customers as intruders.

By five o'clock, Annie was sneezing from the dust and had developed a dull ache in her lower back. The bell at the front door chimed. Annie looked up as Richard entered the store.

"Hi, honey," she called, "we're almost finished."

"Take your time," replied Richard. As Annie looked away, he took a bouquet of flowers from behind his back and placed it casually on a nearby shelf.

Mr. Clark nodded a greeting at Richard. He turned to Annie. "That's okay. There's only a few books left. Run along—I'll take care of these."

Annie got to her feet with a look of mock exhaustion. "I was hoping you'd say that."

As she rushed off to get her coat, Richard knelt down beside Mr. Clark and gingerly examined one of the books.

"You've got good taste," said the older man. "That volume you're holding will go for about $2000."

Richard opened to the flyleaf and whistled softly in appreciation. "1730. Are they all that old?"

"Most of them. These go under lock and key. They're for the trade only."

Richard turned the volume over in his hands. "You know it's a little eerie holding a book this old."

Mr. Clark studied him for a moment with wry amusement. "You get used to it."

Richard and Annie were just outside the shop when he handed her the flowers. They were her favorite kind, baby roses—dark red and giving off a fragrance she had always loved. She had even duplicated the scent in a rosewater made especially for her.

"They're beautiful!" she cried. "What's the occasion?"

"No occasion," grinned Richard, "just pure devotion."

She kissed him. Arm in arm, they started off down the street.

The sun was going down over the Hudson. In a space between two buildings, they caught a glimpse of a weatherbeaten tugboat making its way slowly upriver. A brisk wind was coming off the water. It whipped through the quiet street, sending dust and bits of paper into a madly-swirling dance.

Annie shivered and pressed the roses to her tightly. It was not unlike Richard to surprise her with flowers, but Annie admired his intuition for knowing just when to do it. After a particularly long work day such as this one, a bouquet couldn't have been more welcome.

They drew near to The Treasure Trove, Annie's favorite antique store. Jokingly, Richard put his hands over her eyes and began steering her across the street. Giggling, Annie broke free of his hold and made a dash for the store window.

"How come we never can walk past this place?" asked Richard, throwing up his hands in feigned annoyance. He came up beside her. Together they looked through the glass.

The window was a melange of antique items from around the world. An Italian gilt ashtray nestled precariously against a Japanese silk-screen to which was fastened a souvenir pin from the 1939 World's Fair. Delicate hand-blown glasses stood next to Mason jars filled with yards of antique ribbon. Rings, pocket watches and bracelets were scattered about while portraits of Confederate soldiers, ex-Presidents and silent screen stars looked down on the clutter.

Annie pressed her face to the glass. "There's something new in this window every day."

"How can you tell?"

Annie pointed excitedly. "That clock wasn't there this morning. Or that lamp. Or that ash-tray. Or that vase. Oh, Jesus."

In the corner of the window, wedged between a pair of angel bookends stood a small clay vase. On it, hand-drawn, was a tableau of a young boy being tortured by two goat-like creatures. The boy's head was thrown back in agony as he was being stuffed into a boiling cauldron.

"That looks really old," said Richard, peering at the vase intently.

Annie frowned. "I'm sure it is."

Somewhere in the psyche of Richard Bloch, there was a metallic click as the safety catch of rusted centuries was released. Richard stiffened as a vague flood of primal memories, strange as though not his own, washed over him. He experienced an unsettling sense of deja vu, not in a quick flash as was common, but with a broad, engulfing familiarity that made him instantly vulnerable. For a brief second, it was as if an entire vista of eternity had opened up before him, but in the instant that he struggled to identify what he was feeling, the landscape receded and the safety lock snapped closed.

"I suppose you want to go inside," said Richard, not taking his eyes from the vase.

"What? Giving in this easily?"

"I think I see something I like," said

Richard, sounding strained and oddly determined.

Annie ran the cold water in the kitchen sink. From her utensil drawer, she took a sharp cutting knife. She let the water run gently on the stems of the roses, as she began to cut them, carefully at an angle—the life preserving method her grandmother had shown her as a child.

The stems cut, Annie looked resignedly at the vase. In the fluorescent light of the kitchen, it seemed even more garish and disturbing than it had in the gloomy, darkened antique shop. From the side of the vase, the goat-like creatures glowered at her with a mocking recognition, as though they could see into her mind and were ready to inhabit the landscape of her nightmares. The horror of the young torture victim was vividly etched on his face as his body met the boiling liquid of the cauldron that was about to take his life. Looking at his painfully distorted expression, Annie could almost hear his terrified cries. She shuddered.

It was so unlike Richard to buy something like this, she thought. And, knowing her distaste for the grotesque, it was even more unusual that he would give it to her as a present. When she had opened the bag outside the Treasure Trove, her face had fallen and Richard had been quick to notice.

"It's more than a hundred years old," he had

explained. "The man in the shop said it was one of a kind. I thought you like antiques."

Annie had done a fast recovery. Standing on the cold, wind-swept sidewalk, she made a good pretense of gratitude, though in retrospect, her effusiveness may have been a little forced.

"I guess I'm stuck with the damned thing whether I like it or not," said Annie to herself with a laugh as she placed the flowers in the vase.

She fussed with the arrangement. Then as an afterthought, she dropped an aspirin into the water, another life-prolonging trick that had enhanced her reputation for having a green thumb.

Annie's love for flowers and plants was reflected in the greenhouse-like atmosphere of the apartment that she shared with Richard. When she'd first moved in, the only vegetation there had been a half-dead geranium that Richard over-watered to the point of drowning. Annie had nursed it back to health and gradually surrounded it with leafy companions ranging from an African violet to a five foot high rubber tree—nicknamed Harvey—that nearly obscured Richard's bookcase.

Annie brought the flowers into the living room and placed them at the center of the coffee table. On the floor, Richard was sprawled out, sipping a Scotch and working on a maze of school lesson plans for the following week's classes. Annie kissed him on the top of the head and began preparing dinner.

Annie enjoyed cooking—everything from a simple omelette to the most elaborate gourmet dish. Her natural instincts for cuisine had been supplemented a year earlier by an eight week course at the Cordon Bleu Cooking School. Now she considered herself well on the way to becoming an excellent chef.

The kitchen was very much Annie's domain. Along with several antique utensils that she seldom used were all the latest gadgets and food processors. The large, high-ceilinged kitchen had built-in shelves that were lined with gourmet spices as well as cookbooks of various ethnic styles. Annie had imposed an alphabetized system—which only she understood—on the food items in the cabinets. Even the refrigerator was carefully catalogued.

That Saturday evening was the kind of night Richard and Annie looked forward to after a busy week. Following a light supper, they read for awhile—Richard from Mark Van Doren's "Shakespeare," Annie from the latest Robert Ludlum novel. Later they watched TV, Marlene Dietrich and Cary Grant in "Blonde Venus." They were in bed by eleven.

There was something very special about their lovemaking that night. Richard had never been more tender, more caring; the two of them had never been so much in tune. Afterwards, as he lay sleeping in her arms and Annie listened to his regular breathing, she felt that what they had just experienced had been strangely timeless. It was as if tonight represented the culmination of all their passions.

Annie should have fallen asleep right away. Instead, she tossed and turned for hours.

"Need any help?"

Leslie peeked into the kitchen where Annie was busy preparing a salad.

"No, I'm just about done."

Annie fed a carrot into the top of her La Mecanique food processor and watched at it was caught by the blade. Within seconds, it was completely sliced and deposited in a bowl, after being shot out of the side of the appliance.

"That's a handy little gadget," observed Leslie. "Even I could operate one of those."

"You'd be surprised," laughed Annie. "Richard's afraid of it."

Annie emptied the sliced carrots into a large wooden bowl containing various fresh vegetables. Deftly she added a rapid-fire assortment of exotic spices, topping it off with a specially prepared Greek dressing.

"I wish I could do that," sighed Leslie. "I can't even make a peanut butter sandwich."

"Are you kidding? This is nothing. The hard part is the four hours I spent shopping in Zabar's this afternoon."

"Well, it seems to relax you."

"Yeah, that and jogging. Richard and I were up at the crack of dawn. We ran three miles before he even let me buy the *Times.*"

Leslie smiled. "I don't know where you get the energy."

"I guess you could call it 'marvelously subtle abandonment,' " Annie said impishly.

Leslie shook her head. "Do you believe that critic? He also said I was more appealing than necessary. What the hell is all that supposed to mean?"

"Search me. It sounds positive."

Leslie shrugged. "I guess it is. So far, we've only gotten one bad review. And that guy thought that 'Cat On A Hot Tin Roof' was about the ASPCA."

Richard appeared in the doorway, a large martini pitcher in his hand. Annie jokingly put out her arm to block his entrance.

"Hey," she grinned. "I told you the kitchen was off limits."

Richard ducked under her arm and headed for one of the large cabinets. "I need some olives."

Annie put her hands on her hips. "Well, you won't find any there. That's the pudding and pasta section."

"Pardon me for living."

Leslie winked at Richard. "Try the refrigerator."

"I'm always afraid to try the refrigerator. It's like a fruit and vegetable explosion in there."

Annie threw up her hands in mock exasperation. "Just get your olives and leave. You wanna eat, don't you?"

Richard opened the refrigerator and retrieved a jar of olives. He held them up triumphantly and made a comic run from the room.

"You really have him trained, don't you?" joked Leslie.

"Well, I have control over the kitchen, but other than that Richard is very much his own man."

Leslie nodded. "He always has been. When he was ten years old, he ran away from home just because my mother ordered him to his room. I was only five but I remember all the commotion. My parents called the police and they combed the neighborhood for hours. All the while, Richard was perched in a maple tree in the back yard, watching everyone make asses out of themselves."

"What finally brought him down?"

"It got to be ten o'clock and he never missed 'Twilight Zone.' "

"If they'd had portable TV's in those days, Richard might still be up there, watching over all of us."

Leslie's reply was thoughtful. "Sometimes I think he still is."

Annie admired the antique parson's table that took up most of the dining room area. The soft candlelight seemed to bring out the intricate design on the bone china she used for special occasions. A Beethoven symphony played quietly in the background as Richard and Leslie worked on the Sunday *Times* crossword puzzle.

Feeling content, she added some last minute touches to the roast and came out of the kitchen to join them as they all sat down to dinner. The four course meal was complemented by Richard's favorite wine, a Rhine Valley white, and topped off with a homemade chocolate mousse cake that threatened to make sugar addicts of them all.

Annie enjoyed having Leslie over to dinner. Helped along by Richard and Leslie's brother/sister banter, she felt her customary shyness slipping away. Before long, she was talking with authority on a wide range of subjects, everything from aluminum space purses and the new Al Pacino movie to the recently discovered memory drug, vasopressin, and the upcoming Knicks season. Her occasional glances at the coffee table produced her only moments of uneasiness. The vase was hideous —it just didn't belong.

Leslie noticed it too as she and Annie were clearing away the dishes.

"Where'd you get this?"

"Gruesome, isn't it?" replied Annie, careful to keep her voice down. But Richard had already meandered off to the next room.

Leslie examined the vase's tableau. She made a face. "Reminds me of that old line:

children are fine as long as they're properly cooked."

Annie frowned. "I think it's pretty disgusting."

Leslie pointed to the goat-like figure whose arm was wrapped around the tortured boy's throat. "I think I recognize this one on the left. I went out with him last week and he tried a hold like that on me."

Annie smiled faintly. "Richard gave that to me. *He* thinks it's attractive."

Leslie studied Annie for a moment in silence. "It's only a painting."

"I know," said Annie with a nod, "but it seems so unlike Richard. I mean, he teaches children."

"Shhh," Leslie warned, "here he comes."

Richard emerged from the bedroom carrying a box containing a jigsaw puzzle. Within minutes, he had spread it out on the living room floor and the three of them were absorbed in trying to assemble an 800-piece picture of an anchovy pizza.

Annie broke out the after dinner brandy and replaced Beethoven with a Smokey Robinson cassette.

Richard examined the puzzle box, which showed the completed picture. He ran his fingers through the assortment of multi-shaped fragments. "What happens if there's a piece missing?"

Leslie took a sip of brandy and feigned alarm. "That's not funny, Richard. Don't even joke about that."

Annie stared at the nearly-completed border of the puzzle. She searched through the box for the remaining pieces, but to no avail.

"Leslie, the next time you come over, do me a favor, bring wine—it's a lot easier."

An hour passed. The puzzle began to take shape. Smokey Robinson gave way to Billie Holiday and the volume was turned down so as not to disturb the neighbors.

Richard looked at his watch. It was nearly eleven. He felt oddly restless.

Getting to his feet, he stretched. He stepped gingerly over the puzzle and crossed the room to the antique icebox which had been converted to a bar. He poured himself a good-sized shot of Remy Martin.

Tomorrow was going to be hectic. The first day of school drama rehearsals was never easy. Last year's production of "The Glass Menagerie" had been fraught with difficulties and, Richard guessed, there was no reason to expect "Romeo And Juliet" to go more smoothly.

Richard looked over at Leslie. Having her there tomorrow would be a great help. The fact that she was starring in a newly-opened hit play was an added bonus—the children were sure to be enthusiastic and on their best behavior.

Sipping his brandy, Richard wandered over to the window. He parted the curtains and looked out into the night.

The Woman had been waiting for him.

Standing on a terrace across the courtyard,

she was a brilliantly glowing embodiment of Richard's wildest erotic fantasies. She fixed him with her eyes. He felt magnetized, pulled toward her by an overpowering force of energy. It was as though something was being sucked right out of his body.

The chatter and music behind him faded from his consciousness as he drank in the luscious curves of her inviting body. Clad in a diaphanous white robe that left her fully revealed for him, she smiled fetchingly at Richard, who stood paralyzed with longing.

A wispy cloud of smoke swirled around the terrace on which she stood, seeming to emanate from the room directly behind her. In the dimness of that room, flickering votive candles hinted at ceremonies that called out to Richard in voices of alluring urgency.

The Woman's dark hair fell in folds along the contours of her perfectly formed neck and flawless shoulders. Cupping her firm breasts in her hands, she began to caress them with a lingering circular motion, bringing the nipples to an enticing hardness.

Temptingly, she ran her hands down her body to her thighs. Spreading her legs ever so slightly, she began to sway to and fro in a gently thrusting fashion. Her hand glided upward along the inside of her thigh . . .

Richard felt himself grow hard with desire. In his mind's eye, he was already lowering her to the floor of the terrace, as she pleaded with him to take her by force, to ravage her, to make her scream in surrender.

His heart raced. He breathed heavily. He could not take his eyes away.

The Woman paused. She brought her hands back to her sides. She stared knowingly at Richard. Their eyes locked.

Suddenly, she turned away. With an imperious sweep of her robe, she left the terrace.

Richard blinked and shook his head. The brandy glass fell from his hand, noiselessly to the carpet. He closed the curtains.

Turning, he caught his reflection in a mirror on the living room wall. The eyes that stared back at him were vacant and afraid.

Richard felt like he was looking at a stranger.

CHAPTER THREE

"BUT GOD bless the child that's got his own,
That's got his own . . ."

Annie's voice was slightly off-key and, since she was brushing her teeth, a little underwater. Her wrist watch, balanced precariously on the edge of the bathroom sink, showed five minutes to midnight.

"Hey, Richard," she called, "do I sound like Billie Holiday? I can't get that song out of my head."

She turned off the water and listened for a moment. There was no answer from the adjoining bedroom.

He's probably still concentrating on the

Times crossword, thought Annie. In the two years she'd known him, he'd never gone to sleep on a Sunday night without completing it. She'd grown used to her remarks falling on deaf ears, particularly when he was down to the last few words.

"No fair using the dictionary," she shouted goodnaturedly. Again there was no response.

Annie applied cold cream to her eye makeup and began to tissue it off. She smiled at herself in the mirror. Tonight had been fun. Dinner had been an unqualified success. The cake had been a gamble, since the recipe had been jotted down quickly while watching "Good Morning America." But the requests for second helpings dispelled any doubts she might have had.

Leslie had never seemed more buoyant. Being in a hit show must do that for you, mused Annie as she crumpled up a Kleenex and tossed it into the wastebasket. It had been nice seeing Leslie again. The previous six weeks rehearsal period had given the actress precious little time for socializing. For Annie, Friday night's cast party had been nice, but she preferred seeing Leslie away from the crowd, in the comfort of her own home.

"Don't you doze off on me, Richard," Annie called out with a laugh. "I'll be in there in a minute to jump on your bones."

Annie opened her robe and stood nude before the bathroom mirror. Tall and slender, her figure had often been called model-like, but Annie wouldn't have minded an extra four inches in the bust department and a few more curves further down.

She took one last look at herself in the mirror. I guess I'll do, she thought. A dab of Opium perfume behind each ear provided the finishing touch.

Annie went into the bedroom. Before her, his head buried under the covers, Richard was fast asleep.

"Terrific."

Annie smiled. It had been a long day. She climbed into bed, kissed Richard lightly on the forehead, taking care not to wake him. She turned off the light.

She never noticed the unfinished crossword puzzle on the floor beside the bed.

"Aren't you hungry?"

Annie looked at Richard across the breakfast table. Monday morning sunlight streamed through the casement windows, casting the shadows of Annie's hanging plants across the expanse of the living room. She stabbed at the last piece of French toast on her plate and pointed to Richard's untouched omelette.

"I'm eating," he protested.

"No, you're not," said Annie gently, "you're picking."

She stirred her coffee and opened a copy of *Better Homes & Gardens.* At low volume, the radio played a Chopin sonata.

"Richard?"

"Huh?"

"Can I get you something else?"

"What do you mean?"

Annie peered over the top of the magazine, "You've hardly touched your food."

Richard took a bite of his whole wheat toast. "I'm eating."

"Richard, there's a whole omelette in front of you. You like omelettes. Usually you demolish them in five minutes."

There was no answer. Annie shrugged. She resumed reading an article on the repotting of plants. After a moment, she glanced over at one of her newest acquisitions, an amaryllis that had been floundering. Beside it, on the coffee table, Richard's roses were beginning to wilt. They'd be lucky to last another day, thought Annie regetfully.

She stole another look at Richard, who was still toying with his food. She reached for the coffee pot. "I think what you need is some more caffeine."

Richard stared at her quizzically. "What's that supposed to mean?"

"Best thing for a hangover," she said teasingly.

She reached for his coffee cup, but Richard put his hand over it. His reply was measured and edged with annoyance. "I don't have a hangover."

Annie paused. She put down the coffee pot. "You should. You had enough to drink."

Richard's eyes flashed. Annie patted his hand reassuringly. "It's okay. It was a party. I have a hangover too."

Richard snickered derisively. "Don't be condescending with me. You had two drinks. You couldn't have a hangover. And don't get critical. I didn't have too much to drink."

"Richard, I didn't say that."

"Yes, you did."

"Too much is not the same as enough."

"Oh, now we're getting into quantitative judgments? You're going to tell me what is enough?"

Annie sat back in her chair for a moment. I don't believe this, she thought to herself. Richard was being just plain childish. Maybe he was coming down with something. He had been sick on Friday night, and there was a flu virus going around. But what if it wasn't physical?

"Richard," she asked softly, "did I do something to upset you? If I did, I'm sorry."

Richard lit a cigarette and inhaled deeply. "I don't feel like arguing with you."

"I'm not arguing, honey."

Richard stood up and took his jacket from the back of the chair. "It's late. I've got to leave."

"It's only ten to eight. You've got a little time."

Richard buttoned his jacket. "Annie, I just told you," he said evenly. "I've got to leave. Do you want me to be late?"

Annie looked away. "No, of course not."

She stared into the magazine, feeling the tears begin to well up in her eyes. As the glossy photographs of exotic house plants became blurry in front of her, she heard Richard's purposeful footsteps as he walked to the front door. A second later, she heard the door close behind him.

"Well, at least, he didn't slam it," she said aloud.

Annie put down her magazine and gave a start. Across the breakfast table, Richard's half-smoked cigarette was embedded in her lovingly prepared omelette.

The Evil laughed an ancient cackle like dried leaves being trod upon. Whispers ran through and around its twisted mass, caressing hidden corners, secret places that even The Old One didn't know about. It waited. Stinking corruption. Unspoken voices said it wouldn't be long now . . .

Leslie's phone rang. Drowsily, she reached out of bed to the night table and picked up the receiver. The voice at the other end of the phone was impossibly chipper for eight o'clock in the morning.

"It's your wake-up call, Miss Bloch. Rise and Shine!"

Leslie laughed. "Hi, Jill. Thanks for calling. I was afraid I'd sleep right through the alarm clock."

"And miss school?"

"Richard asked me to be there by nine-thirty. I'd better move my ass if I'm going to play a pubescent virgin in Verona."

"Good luck," said Jill with a giggle.

"Thanks, I'll need it."

Leslie hung up the phone. Jill was more dependable than an alarm clock. Up every morning at seven, she occasionally called Leslie to wake her for an early appointment, particularly if Leslie was anxious about being on time. Helping Richard's students with "Romeo And Juliet" was as important as any audition.

The sun was already warm on her face as she hurried up the avenue to the bus stop. It was useless to look for an available taxi between eight and nine on a weekday and the bus would move quickly enough once it passed the 59th Street Bridge traffic.

Leslie stood all the way to 72nd, then grabbed a seat next to a small, dapper man with a goatee who was muttering to himself about parakeets. Ignoring him, she paged through her Folger's Shakespeare paperback, as a gigantic portable radio, equipped with the power of a hydraulic drill, blared out the latest Donna Summer single.

Leslie was amazed at how much of Shakespeare's famous tragedy was coming back to her. She closed her eyes and suppressed a laugh. Once again, she was on the stage of a high school auditorium in Southern Vermont, playing a gawky Juliet to Vinny Nunzio's Romeo.

Maybe I'll hear from Vinny, she thought to herself, if they get theatre reviews in the Merchant Marine. Over the weekend, ever since the critics had handed down their words of approval for "Straw Hat," Leslie had been surprised by phone calls and telegrams from quite a few long lost acquaintances, ranging from her seventh grade math teacher to a gay gynecologist she'd visited once in summer stock.

Richard's school was a newly refurbished four story edifice on 97th Street, not far from the East River. Leslie checked her watch as she ran up the front steps. Nine twenty-eight. She was right on time.

Richard was just finishing up first period when Leslie opened the door to his classroom. She glanced around the room. As always, she was taken aback for a moment by the absence of blackboards.

Donald Carter, a tall good-looking black student of about fourteen, was reading aloud from a text on the Thirty Years War. His voice was firm and assured as his strong, tapered fingers moved carefully over the page of Braille characters.

He's got presence and vocal projection, thought Leslie. I wonder if he's my Romeo.

Leslie was a little nervous. Standing on the makeshift balcony Richard had fashioned from some orange crates, she felt that, even though the children couldn't see her, they could sense her every move and read her every emotion. But the applause that followed her first speech put her at ease.

Leslie marveled at Donald's quick grasp of

the role. He was going to be a splendid Romeo. She hoped that the girl chosen to play Juliet could match him.

Leslie's time spent with the students was over before she knew it. She was surprised when the noon bell rang for lunch.

"I'm starving," she confided to Richard as they stood outside the classroom. The children filed past them on their way to the school lunchroom. Hearing her voice, they smiled in her direction. Several came closer to embrace her.

Donald was the last to exit the classroom. Richard put an arm around the boy's shoulders paternally. He turned to his sister.

"Why don't you two save me a place in the cafeteria? I'll join you in a minute."

"Great," said Leslie, taking Donald by the hand. They started off down the corridor. Richard rummaged in his pockets for coins, then called out to his sister. "Les, do you have a dime?"

Leslie paused uncertainly. Gently, Donald took his hand from hers. "Go ahead back, Miss Bloch. I know where the cafeteria is. I can smell the meatloaf from here."

Leslie rejoined her brother. She fished in her purse and came up with some change.

"I want to call Annie," explained Richard. "We had a little fight this morning."

"Anything serious?" asked Leslie.

"Not really. I just acted like a shit. I don't know what came over me."

"Here, take two dimes, you shit."

"I'm not a shit," Richard protested with a laugh.

"You said it, I didn't," replied Leslie. "I think you're terrific."

Richard hurried off down the corridor. "Meet you in the cafeteria," he called back over his shoulder. "Order me a health salad. And stay away from the special—whatever it is!"

At the store, Annie was at the top of a ladder, balancing an armful of books, when the phone rang. "Never fails," she sighed. Gingerly, she began to make her way down the steps. She got to the phone in the middle of the sixth ring.

"Forgotten Lore," she said, her voice a little breathless.

"Annie, hi, it's me."

Annie brightened. "Hi, Richard, sorry I took so long to answer. Mr. Clark's out to lunch. I was on the shelves."

"I won't keep you. I just wanted to apologize for this morning."

"Oh come on, I'd already forgotten about it."

"No, really, I acted like a Class A shit. Forgive me?"

"There's nothing to forgive."

"Yes, there is. I'm sorry. You should have slugged me one."

"Next time maybe I will," she laughed.

"You're beautiful."

"How'd the rehearsal go? How was Leslie?"

"She was beautiful too."

"Great, I knew she would be."

The bell rang at the entrance of the book shop. Annie looked up to see a deliveryman carrying a large crate.

"Got to run, Richard. A delivery just came in. I'll see you at home."

"Bye, darling, see you later."

"Oh, and Richard?" said Annie, lowering her voice. "I'm glad you called."

She put down the receiver and signed the packing slip the deliveryman was waving impatiently in front of her.

"Watch out for that crate, lady," he said, pocketing the signed receipt. "You'll get splinters."

Annie took a hammer from the front desk drawer. "Don't worry, I'm used to it."

Alone once again, Annie eyed the crate with anticipation. The address was intriguing. Bad Salzuflen, West Germany. Going to the desk, she checked the incoming orders. There was nothing listed for Germany. It must have slipped Mr. Clark's mind, she reasoned.

Wrenching upward with the pronged end of the hammer, Annie expertly pried the cover from the crate. She peered into the box.

Wrapped snugly within a protective blanket of canvas were two stacks of books. Annie drew aside the canvas and began removing the volumes. She coughed as their mildewed pages released countless years of dust.

Taking a clean white rag from her work smock, she carefully dusted off several of the books. A title leaped out at her in German. She recognized the name "Satan."

She opened the book. Gently she turned the pages, searching for German words that had an English counterpart. Finding none, she was about to close the book when a full-page drawing brought her up short.

In vivid detail, the drawing depicted a gathering of thirteen hooded people, praying in supplication to a horned, cloven-hoofed figure whose countenance of undiluted evil made Annie give a quick involuntary shudder.

Curious, Annie began removing the remainder of the volumes from the crate. There were thirteen books in all, she noted, as she held the last one in her hand. It was in English.

" 'Rites of Devil Worship,' " said Annie, reading the title out loud. She opened the book to the first page.

The deliveryman had left the front door slightly ajar, so there was no warning bell as Mr. Clark let himself quietly into the book shop. Frowning, he crossed the room and stood behind Annie.

She thumbed through the pages, with curiosity and distaste. Mr. Clark watched her in silence.

Annie was staring at an engraving of Lucifer Triumphant, casting souls into hell fire when she felt Mr. Clark's bony hand on her shoulder. Startled, she spun around.

"Oh, you really scared me," she gasped.

"I'll take care of those," he said severely. Then realizing her alarm, he placed a comforting hand on her shoulder.

Annie gave a nervous twitter. "I must have jumped a foot!"

"I'm sorry," said Mr. Clark kindly. "It's just that those books are quite old and extremely delicate."

"They weren't on the incoming list."

"They won't be here long enough. Someone's picking them up tonight. I already have a buyer for the whole lot."

"Good, 'cause they really gave me the creeps."

"I just sell them," Mr. Clark shrugged. "I don't inquire about the contents."

"I was raised Catholic," explained Annie. "I'm not used to seeing books like that."

"That's interesting," said Mr. Clark. "Catholics usually find them the most fascinating."

Mr. Clark watched from the doorway until Annie had rounded the corner on her way to lunch. He placed a "Will Return In 30 Minutes" sign in the front window, then stepped inside the shop. He locked the front door securely and pulled down the shade.

At the desk, he picked up the phone. Glancing at the newly-arrived crate of books, he removed a list of names from his shirt pocket. He dialed the first number on the list.

A voice answered. As Mr. Clark spoke, he could barely contain his mounting fervor.

"The books have arrived from Germany. They're very fragile but quite readable. I think they'll serve very nicely at our next meeting."

He hung up the phone. There were eleven more numbers to call.

CHAPTER FOUR

THE TAXI wheeled to a screeching halt. Standing outside the school entrance, Leslie watched in admiration at the New York City phenomenon known as Three Cabs Racing for the Same Passenger. The two losing vehicles nearly collided, then drove off morosely, drivers' invectives trailing in the air. Leslie got into the winning taxi.

As she settled into the back seat, she stole a glance at the driver in the rear view mirror. Though only his eyes and forehead were visible, Leslie liked what she saw.

"Do I need a crash helmet to ride with you?" she asked facetiously.

"Are you kidding?" he replied in a voice Leslie found surprisingly resonant. "I haven't had an accident yet. 'Course I've only been driving for three days."

Leslie feigned alarm, putting her hand to her heart. "Oh my God, let me out right now!"

The driver turned around and smiled. Dark haired, about thirty years of age, he was strikingly handsome in a way Leslie found instantly appealing.

"No, I mean driving a *cab,*" he said. "I just started. It's not exactly my chosen line of work."

His eyes took in Leslie with a glimmer of appreciation. He pushed down the flag on the meter. "Where to?"

"Fifth Avenue and Eleventh Street," replied Leslie.

The driver gunned the engine and the cab surged forward, neatly merging into the heavy avenue traffic.

"What is your line of work?" asked Leslie. "Let me guess, you're a brain surgeon on a sabbatical."

"No, but you're close," he laughed. "I almost played a doctor last year on 'General Hospital.' I'm an actor. Currently, as we say, between engagements. I'm out of work. Unlike you."

Leslie was momentarily taken aback. "I beg your pardon."

"You're Leslie Bloch, aren't you?"

"Yes."

"I'm Michael Wingate. I saw your picture in the papers. Congratulations. It looks like you're in a hit."

"Yeah, my first one. I've even got heat in my

dressing room. You wouldn't believe some of the dumps I've played in."

The traffic light at 86th Street turned yellow. Michael put his foot down heavily on the brake.

"Like the Theatre of the Seventh Sense in Soho?" he asked. "I saw you there in an all-female version of 'Twelve Angry Men.' "

"You saw that? I don't believe it! We used to outnumber the audience every night."

Michael grinned. "I thought you were pretty good."

"Thanks," said Leslie. She closed her eyes, feeling herself beginning to relax as the cab resumed its trip downtown. It wasn't like her to strike up a conversation with a taxi driver but this guy hardly seemed your stereotypical New York cabbie.

Leslie found herself exchanging show business gossip and critical evaluations with him. They both had loved "Amadeus" on Broadway and shared equally strong reactions to Werner Herzog films. Both were fans of Southern Gothic novels.

They traded embarrassing audition stories. The tale of Michael's introduction to the New York audition scene, told against the backdrop of blaring midtown traffic, had Leslie smiling appreciatively.

"So there I was," he said, "in the middle of the stage, right? The theatre is totally dark. I can't see anybody in the house. Suddenly, I hear the director, with this booming voice, coming out of the darkness, and he says, 'Would you mind dropping your pants?' Do you believe I had mixed up my auditions? I thought I was auditioning for Franco Zeffirelli and it was the road company of 'Oh Calcutta!"

Leslie leaned her head back on the seat and laughed. She didn't notice the cool way Michael studied her in the rear view mirror.

"I've done the same thing," she giggled. "I mixed up 'Trojan Women' with an 'Annie Get Your Gun' audition and showed up in Ancient Greece wearing a cowgirl outfit."

"Oh, that's even worse."

Leslie considered. The company manager for "Straw Hat" had promised her passes for any performance. She felt a strong impulse to have Michael see her onstage. She wasn't in the habit of picking up strange men, but she thought, there's always a first time.

"What are you doing tomorrow night?" she heard herself asking.

It was 1:30 when Annie paid her check at Pedro's, the health food restaurant on Hudson Street that she'd recently discovered.

Bundling up against the cold, she headed off toward Grove Street, resisting the temptation to browse among the many junk stores that lined the sidewalk.

The books shop was closed when Annie arrived there. A note on the door informed her that Mr. Clark had already left for lunch. Annie unlocked the door and entered the shop to the sound of a ringing telephone. She unbuttoned her coat as she hurried across the room to pick up the receiver.

"Forgotten Lore," she answered.

She heard the familiar high-pitched voice of Mr. Powell, one of the store's oldest and most loyal customers. Once again, he had lost his gloves—the third time this month—and Annie promised to search for them.

"I'll call you back if they turn up," she said. Putting down the phone, she made a hasty perusal of the front room. No gloves here, thought Annie, but if Mr. Clark found them they're liable to be anywhere.

She went into the back room and paused before Mr. Clark's large Victorian desk. The gloves were not on top. They're probably in one of the drawers, thought Annie, and that means forget it. Only Mr. Clark would lock up a pair of gloves.

Her employer's desk was an amusing source of speculation for Annie who had never managed to get a glimpse inside any of its seven drawers. Under lock and key, the desk had even earned the nickname of The Inner Sanctum, coined by Richard who believed it contained Mr. Clark's private collection of *Bitches in Bondage* magazines.

Annie shrugged and gave a nonchalant tug to the top drawer as she had done many times before. To her surprise, the drawer slid open easily.

"I don't believe it," said Annie aloud.

Leaning down for a closer look, Annie was

disappointed to see nothing more interesting than a pile of ledger books. Moving them aside, she noticed a clipboard filled with receipts and invoices. She was about to close the drawer when something shiny caught her eye.

She hesitated. Mr. Clark might return at any minute. If he found her rummaging in his private desk, she'd be mortified. Besides, from what she could see, Richard's humorous theory of Mr. Clark's pornographic bent was totally unfounded.

Still the glint at the bottom of the drawer was very tempting.

Annie pondered. As long as the bell at the shop's entrance didn't ring, the coast was clear. She would have more than enough time to check out this little treasure.

Curious, she moved aside the clipboard to reveal a beautifully carved antique gold box measuring about six inches by twelve. With extreme caution, she put both hands underneath the box and lifted it from the drawer. Weighs a ton, she mused, as she held it up to the light admiringly. Wonder what's inside.

The box was intricately engraved with swirling curlicues and geometric patterns of varying density. Annie ran her index finger lightly along the surface. From the texture of the box's dappled exterior, she guessed that the gold content could be as high as 18 karats.

Not surprising that he locks the drawer, thought Annie. With the price of gold today, this thing must be worth a fortune.

Still listening for the front doorbell, Annie

examined the box carefully but could find no trace of an opening latch.

Probably one of those puzzle boxes that open with a spring, she reasoned, which means it could take hours to find out what's inside.

On the verge of returning it to the bottom of the drawer, Annie inadvertently brushed her finger against a slightly indented portion at the corner of the box. The lid sprang open.

"Oh," exclaimed Annie, startled.

She peered into the box. A vermilion satin cloth was folded across the top of the interior. Annie drew it aside. Hidden beneath it, neatly arrayed in rows of three, was a hoard of gold pieces that left Annie momentarily stunned.

She felt her hand tremble slightly as she reached into the box for one of the coins. Holding the piece up to the light, she felt a quick flash of recognition from childhood.

It's like a medal that the nuns in school used to wear, she thought.

Then she took a closer look.

The gleaming round medal, roughly an inch and a half in diameter, depicted in bas-relief, a close up of a young woman's face, infused with a look of beatific serenity. But the heart-shaped face, with its high cheekbones and beautiful almond eyes, exuded a ripened and knowing sensuality that Annie recognized as far from saintlike. The woman's lips, full and sensuous, and her expression of majestic triumph gave Annie an uneasy feeling. She had never seen this face on any nun's medal.

She turned over the medal.

"Oh, my God."

The other side presented a full-length portrait of the same woman, naked with a serpent crawling up her thigh. Full-figured and voluptuous, with long shapely legs, the woman stood expectantly poised to receive the serpent's flickering tongue which was about to enter her.

Annie shuddered as she felt a strange sensation of excitement and longing. Staring at the snake's powerful, sinewy bulk, she blushed, as she imagined it thrusting itself between her own legs. A warm tingle invaded her loins.

The front doorbell chimed.

Mr. Clark's voice called out from the other room.

"Annie? It's only me."

Flustered, Annie closed the gold box and shoved it back into the desk drawer, quickly covering it with the ledger books and clipboard.

"I'll be out in a minute, Mr. Clark," she cried, a trifle too loudly.

"It's all right," Mr. Clark replied, "I'm on my way back."

Clumsily, Annie tried to push the drawer closed but one of the ledger books got in the way.

"Shit!"

"Did you say something?" asked Mr. Clark cheerfully, his voice growing nearer.

Annie pressed down on the ledger book and jammed the drawer shut. She hurried across to the doorway, where she nearly stumbled into Mr. Clark.

"Oh, excuse me," she exclaimed.

Mr. Clark paused. He studied her for a moment. Annie felt her heart racing as she realized her fingers were still wrapped tightly around the gold medal.

"That's okay, Annie," said Mr. Clark with a slight chuckle. "It's a wonder we don't collide in here more often."

With an inward sigh of relief, Annie casually dropped the medal into her pocket. Thank God he didn't catch me! she thought. Now how do I return it to the box?

The roast from the night before had been transformed into overstuffed sandwiches topped with a Russian dressing Annie had flavored with dill. Sliced pickles, potato salad and cole slaw provided the side dishes and Annie planned to start off the meal with her homemade tomato bisque.

The vegetables in the frying pan had begun to simmer and Annie gave them a quick stir. With her free hand, she opened the refrigerator; a six pack of Heineken would be more than enough for the evening.

She heard the front door open. Richard's hello was barely audible over the Sibelius. Annie went into the living room and embraced him.

"There was a midget on the elevator," said Richard, taking off his coat. "He was going up to the penthouse. I had to press the button for him."

Annie laughed. "That was big of you."

Richard rolled his eyes toward the ceiling and groaned. He kissed Annie and went to the closet to hang up his coat.

"Are you cooking tonight?" he asked.

"Sauteed leftovers."

"I could use a beer."

"Coming right up, master," said Annie jokingly. Richard loosened his tie and sank down onto the sofa. He closed his eyes wearily. Annie brought him a beer and began clearing the coffee table. Taking Richard's wilted roses from the vase, she started toward the kitchen.

Richard's eyes opened. "Where are you going with those?"

"They're dead," she said matter-of-factly. "I'm going to throw them out."

"They're not dead. Put them back."

Annie flicked one of the lifeless petals. "Richard, they're most definitely dead."

Richard eyed her deliberately. "Annie, I said put them back." His tone was clipped and measured.

Puzzled, Annie searched Richard's face for signs of humor. She didn't find any.

"Are you crazy? Look at these," said Annie holding the flowers up to Richard's face.

"I like them," said Richard vacantly. "Roses live longer than you think."

Richard took the flowers from her hand. Lovingly he began to arrange them in the vase. Annie stared at him in disbelief.

"You know something?" she said, striving for a light-hearted tone. "You're getting weird."

Richard leaned forward. "You know something? You're a pain in the ass!"

Annie took a step backward. This is silly, she thought. The flowers were dead and Richard would just have to admit it. Annie folded her arms.

"I'm not serving dinner on a table with dead roses."

Richard go to his feet abruptly. "Good, I'll serve myself. You can eat in the kitchen for all I care."

"I may do just that," replied Annie, surprised at her own defiance. She turned on her heel and started toward the kitchen.

Hard day or not, she thought, Richard's being an asshole. This morning was bad enough—now he's picking another fight. She whirled around, suddenly angry.

"Not only are the flowers dead," she snapped. "That vase is absolutely revolting."

Richard smiled sardonically. "Oh, I see. Is there anything else around here that you don't like?"

"Yes, *you* when you're like this."

"Like what?" he asked, traces of a smirk on his face. "How am I?"

"At the moment, you're being totally irrational." Annie paused, trying to find the right words. "You're behaving like a child."

"Oh, is that so?" he asked sarcastically.

Annie put her hand on Richard's shoulder.

"This isn't like you. I don't know what's wrong, so I don't know what to say."

"Don't say anything," he said harshly. "I'll make it easy for you."

She watched incredulously as he brushed her hand from his shoulder, grabbed his jacket from the closet and walked calmly to the front door.

"Where are you going?" she called.

The slam of the door was the only answer.

Frustrated and hurt, Annie scooped up the wilted roses, hurried into the kitchen and threw them into the garbage.

It was nearly midnight when Annie awoke to Richard's touch.

He kissed her on the lips. Annie smiled.

"Richard? Could we just not fight anymore?"

"Come here."

Later as she lay in his arms, Annie felt a vague uneasiness. Something was wrong. Their lovemaking had been cold and mechanical. Richard had been distant.

Eyes closed, Annie cleared her mind for sleep. She never noticed Richard's empty gaze as he stared into the darkness.

In the living room, back in their vase, bits of egg shell and tea leaves clinging to their petals, Richard's roses kept an all-night vigil.

The madness had begun.

CHAPTER FIVE

"IT'S RICHARD. I'm a little concerned about him."

Annie faced Leslie across the table in the Chinese restaurant where they were having lunch.

"What do you mean?" asked Leslie, blowing on her wonton soup.

Good question, thought Annie. What *did* she mean? Ever since this morning, when she'd found the dead flowers, she'd been apprehensive. She hadn't brought it up to Richard but, seconds after he'd left for work, she'd been on the phone to Leslie. Now as she sat opposite her, Annie wondered: am I blowing this out of proportion?

"Well," she began, "we've been having these

arguments over nothing. Richard initiates them. We had two fights yesterday that came right out of the blue."

"So?" laughed Leslie. "Welcome to the wonderful world of longterm relationships."

"Leslie, I've lived with Richard for two years. Sure we've argued but never over nothing."

"Maybe he's just been working too hard. You know how dedicated Richard is. He's the Dr. Kildare of private schools."

"I know," said Annie with a faint smile, "but it gets worse. He pulled a little stunt last night that made no sense at all. I'm almost embarrassed to tell you."

"Oh, come on, don't be silly."

Annie sipped her tea. "Richard bought me flowers the other day. You might remember, they were on the dinner table."

"The roses, right? In the disgusting vase?"

"Exactly," nodded Annie. "Well, I kept them for a few days until they wilted. Last night I went to throw them out but Richard wouldn't let me. He made an issue of it. He stormed out of the apartment. So I threw them out. I wake up this morning and they're back in the vase with pieces of garbage all over them. He went and fished them out of the garbage!"

Annie lowered her head uncomfortably. Leslie smiled back at her.

"You know Richard. He's always had a stubborn streak. When we were kids, he used to do the same thing with his broken toys. Mom would throw them out and Richard would retrieve them from the garbage. He wouldn't part with them until *he* was ready."

"But, Leslie, dead roses?"

Leslie shrugged. "Maybe he's going through male menopause a little early."

"I'm serious," said Annie. "He's been acting very strange toward me."

"Oh, really? I haven't noticed anything. He seemed fine the other night."

"He *was* fine the other night. He's okay with other people. It's when the two of us are alone that something seems to come over him. I don't know. Maybe it's me."

"What do you mean?"

Annie's voice was little more than a whisper. "Do you think he's seeing another woman?"

"Richard?" said Leslie, surprised. "He doesn't even have *time* to see another woman."

"I'm not so sure about that. He disappeared for a few hours last night."

"Annie, you're talking about a few hours. He probably went to a movie. Besides, Richard's devoted to you. He adores you. Everybody knows that."

Annie lowered her voice even further. "I know I'm not imagining this. Can we talk frankly for a minute?"

"Of course."

"Well," said Annie, "last night when Richard made love to me, it was like he was . . . going through the motions. He was . . . I don't know, mechanical. He treated me as if I wasn't there."

"Annie, you've been with Richard two years.

These things can happen. You can't judge a person by one night."

Annie paused to consider. "Maybe you're right. I'm probably jumping to conclusions. It's just that . . ."

"Maybe he's tired," interrupted Leslie. "You know how guys are. I had one who couldn't do it unless the phonograph was playing 'Stars and Stripes Forever.' "

Annie threw back her head and laughed. "Well, it's not that bad yet."

Leslie patted her hand encouragingly. "Give it a few days. It'll blow over."

"I hope you're right," said Annie, her voice a little uncertain.

On the walk back to the Forgotten Lore, Annie felt relieved. Though some doubts still remained about Richard's behavior, she had been comforted by Leslie's words of assurance.

As they walked along Bleecker, Annie turned to Leslie. "Well, now that I've talked your ear off, what's happening with you?"

Leslie grinned. "I thought you'd never ask."

"Oh, is this going to be juicy?"

"I don't know. I met this really cute guy. You'll never guess where."

"Oh, don't make me guess—I can't wait to hear."

"In a Checker cab. He was driving."

"What's he look like?"

"Would you believe a cross between Warren Beatty and David Bowie? He's an actor."

"Looking like that," laughed Annie, "he'd better be."

"I only spent twenty minutes with him," said Leslie, "but he seemed really intelligent and very funny."

"Sounds great."

"It's too early to tell. But he is coming to the show tonight. I invited him."

"I can't wait to meet him."

They turned onto Grove Street and approached the book shop. As they stood outside the front door, exchanging goodbyes, the bright rays of the sun bathed the Forgotten Lore in a vivid glow.

Looking through the window, Annie was the first to see it.

Over Leslie's right shoulder, visible near the store's front desk, the sparkle of gold had caught Annie's eye. An oval medallion, connected to a chain, was being lowered by Mr. Clark onto the neck of a blonde, middle-aged woman.

"Look quick," Annie urged.

Leslie turned around just in time to see Mr. Clark as he grasped both of the woman's hands and kissed her on each cheek. The woman gave Mr. Clark a slight bow, almost formal in nature, then hurried toward the front door. She opened it and brushed past Annie and Leslie rudely, but not before Annie had glimpsed the shining gold medal which nestled on her breast.

"What was that all about?" asked Leslie.

Annie blushed knowingly. "I'll bet I know what that was." She reached into her blazer and frowned. "Shit, it's in my other jacket."

"What is?"

"I'll tell you later," replied Annie. "Mr. Clark just spotted me."

Annie hugged Leslie. "Thanks for everything, really. Thanks for listening."

"Are you kidding?" laughed Leslie. "Thank you for lunch. Don't worry too much about Richard. I lived with him for eighteen years and he's a pretty good guy."

Annie squeezed her hand gratefully. "I know."

She watched as her friend went off down the street. Leslie turned the corner and disappeared from view.

Annie thought about the medal. I forgot all about it, she realized. There were a couple of dozen in the box, so Mr. Clark probably hasn't missed it. But I'd better get it back tomorrow or there'll be hell to pay.

Suddenly Annie felt an inexplicable chill. For an instant, she was overtaken by a nameless dread. Something evil was in the air.

It was seven fifteen. Leslie walked down Fifth Avenue toward Washington Square Park. This was her favorite part of the Village. Growing up in Vermont, Leslie's teenage years had been filled with Henry James tales of Washington Square and its stylish residents back in the time when this area of New York represented the center of elegance.

As she entered the park, Leslie could almost imagine herself back in nineteenth century New York. The buses and taxi cabs vanished, replaced by horse-drawn carriages. Instead of jeans and turtlenecks, Leslie wore a floor length taffeta dress, high button shoes and a floral bonnet. In her hand, she carried a ruffled-edged parasol. She felt herself the picture of a Henry James heroine in an age of charm and refinement.

"Loose joints, acid, cocaine?"

Leslie was jolted back to reality by the sales pitch of the grinning street pusher who lounged at the side of the fountain. Leslie blinked and walked by him wordlessly.

As she approached West Fourth Street, she reflected on this afternoon's conversation with Annie. Leslie had been surprised by Annie's frankness—in the past, she had seemed shy, even reticent about discussing her relationship with Richard. Today, despite her candor, Leslie couldn't help feeling that Annie was exaggerating the significance of Richard's actions, especially with regard to the roses. Richard had his quirks, Leslie would admit, but they were nothing more than that—just harmless eccentricities that Annie ought to be used to. An entire lunch devoted to such a trivial incident—ridiculous!

Sometimes Leslie felt Annie loved Richard a little too much. Being sensitive was one thing —Annie took certain actions and remarks too personally. It was as if, in her devotion to Richard, she examined everything he did and said in search of hidden meanings that might indicate displeasure with her, or even worse, a lessening of affection.

Leslie had seen enough shaky relationships and had even been in a few to know that Richard's and Annie's was built on a solid foundation. If only Annie would relax and feel secure in Richard's love for her. She had a good man there and should consider herself lucky.

Nearing the theatre, Leslie decided to have a talk with Richard. Keeping dead flowers around *was* a little weird, particularly when Annie had made a point of throwing them out. Perhaps something was troubling him. In any case, Leslie would find out. It couldn't be that serious.

Leslie entered the lobby of the theatre and paused at the box office window.

"Shirley?"

An elderly, grey-haired woman, sporting a pink carnation in her lapel, peeped through the box office bars.

"Good evening, Miss Bloch. Congratulations. We're getting mail orders through January. Today we must have sold five hundred tickets right here at the window."

"They're going to miss me at unemployment," laughed Leslie. "I practically have my own engraved chair in Section C."

"Listen, I've been there myself. I think we're in the clear for a while now."

"From your mouth to God's ear, Shirley. Hey, can you do me a favor? Would you put aside a ticket—something down front if you've got it—for a friend of mine tonight?"

Shirley checked the available tickets for that evening's performance.

"You're in luck," she said. "I've got a single, row D, right on the aisle."

"Terrific. His name is Michael Wingate and he'll probably have his cab double parked outside."

"Cab? Two to one he's an actor, right?"

"Is he out there?"

Leslie and Jill peered through a hole in the stage curtain, which afforded them a sweeping view of the audience. At two minutes to eight, the house lights had begun flashing to summon the crowd in from the lobby.

"There he is, fourth row, center aisle."

In a dark suit with a black silk shirt, Michael looked stunning. As he paged through his program, his delicately sculpted face seemed to reflect an intelligence and perception far beyond his years.

"You found *that* in a cab!" whispered Jill in mock disbelief. "He's gorgeous!"

"He looked good in the cab, but I must admit I'm impressed," said Leslie.

"If you'll pardon my French, he's tres chic."

Leslie stole another look through the curtain. A lock of Michael's hair had fallen down over his forehead, giving him a tousled look that bordered on innocence. Jill gave Leslie a playful jab in the ribs.

"How come when I take a cab, the driver

usually looks like The Werewolf of London?"

"Places, please."

Behind them, the stage manager was assembling the actors for the beginning of the play. Leslie and Jill hurried off to the side of the stage and took their positions for Act One.

"One minute to curtain," announced the stage manager.

"I had lunch with Annie today," said Leslie under her breath.

"How is she?" asked Jill absently.

"She was upset. She had a fight with Richard, but I think she's blowing things out of proportion."

Jill saw a hand come over her shoulder and reach to encircle her breast. Deftly, she sidestepped a leering Burt Shulman.

"Break a leg, you sexy thing," he whispered loudly, giving her a broad wink.

"Oh, Christ," said Jill, making a face. "Leave me alone. I'll break *both* your legs."

The curtain rose. Jill walked briskly onto the stage.

"Jill Martin, I'd like you to meet Michael Wingate."

Jill looked up from her dressing table to see Leslie and Michael standing in the doorway. Leslie was already out of her makeup and changed into her street clothes.

Michael extended his hand almost shyly. "Pleased to meet you, Jill."

Jill shook his hand. His grip was firm yet

gentle. Seeing him up close for the first time and clasping his hand, Jill felt an unexpected flutter of desire, mixed instantly with embarrassment. He certainly is attractive, she thought, too bad Leslie saw him first.

"I enjoyed your performance," said Michael, smiling at her warmly. Jill blushed.

"I wish you'd seen it on another night. The audience was a bit solemn tonight. Present company excepted."

Leslie was buttoning her coat. Jill laughed to herself at how quickly her co-star was spiriting Michael off the premises. Not that I blame her, she thought. If he were with me, I'd do the same thing.

Ten minutes later, Jill was still taking off her makeup when there was as soft knock on the dressing room door. It was Richard.

"Hi," said Jill, a little surprised.

Richard kissed her on the cheek. "How'd it go tonight?"

"You know that line: 'Are you an audience or an oil painting?' Tonight they were an oil painting."

Richard looked around the room uncomfortably. "Where's Leslie?" he asked.

"You just missed her," replied Jill, removing the last of her stage freckles. "She had a hot date."

"Oh," said Richard, his face showing disappointment.

"She broke the house record for getting out of here. I think she even beat out some of the people in the audience."

Richard smiled half-heartedly. "I'm sorry I missed her. I should have called first."

Jill splashed water on her face. Rubbing herself dry with a towel, she looked up. Richard was pacing uneasily.

"Is something the matter?" she asked.

"Why?"

"You're wearing a path in my carpet."

Richard stopped pacing and sat down on the edge of the dressing table. "I don't know. I've been feeling restless. I was hoping Leslie would be here. I feel like talking."

Jill studied him for a moment. "Where's Annie?"

"She's home."

"Is she okay? Is anything wrong?"

"She's fine. I just wanted to get out."

"So," smiled Jill, "let's get out."

It was nearly midnight when they ordered their third cup of espresso at the quaint and crowded Greenwich Village cafe nearby. Richard had unbuttoned his shirt and seemed more relaxed. Jill glanced at the clock. She hadn't expected to play Dear Abby on the subject of Richard and Annie for nearly two hours.

Richard lit a cigarette. "I really can't put my finger on it. I love Annie but she's bothering the hell out of me. I find myself getting aggravated by things that don't mean anything."

"What sort of things?"

"A random remark. A suggestion. But it's more than that."

"How do you mean?"

"Well, we'll be together for two minutes and I just want to be somewhere else. I never felt that before—not about Annie. It isn't even anything that she does—it's just a feeling that comes over me. It's kind of eerie, like I'm not in charge of my own emotions."

Jill paused. She took a sip of espresso. "That's silly, Richard, you're probably the most 'in charge' person I know. You wouldn't be here talking to me this way if you weren't."

"I don't know," said Richard, looking unconvinced. "I feel stifled."

Jill decided to try another tack. "How long have you and Annie been living together?"

"Just over two years."

"That's a long time, Richard. Maybe you need to get away by yourself for a week or so."

"Where would I go?"

"Take a cruise. Go to Bermuda. Go to the country."

"Maybe," said Richard, looking vaguely out the window. "I'm not sure that's the answer."

Leslie didn't know what was wrong. All day she'd been full of energy but now as she sat in the back booth of the Corner Bistro on Jane Street, she felt curiously drained, almost inert.

A Bunny Berrigan jazz standard blared from the jukebox as Michael handed the waiter a twenty dollar bill. The waiter cleared off their dinner plates and went to the bar to get change. Leslie cupped a hand over her mouth, hoping to conceal a yawn.

Tremendous, thought Leslie to herself. Here I am sittiing opposite this beautiful creature and I'm falling asleep. And it's not that he's boring. He's one of the most fascinating men I've ever met. Bet he's not used to this. I've been smothering yawns for an hour but I think he's noticed. Guess it was a fuller day than I thought. I'm exhausted. I'd better just tell him before I fall asleep in my wine spritzer.

"Michael, I don't know why I'm so tired," she said apologetically.

"That's okay. I understand. Why don't I take you home?"

"Oh, I'll just get a cab."

"Sorry," said Michael with a laugh, "mine's at the garage tonight."

"I hope they're fixing the shock absorbers."

"You hope. I bounce around in that cab so much I've got battle scars on the top of my head. Next week I'm putting in for the Purple Heart."

Outside on the street, Michael expertly flagged a taxi. He opened the door and helped Leslie into the back seat.

"Sure you'll be alright?" he asked.

"Positive."

He closed the door. Leslie rolled down the window. Michael took her hand.

"Thank you again for the ticket, I'll call you soon."

"I'd like that, Michael."

He leaned into the cab and kissed her gently but lingeringly on the lips.

Moments later, as the cab was racing east on

14th Street, Leslie, unaware of what she was doing, ran an index finger along the contours of her mouth.

"My, oh, my!" she said aloud.

The crowd at the espresso cafe had thinned out considerably as the hour approached one o'clock. Jill had given up on coffee and switched over to Amaretto but now the almond taste of that drink was beginning to get to her too.

Jill glanced at her watch. This is the last time I let Richard cry on my shoulder, she thought to herself. He's obviously troubled, but the incidents he's been rehashing for two hours hardly seem to warrant the emphasis he's giving them. A few arguments with Annie, and Richard's blown it up to the point where he thinks he's lost control of his own emotions. Jill smiled to herself. He should meet some of the actors I've worked with—that would show him what Out of Control really means.

Still, Richard was a dear soul and Jill knew that if the situation were reversed, she couldn't ask for a more sympathetic ear. And it wasn't as if he did this every day. As a matter of fact, Jill mused, this was the first time she'd seen him like this.

The waiters in the cafe began stacking chairs on table tops. A party of four exited the restaurant, leaving Richard and Jill as the only customers.

" . . . It's not that Annie is provoking me, maybe I'm overreacting. It's just that . . ."

Jill took Richard's hand. "It's getting late. Maybe you should call her."

"Annie? She's probably alseep by now."

"Richard," said Jill gently as the waiter brought the check, "I think you should sit down with her tomorrow and have a good long talk."

"You're probably right," said Richard, nodding his head thoughtfully, "but I really don't know what I want to say."

"That shouldn't be difficult," Jill replied. "You're the most articulate person I know. Tell her everything you've been telling me."

A new moon was high in the cloud-strewn October sky as Jill and Richard walked, arm in arm, through the near-deserted streets of the Village. As they reached an intersection, Richard turned to Jill.

"You're not far from here, are you?"

"Just a few blocks."

"I'll walk you."

"That's okay. You don't have to. I walk around down here at all hours and nobody's bothered me yet."

"It's late," said Richard. "I'd feel better seeing you home. And I can use some air myself. Besides, it's the least I can do after talking your ear off all night."

"You'll get my bill in the morning," laughed Jill.

"Oh," said Richard, raising an eyebrow. "What are you charging for consultations these days?"

"Fifty dollars an hour. But it's tax deductible."

"I'm glad we didn't stay for another espresso."

"If we had, Richard, the waiter would have poured it over our heads."

Richard grinned sheepishly. "I guess we were in there a long time."

"Are you kidding? They're naming the table after us."

Richard's laugh echoed through the quiet streets. Jill felt gratified. A couple of wisecracks never hurt, she thought.

Noiselessly, in the soft autumn night, the sleek black limousine drew even with them, then inched forward toward the corner.

Jill paid the car no notice. Richard's laughter ended abruptly, leaving a strained emptiness that sent a shiver down her spine. Jill turned to Richard but his eyes were following the limousine's progress. The car reached the corner and stopped for a red light.

"Is something the matter?" asked Jill.

Richard didn't answer. He had paused stock still on the pavement, three paces behind where Jill stood, a look of curiosity on her face.

Everything in Richard's field of vision fell away except the sombre lines of the hearse-like limousine. His eyes focused on the automobile's side-view mirrow which reflected a chrome framed cameo of terrifying loveliness.

The Woman had made her lips blood red just for him.

Her eyes seemed to drill directly into Richard's soul, laying bare his most primitive emotions. She licked her lips, running her tongue suggestively along their delicate outline, intimating a promise of savage passion that Richard had only allowed himself to dream about in his most private moments.

As he stood there like a sleepwalker, Richard sensed the extraordinary power that The Woman was exerting. Unlike the previous occasion, when she had used her luscious body to bring him to a state of arousal, she was now having a similar effect though all he could see was her face.

"Richard, is something wrong?"

Jill's voice seemed to come from a vacuum traveling down an endless corridor of deadening silence.

Richard continued to stare at The Woman. She smiled and nodded a wordless agreement. Richard trembled with desire.

"Richard, what the hell is it?"

Standing at his side now, Jill followed his gaze to the car's side-view mirror. The traffic light changed to green. The limousine began to turn the corner, but not before Jill caught a brief glimpse of its lovely passenger. The car disappeared from view.

"Who is that?" Jill asked.

Richard seemed to notice Jill for the first time. His expression was blank, almost dazed.

"I asked you a question," said Jill, making no effort to disguise her annoyance.

Richard looked away. "I've got to go home,"

he said, his voice barely above a hoarse whisper.

A baffled Jill watched as he lurched off down the sidewalk.

"Richard?" she called after him. There was no reply.

For the first time in her life, Jill felt afraid to walk down the street.

CHAPTER SIX

The Evil remembered death. And blood. Shivering in anticipation, it went back in time. It was of time itself. The cackling turned to demonic laughter and shook its soulless form. The Evil could taste the blood now. Its breath smelled of decay, its lips split open in an endless gash . . .

"So THERE I was, standing on the corner like an asshole," recounted Jill. It was early the next afternoon and she was just winding up her description of last night's peculiar events.

On the other end of the line, she could hear Leslie trying to suppress a laugh. "Oh come on, Jill, you sound like you were stood up on your first date."

"Leslie, I'm serious. It wasn't just that he was staring at this woman. It's like some kind of change came over him. I don't even think he heard me calling his name. And once the limo turned the corner, he just walked off and left me there. It was spooky. I hate to say it, but he acted like he was nuts."

"You're saying my brother is bonkers?"

"No, I'm saying that one minute he was Richard, the next minute he was acting like someone I've never seen before."

"It definitely had something to do with this woman?"

Jill paused. She stroked the fur of Kisser, her long-haired Persian cat which lay curled up on her lap. "I can't say for sure, but . . . yes, I think so. There was no one else he could have been staring at."

"Did you get a good look at her?"

"Well, the car was already moving by the time I spotted her, but she was very beautiful."

"Do you think she was someone famous? A celebrity?"

"Leslie, that wouldn't explain Richard leaving me there on the street. I mean he walked off like a zombie."

"A zombie?"

"Leslie, it all ties in. Earlier he was telling me he felt like he wasn't in control of his own emotions. And we know he's been arguing with Annie."

"And you think he's seeing this woman? Is that what you're saying?"

"I don't know. Maybe. But that's not even the point. The way he acted last night was enough to make me worry."

Leslie considered for a moment. "Annie's a little worried about him too. Maybe I should give him a call."

"Isn't he in school?"

"It's lunch time. I might be able to catch him."

"I hope I didn't alarm you," said Jill. "There may be a logical explanation for what happened."

"I hope so."

"By the way, how did it go with Michael last night?"

"I was waiting for that. Well, let's just say I was in bed by twelve fifteen."

"Oh, really?"

"And asleep by twelve twenty."

"That doesn't sound good," laughed Jill.

"It's not what you think, dearie, but I'll give you all the details when I see you."

"I can hardly wait."

"See you later."

Leslie hung up the phone. Now what, she thought. I've got two people telling me my brother's losing his marbles. And according to Jill, Richard himself is talking about having emotional problems. Leslie felt a pang of guilt. Maybe Annie hadn't been exaggerating yesterday.

Leslie picked up the receiver and dialed Richard's school. A woman in the registrar's office answered with academic efficiency.

"Brent School."

"Hello. Is Richard Bloch there? This is his sister."

"No, I'm afraid he's left for the day."

"But it's too early."

"He felt ill. He went home about an hour ago."

"Okay, I'll reach him there. Thank you."

Feeling anxious now, Leslie hurriedly dialed Richard at home. The phone rang seven times. On the eighth ring, someone picked up the receiver. There was silence on the other end.

"Hello? Hello, Richard?" asked Leslie apprehensively. The phone clicked in her ear.

"Jesus Christ," she muttered angrily.

When she redialed Richard's number, the line was busy.

"Please hang up. There appears to be a receiver off the hook. Please check your main telephone and extensions, then try your call again. Thank you. This is a recording."

Seated cross-legged on the floor of his living room, Richard scowled at the telephone, from the ear piece of which blared the insistent, condescending request of the phone company pre-recorded message tape.

"I'll hang up when I'm goddamn good and ready," said Richard aloud. "I don't need some public utility flunky telling me what to do."

Taking a throw pillow from the sofa, he smothered the receiver. The room was quiet again. If only, mused Richard, it was that simple to get rid of every annoying interruption. First my goddamn sister, than a New York Telephone tape. Won't anybody leave me alone?

His mind flipped back to the previous evening. Annie had been ridiculous. Trying so hard to be "understanding." What was there to understand anyway? A man needs his privacy and Annie, with that perpetual smile and overly supportive attitude, was enough to make you sick. Why couldn't she just let him be?

Then Jill. I never wanted to have coffee with her in the first place. All those prying questions of hers. She couldn't wait to get all the gossip on me and Annie. She missed the point of everything I was saying about what's going on in my head. And her final suggestion? A trip to Bermuda. Brilliant. But what can you expect from a second-rate, fucked up actress?

Now Leslie's on my case. Jill must have called her. Women really stick together, especially when they see a man trying to assert himself. They're all so concerned about Annie, but what about me? I love Annie. I just want some breathing room.

Richard was pacing now. He glanced at the digital clock on the book shelf. One thirty-seven. If he'd stayed at school, he'd have eaten an hour ago. No wonder he was starting to get hungry.

He cracked his knuckles nervously. Standing before the window curtain, he suddenly felt a twinge of excitement. He hesitated, then moved the curtain slightly, enough for him to peek out without being seen.

The terrace across the courtyard was deserted. The glass doors of that apartment were shut. The shades were drawn.

Richard's heart sank but he checked himself. I didn't really expect her to be there, he thought. The other night when I looked out it was like a dream. I wasn't even sure it was the same woman I saw on the corner in the rain. But last night was different. She was in that limousine. Jill saw her too.

Jill probably thinks I'm an inconsiderate bastard. Leaving her like that on the street. Too fucking bad about her. If she doesn't like it, let *her* go to Bermuda.

Richard mopped his brow. Funny that he should be feeling feverish and hungry at the same time. He drifted across the living room toward the kitchen.

The refrigerator was packed to overflowing, just as Richard had expected. "Goddamn Annie and her fucking health foods!" he exclaimed, as the opening door dislodged a box of red dates from one of the shelves. Richard caught the box and tossed it angrily onto the kitchen counter.

Poring over the carefully labeled plastic containers of sprouts, beans, rice and the like, Richard could feel his irritation growing. Annie's certainly staked out her territory here, he fumed. A man had to have the hands of Houdini to maneuver his way through this nutritional shit to get at something good.

Carefully, Richard extended his hand, reaching past a quart bottle of cranberry juice and over an aluminum foiled assortment of leftovers. His fingertips touched the cellophane of the bakery carton he'd been looking for.

"Jesus," muttered Richard, as he slid the

carton out of the refrigerator. "What a man won't do for a nice sloppy eclair!"

Tucking the box under his arm, Richard returned to the living room. He flopped down onto the floor, leaning his back up against the sofa. He reached into the box and took out a creamy eclair. He stuffed it into his mouth and licked his fingers greedily.

God, do I like to eat alone, reflected Richard. No utensils. I can chew with my mouth open. I can make as much noise as I want. I can get the icing all over me. It doesn't matter. Nobody cares.

Richard crammed another eclair into his mouth. The custard dripped down his chin onto the carpet. He chewed mechanically, smacking his lips.

"This is delicious," said Richard aloud. "Who needs Annie's fucking turnip surprise when I've got my eclairs? And I've still got four more to go!"

Custard feels so good in your mouth, thought Richard. It's creamy, sweet and cold. It even smells nice. But not as nice as roses.

He ran his fingers lightly along the surface of the antique vase that rested on the coffee table. Gently he lifted the dead roses from the vase, stroking them lovingly. He brushed the flowers against his face, breathing deeply of their stench. Tea leaves dripped from the petals onto his shirt. Richard didn't notice.

"You're such beautiful roses," said Richard. "Annie doesn't appreciate you but I do. She says you're dead but I say so what?" He chuckled giddily. "Dead things have a right to live too."

He stuffed another eclair into his mouth.

"Why did you hang up on me?"

Leslie brushed past Richard into his apartment. She tossed her hat and purse onto a chair and fixed her brother with a hard stare. Richard closed the apartment door and turned away.

"I don't feel well," he said, his voice barely above a whisper. "I've got a headache and I think I'm running a temperature."

Her vexation giving way to concern, Leslie placed a hand on Richard's forehead.

"You feel warm. Have you taken any aspirin?"

"No, I haven't taken anything."

"Go in the bathroom and take two aspirin."

"Do you really think so?"

"Richard, don't be silly."

"I'm not being silly."

"Take two aspirin."

"Okay."

Richard left the room, moving in a curious, wooden way Leslie found disturbing. I wonder if he's coming down with the flu, she thought —he looks like he's in pain just walking.

Leslie surveyed the living room. Noticing that the phone was off the hook, she replaced the receiver. The dead roses, laid out neatly in a circle on the floor, clamored for her attention.

"God, Annie wasn't kidding."

Making a face, she scooped up the flowers. The smell was almost overpowering. Bits of tea leaves and eggshell clung to her fingers as she hurried off to the kitchen area. She buried the roses deep in the trash basket.

No wonder Annie said he was strange, thought Leslie, as she rinsed her hands in the sink. Arranging those nauseating flowers in a circle—what's that all about?

"How did you know I was here?" asked Richard from the doorway.

Leslie glanced up. She toweled off her hands. "I called the school."

"Of course. How logical of you."

"There's no need to be sarcastic. I just wanted to talk to you."

"What did they tell you?"

"At school?"

"They didn't even miss me, right? The kids probably still think I'm there. They don't know the difference. They can't see me anyway."

Richard cackled derisively. Leslie frowned at him.

"Richard, that's an awful thing to say."

"It's gonna be a scream at rehearsal today. Juliet will probably fall off the balcony. Sword fight ought to be hilarious."

He laughed giddily, doubled over with a comic image of his students that Leslie couldn't share. She glowered at him reprovingly.

"I don't believe you said that! You love those children."

"How do you know who I love? I'm a teacher, Leslie. They're just a bunch of idiotic blind kids."

"That's sick," said Leslie evenly.

Richard rolled his eyes in mock frenzy. "Well, I *am* sick!" he bellowed dramatically.

Leslie paused, then ran the water in the sink. "I'm going to make you some hot tea."

"I don't want any tea."

"How about some hot soup then?"

"No, I don't want any. I've got food."

He turned abruptly and disappeared into the living room. Leslie filled the tea kettle. I could use a cup myself, she decided.

This was more serious than she had imagined. Flu or no flu, Richard had never spoken like this before. He doted on those students. He lived for them. Annie hadn't exaggerated. Something was definitely wrong. Very wrong.

She returned to the living room. Richard was spread out on the floor, looking dreamily at the ceiling. Leslie sat down on the couch.

"Have you called a doctor?" she asked.

"What for?"

"Richard, for God's sake, you just told me you were sick. If you don't feel well enough to go out, there's a doctor's service that will make housecalls. I think I've got the number in my bag."

"I don't need a doctor." Opening the cardboard box, he removed a chocolate eclair. He bit into it hungrily. "Do I look like I need a doctor?" he asked, chewing noisily.

"Yes, as a matter of fact, I think you do. You're running a fever. You look pale. You're saying things that don't make any sense. Things that are totally uncharacteristic. Richard, what are you eating? You're getting that stuff all over you."

"Haven't you ever seen an eclair before?"

"Yes, I have. But I don't think it's what you should be eating if you're feeling ill. Richard, you're making a mess!"

"Am I? Well, it's my apartment. I live here. I can make a mess if I want to. I can do anything I goddamn please!"

Playfully, he lobbed a handful of custard against the wall. It splattered and began dripping to the floor.

Richard grinned mischievously. "That looks good on the wall. I think I'll leave it."

"Have you lost your mind?" Leslie asked, struggling to remain calm. She made a grab for the eclair box but Richard was too fast for her. He pushed the box under a chair, out of her reach.

"Give me those! What are you, crazy?" Leslie was growing alarmed.

"I think you'd better go now. You're getting on my nerves."

"Oh, is that so? Well, *you're* the one who's behaving like a child—like some kind of crazy slob. I think you need help. I think you're freaking out."

Richard looked at her coldly. "I don't care what you think. I don't need you around. What are you doing here?"

"Richard, I'm your sister. I love you. Something's the matter. I'm concerned. And I'm not the only one."

She reached out to touch him but Richard moved away. "Just get out of here, Leslie, and don't pull that kid sister shit."

"It's not shit. Jill told me about last night. She thinks you're nuts."

Richard smirked. Custard trickled from the corner of his mouth. "Did that cunt also tell you she wanted me to fuck her?"

Leslie was shocked into silence. A tremor of fear ran down her spine. This man sitting across from her was not the Richard she'd always known.

She didn't begin crying until she was in the elevator.

Leslie tried three pay phone booths before she found one that was working. Her hand shook as she dialed Annie's number.

"Forgotten Lore Book Shop."

"Annie, it's Leslie. I think you'd better get home and see about Richard."

"What's wrong?" Annie asked anxiously.

"He's sick. He left school early. I just saw him and I think he needs help."

"You just saw him? I don't understand."

"Look, I'm standing on the sidewalk. I don't have time to explain. Just go home. Maybe you can do something for him. I couldn't."

"Leslie, don't just say that and hang up. What's going on?"

"Richard's not acting right. He's got a fever,

but I think his problem is a lot deeper than that."

"What do you mean?"

"Remember what you said the other day? That he was only strange when the two of you were alone?"

"Yes."

"And he was okay with other people?"

"Yes."

"Well, he isn't anymore."

"I was wondering when you'd get here."

Richard opened the front door wide for Annie and waved her into the apartment. She nearly tripped on the cord from the vacuum cleaner.

"Yeah, I know," said Richard. "Leslie told you I was sick. It was just a headache. It's gone now. I thought I'd do some cleaning."

Annie kissed him on the cheek. "A headache? You left school."

"I took half a sick day. I'm entitled. It's the first one I've taken this term."

"What's with the cleaning? I just vacuumed yesterday."

"Leslie's not exactly the neatest person. She even got custard on the wallpaper."

Annie sat down and kicked off her shoes. "I find that hard to believe," she said good-naturedly.

"Are you calling me a liar?" Richard snapped. He pointed across the room. "There's the fucking stain. Go look at it yourself."

"I see the stain, Richard."

"Good. Don't call me a liar."

Annie reached up and playfully pulled Richard down onto the sofa. Taking his hand, she cuddled up against him.

"Let's not fight. We've both got the afternoon off. We can make wild, passionate love. I'll wear that Frederick's of Hollywood number you gave me for Christmas. How's that?"

"It's about what I'd expect from you," said Richard, getting to his feet. He lit a cigarette. "You women think everything can be cured by a good fuck. Well, life's a little more complicated than that. If you want to get laid, why don't you go stand on 42nd Street? You might even make a few dollars."

Hurt and bewildered, Annie blinked away tears. For the past few days, she thought to herself, Richard has been argumentative. Now he's turning absolutely cruel. Here was the person closest to her in the world and suddenly she felt uncomfortable—even a little scared—to be with him.

"I know you're troubled about something, Richard. I just want to help."

"Sure," Richard cut her off. "Like Leslie wants to help. Like Jill wants to help. Maybe the four of us should have a good roll in the hay and everything will be alright, huh? Jill propositioned me last night and Leslie's been hot for me ever since we were kids."

Tears flowing freely now, Annie stood up. Cautiously she approached him. Richard puffed on his cigarette resolutely. Annie put her arms around him.

"Please don't talk like that, Richard. It frightens me. You know I love you. Let me help."

At first when Richard lifted her off the floor, Annie thought he was going to kiss her. Then she felt herself flying through the air. Her head crashed against the coffee table as she fell, knocking an antique lamp to the floor. A sharp spasm of pain shot from her ear to the back of her neck.

Richard was already on his way to the door. As he put on his jacket, he looked down at Annie. She saw shock and confusion in his eyes.

"See what you made me do," he said helplessly. "I've got to get out of here. I've got to get away from you."

There was something very final about the way the front door closed. Annie had the terrifying feeling she would never see Richard again.

But that was ridiculous, she reasoned. Richard would probably be back in a few hours and everything would be alright.

Still, Annie had never felt so alone.

There were two bars in Richard's neighborhood that he liked to frequent. The Blue Grotto, around the corner on Broadway, was posh and relaxing, with soft leather booths, lazily turning overhead fans, and imported beers on tap. Richard liked to drop in there for a drink or two when he was feeling sociable. The other bar, Burke's Lounge, a block further east, near a gutted-out building on Amsterdam, was dark and stuffy, a no-nonsense working class saloon. Richard ventured in there when he wanted to be alone.

Today was definitely a day for Burke's Lounge.

Richard sat at the bar, nursing a Budweiser. It was too early for the evening rush and there were only two other patrons on hand, one of them slumped down over the daily racing form. The television above the bar was turned to the 4:30 movie, a Godzilla picture that was being watched with casual amusement by Johnny, the ruddy-faced, formidable bartender.

"Don't look now, but Tokyo's in trouble," Johnny remarked, taking a sip of coffee.

Richard didn't answer. He traced a pattern in the wet ring which his glass had left on the bar.

"I always root for Godzilla, don't you?" chuckled Johnny.

Richard drew a series of connecting squares. He made no response.

Johnny glanced at the Budweiser bottle. "Can I get you another beer, Rich?"

"What?" asked Richard, looking up vaguely.

"Do you want a beer?"

"I'm fine, Johnny."

The bartender studied him a few seconds, then lumbered off down the bar.

That was the nice thing about Burke's, Richard had learned long ago. The people who worked there could read your signals. They'd initiate casual conversation and give you the opportunity to join in. But if you remained silent, they were perfectly happy to leave you alone with your thoughts.

Richard's thoughts had never seemed so tangled. He felt as if his brain were pounding with sharp images, random bits of conversation, flashes of insight—creating a jam-up that made it virtually impossible for him to concentrate on anything for more than a few seconds.

What was happening to him, anyway?

Jill's wanting to sleep with him was a total fabrication. Leslie had never spread custard on the wall. He was making up lies for no reason concerning people he really cared about. It's as if I'm trying to alienate them, he thought.

And those sadistic remarks about the students. Even as he heard himself speaking those insensitive words, he'd felt like an outsider, eavesdropping on his own existence.

Then the topper. Throwing Annie across the room. He'd never committed a violent act before. But he'd done it without hesitation and felt an odd sense of power at seeing Annie defenseless on the floor.

Then there was The Woman.

He had seen her three times now and on each occasion she had stirred him in a different way. Somehow, in some mysterious fashion, she had imposed her sensuous presence on the very fiber of his thinking processes.

Ever since that first night, on the rainy corner, Richard had found himself searching for her, hoping to see her at any moment. Her appearance on the balcony had left him eager for another encounter. And the glimpse he'd caught of her last evening was enough to make him feel he was in the grip of an obsession.

He had to possess her. She couldn't tease him like this. The next time they met, she wouldn't get away. He would have her. No matter what the cost.

"Need a refill, Rich?" called Johnny from the end of the bar.

"I'm okay," Richard replied.

That's a joke, he thought to himself. I've never been so fucked up in my life.

When it returned, The Evil would be beautiful, with a loveliness that none would be able to resist, yet none would be able to speak of. Its rotting filth would reach out with the caress of the damned. The night wind sang of The Evil's existence. In the dawn of the next day, the sun would mourn for its children.

"What's wrong with him, Leslie? What's *wrong* with him?"

On the other end of the phone, Leslie tried to sound reassuring. "Listen, Annie, calm down. I'll be over as soon as I can."

"Please hurry."

"I will. Bye."

Annie hung up the receiver. She felt a little relieved. Given Leslie's busy schedule, it had been a stroke of luck to catch her at her dance class. She needed a good friend to talk to and, maybe with Leslie's help, she could arrive at some plan of action that would convince Richard that he needed psychiatric care.

She glanced at the antique grandfather clock in the corner. It was nearly five. Richard had been gone for over an hour. Probably out for a long walk—maybe down to the boat basin for a bit of air.

Annie looked around the apartment. Fortunately, Richard's outburst hadn't done any damage. With all these collectibles in here, it could have really been a mess, she realized. She rubbed the side of her head. Even the stinging pain that she'd felt on hitting the coffee table had completely disappeared.

She put her shoes in the closet and stepped into a pair of house slippers. She was hanging up her blazer when a faint thought jolted her memory. She stood still for a moment, trying to recall something.

"The gold medal," she said aloud.

She reached into the pocket of the blazer. Her fingers touched the strangely cold embossed surface of the coin she had taken from Mr. Clark's drawer.

She held it up to the light. This, she considered, has got to be the most peculiar medallion I've ever seen in my life. And I've got to figure out a way to get it back into the desk before Mr. Clark misses it.

Again she examined the portrait of the beautiful woman. The serpent, in all its seductive splendor, filled her with the same mixture of excitement and desire.

"A snake crawling up your naked thigh. God, that's a hot image!"

Annie switched on a high-wattage lamp on a table near the window. She peered at the coin curiously. No names or dates, she observed. What kind of culture could have produced something like this?

Annie found herself wondering: was the woman on this coin drawn from life or was she the product of some artist's imagination? If she really existed, Annie thought with a giggle, that must have been some sexy modeling session!

Annie didn't know how long she stood there in front of the window before the shivering began.

An uneasiness, a dread, descended upon the room. Annie's heart beat wildly. Someone was watching her.

She turned. Her eyes darted about the room. The front door. Richard had closed it behind him. Had *she* remembered to lock it?

Suddenly the medallion was like a weight in her hand. She dropped it onto the table. It landed noiselessly on the crushed velvet doily.

The silence was shattered by a chime that brought a cry of fear to Annie's lips. Four more rings from the grandfather clock reminded her of the time.

"God, I'm a nervous wreck," she said with relief. She walked across the room and checked the front door. It was locked.

Well, that's the only entrance, reasoned Annie, if there's someone in the apartment watching me, they must have flown in through the window.

The window.

Annie whirled around. Standing on the terrace across the way, bathed in the late afternoon sunlight, with a startling beauty incongruous against the backdrop of a conventional West Side apartment, was The Woman.

Annie crossed to the window with no sensation of walking. She seemed drawn, almost magnetized by The Woman's very presence.

Her face pressed against the glass, Annie drew a deep breath, feeling the impact of The Woman's tempting appearance.

She stood, legs apart, in a revealing blood red net-like garment which clung to her voluptuous figure. Her jet black hair was tossed about by a slight breeze, giving her a look of playful innocence that was belied by her sharp, cunning stare.

The woman on the coin, thought Annie with a shock of disbelief. But that's impossible!

The Woman's smile, as if inspired by a direct line to Annie's thoughts, told her it was very possible.

Annie let out her breath. Trickles of cold sweat were beginning to flow. She grew tense.

She felt the first stirrings of an unexpected attraction.

Never taking her eyes from Annie, The Woman began to rub her body suggestively against the balcony railing. With each gentle movement, her knowing smile broadened. Teasingly, she eased down the zipper of the netted garment, letting it fall away with a flourish. Totally exposed now, The Woman licked her fingers tantalizingly with her tongue. She brought her moistened hands slowly down the length of her body, caressing her full, rich breasts, pausing dramatically just as she reached her parted thighs. As her hand went between her legs, she smiled wickedly across the courtyard at Annie.

With an embarrassed start, Annie realized that her own hands had followed a similar path. Her fingers were poised at the front of her jeans expectantly. She pulled down the zipper.

As Annie began to masturbate, an unspoken bond was born. It was as if The Woman were there in the room, next to her, coaxing her along, nodding her silent approval. Annie began breathing heavily, touching herself imitatively, with a gently rocking movement that was in intimate accord with what The Woman was doing fifty yards away.

Annie had never brought herself to such quick excitement. Her fingers, inside her silk panties, grew wet with urgent desire. She moaned aloud with pleasure.

She was nearing orgasm. She leaned back

against the couch, arching her body invitingly, giving herself up to The Woman's exquisite domination.

"Oh, God," Annie cried.

With a mocking, superior air, The Woman laughed, issuing a jubilant, ringing indictment of Annie's powerless situation. She threw back her head in delight, breaking the eye contact that linked Annie to a sexuality as frightening as it was irresistible. She glided from the terrace, disappearing into the apartment with a finality that left Annie jolted and unfulfilled.

She blinked her eyes as if awakening from a dream. Guiltily she drew the curtains and zipped up her jeans. She dropped down onto the sofa.

She stared at her hands which were still wet from her excitement. Seconds ago a woman had brought her to near orgasm; now all she felt was foolish and ashamed.

What in the world did I just do? Annie asked herself. That strange woman—how did she make me act that way?

She glanced at the gold medallion. I can't get over the resemblance, she thought. What's happening, anyway?

Annie could feel her puzzlement turning to anxiety. I need to calm down, she decided, reaching for her purse. She took out a bottle of Valium and shook one tablet into her hand.

"Everything's alright," she said, surprising herself with the sound of her own voice. "I'll just go get a glass of water, take a tranquilizer and I'll be fine."

She moved unsteadily across the room into the kitchen. She ran the water in the sink, letting it wash over her hands soothingly. She dampened a dish towel and pressed it against the back of her neck. She took the Valium.

Leaning against the refrigerator door, Annie tried to collect herself. What she had just done, standing there brazenly in front of the window, was insane. What if someone had seen her, masturbating like that? Someone from the other building. What if they told Richard?

Leslie would be here soon. Should I tell her what happened, wondered Annie. She'd never understand. She's coming over to talk about Richard's craziness, not mine. Suddenly Annie's fight with Richard seemed ages ago.

Annie closed her eyes. Whoever that woman was, this couldn't happen again. She must live in that apartment. Oh, God, she thought, I could run into her on the street.

I won't even think about that right now, resolved Annie, not with Leslie on her way. Richard may come home too. I'd better get my act together or they're going to wonder about me.

Without really thinking, Annie reached into a cookie jar on the counter. She bit into an oatmeal cookie, then snapped her fingers decisively.

Food! That was the answer. Puttering around the kitchen, putting together a meal, never failed to make her feel relaxed.

She opened the refrigerator and studied its

contents. Fish, she thought, no we had that the other night. Lamb chops—no, Leslie doesn't like lamb. Chicken—too boring. Maybe some vegetables. Let's see what's here. Broccoli, carrots, lettuce, tomatoes, cucumbers. That ought to be enough for a really nice salad. I'll top it off with some vinaigrette dressing. Three portions. Me, Leslie and Richard. If Richard doesn't make it home for dinner, it'll keep. He can have it later. Oh, please, just let him be alright.

Annie set up the vegetables on the counter and took a large salad bowl from the cabinet. With a slicing knife, she began cutting up the tomatoes.

That's better, she observed, I'm only trembling slightly now.

She broke apart some lettuce and placed it in the salad bowl, arranging the sliced tomatoes on top. She plugged in her La Mecanique food processor and lined up the salad bowl directly underneath. She fed a carrot into the top of the processor and watched with satisfaction as it appeared, fully sliced, in the salad bowl an instant later. She looked at her hands. The trembling had stopped.

Taking a large cucumber, she tried to insert it in the machine. Too thick, she noticed right away, the blade isn't catching. With her knife, she trimmed away some of the cucumber. She fed the remaining portion into the processor. It caught immediately and Annie pushed it further in. She exerted more pressure as the blade began its slicing.

"Get in there, you little bastard!" Annie chided.

The cucumber disappeared into the top of the machine.

"Next," she laughed.

She went to take her fingers away but the machine would not allow it. Her hand was being drawn into the opening and was only inches away from being wedged inside. With a cry of panic, she tried to free herself. Her fingers wouldn't budge.

Annie watched in horror as the rotor blade sliced off the top of her middle finger. She screamed with excruciating pain. A second later she recoiled as the fingertip shot out the side of the processor into the salad bowl.

She tugged violently but the machine seemed possessed by a magnetic force all its own. It whittled away at her fingers as she shrieked in agony. Blood and bits of severed skin flew into the salad.

"Oh, God," Annie pleaded, "help me!"

The machine had done its work. Annie's hand, reduced now by a third, was becoming too lean to remain wedged. She wrenched it free as blood splattered the kitchen walls.

She stared dumbly at the mutilated stumps of her fingers. In a state of severe shock, she never noticed that the machine, which should have clicked off automatically, was still going.

The horror was not over.

With a loud, whirring noise, the top of the machine flew off, seemingly of its own power, unleashing the deadly rotor blade. Spinning faster now, the blade rose up off its axis, aiming itself for Annie.

It shot forward, severing her throat. Blood was everywhere.

Annie was dead before she hit the floor.

The doorbell rang. Leslie was too late.

Part II

THE PRIEST

CHAPTER SEVEN

LESLIE SAT dazed, crying softly in a chair near the phone table. Her initial hysteria had given way to an overpowering sense of sadness, a feeling that she was lost and alone in a world of insensitive official activity.

Annie had been dead for less than an hour and already she was being depersonalized, changing into a statistic, another casualty on a sheaf of police records.

In the kitchen, Leslie could see two uniformed patrolmen methodically tagging items on the counter. Probably for evidence, Leslie guessed. Evidence of what? Annie's body, now bundled on a stretcher with a rubberized canvas covering, was all the evidence required. She was gone and that's all that mattered.

If only these people would leave, Leslie wished, glancing around the room at the police officers, morgue attendants and finally at a burly, disheveled looking man of about forty who was chain smoking mechanically, perched on the arm of the sofa.

Detective Davis. She had met him when he arrived. Seeing her state of near collapse, he had postponed questioning her, opting for an interview with the building super instead.

Poor Mr. Santana, Leslie sympathized, eyeing the slight, stoop-shouldered man who sat nervously next to Detective Davis. He was nice enough to let me into the apartment with his key and now look at him, he's almost as freaked out as me.

Detective Davis closed his note pad. Looking relieved, Mr. Santana got to his feet. Without even a nod in Leslie's direction, he scurried out of the apartment.

Leslie tensed. Detective Davis motioned for her to join him. God, she thought as she crossed the room, if only Richard were here—he still doesn't know.

Davis's tone was gentle but authoritative. "Are you feeling any better, Miss Bloch? Do you think you could answer some questions?"

"Yes, I'll try."

Davis reopened his note pad. "How long did you know Miss Mulligan?"

"Two years. She is—she *was*—my brother's girlfriend."

"When did you last speak with her?"
"This afternoon?"
"Could you be more specific?"
"About a quarter to five. She asked me to come over."
"Did she sound upset?"
Leslie hesitated. "What do you mean?"
"Well," said Davis, "you came here, rang the bell and when no one answered, you asked the super to help you gain entry to the apartment. Isn't that a bit unusual?"
"Yes, I suppose so. But Annie was expecting me. She wouldn't have gone out. She was anxious to talk to me."
Davis studied his notes for a moment. "Tell me about your brother—this guy she lived with. Any idea where he is?"
"No. Annie said he went out."
Davis cleared his throat. "Were he and Miss Mulligan getting along? Any problems between them?"
"No. Not that I know of. Why?"
"Well, she was anxious to talk to you. Was it anything to do with him?"
Leslie looked at Davis directly. "They'd had an argument. She was crying. She needed a friend—some sympathy."
"Nothing more than that?"
"No," replied Leslie, shaking her head.
"Was she in the habit of calling you every time she and your brother had a fight?"
"No. She'd never done it before."
Davis jabbed out his cigarette in the ashtray. His eyes narrowed. "Then why this time?"

"You don't think my brother had anything to do with this?" asked Leslie, her voice rising involuntarily. "That machine killed Annie. It was an accident. Anybody can see that."

Davis lit another cigarette. He shifted his heavy frame uncomfortably. "We've never heard of one of those machines doing that."

"I don't understand," said Leslie, fighting to control a sudden surge of anger.

"It just seems very unlikely."

There was a flurry of activity at the kitchen door. Leslie and Detective Davis looked up to see two morgue attendants, their faces indifferent, struggling to maneuver Annie's stretcher through the door.

Leslie felt the tears start up again. Davis pocketed his note pad and stood up. "Thank you, Miss Bloch. That's enough for now."

Leslie leaned her head back, resting it against the cushion. She closed her eyes, trying to blot out the scene that was all too real before her.

Annie's radiant face, with its perky, unaffected grin, swam into her consciousness, taking Leslie back two years to the first time they'd met. The occasion was a Bruce Springsteen concert at the Garden and, minutes after Richard introduced them, Leslie felt she was in the company of an old friend. To Richard's amazement, she and Annie had danced wildly in the aisle, yelled "Bruce" repeatedly at the top of their lungs and puffed from jumbo length Thaisticks that were being passed indiscriminately down the row. Afterwards, they'd commiserated like a pair of schoolgirls about the state of their eardrums, bar-hopped in the Village till 4 a.m., then topped off the evening with scrambled eggs at the Brasserie. Richard had christened them the Three Stooges as they'd lurched, arm in arm, up Fifth Avenue, watching the sunrise.

Something tells me, thought Leslie, Richard fell in love with Annie that same night.

Richard.

How long had he been standing at the front door? Leslie, her eyes open now, stared in shocked surprise at a pale, shaken Richard who wavered in wordless alarm, the door keys still in his hand, his eyes riveted to the rubberized stretcher that blocked his way.

"My God. Annie? Oh, no!"

But even as he spoke, the expression on Richard's face showed that he knew.

Leslie felt weighted as she crossed the room to her brother. It was as if she were trapped in some slow motion dream. She held out her arms to him but he seemed to be receding unalterably from her embrace.

She emerged from this remote void into the reality of holding an uncomprehending Richard as tightly as she could, aware that there was no way she could ease his pain.

On the other side of the room, on the table near Leslie's purse, the gold medallion gleamed menacingly.

Later, back in her own apartment, with Richard under sedation in the next room, Leslie couldn't remember the precise moment she had spied the medallion or even her reason for taking it. But now, as she turned it over in her hand, admiring the workmanship, she knew she had done the right thing.

Annie said it was creepy, thought Leslie, but it's really quite fascinating.

It was a gray, somber morning. In the sacristy of St. Matthew's Church, Father James Hamilton, S.J., was changing out of his altar robes into his priestly black suit. Carefully, he hung up his alb, the long, white linen robe he had just worn while serving daily Mass. He took another hanger from the closet and over it draped the red chasuble, the sleeveless outer vestment which completed his ceremonial garb. Hearing footsteps in the hallway, he turned to see two altar boys who had transformed themselves from cherubic acolytes to rough and ready street urchins in t-shirts and jeans in what seemed like record time.

"You guys are getting faster every minute," Fr. Hamilton observed with a smile. "You're making me feel old."

"Can we go now?" asked the taller of the boys expectantly.

"Did you put everything away?"

"Yes, Father."

"Filled the cruets for the next Mass?"

"Yes, Father."

The boys smiled gleefully as Fr. Hamilton launched into his familiar dismissive routine, in his best James Cagney accent.

"All right, you dirty rats, beat it, get outta here . . ."

Giggling delightedly, the boys disappeared out the door. The priest folded his stole, touched it to his lips and placed it in a drawer.

He flexed his muscles. At thirty-five, robust and in good health, he felt in top physical condition. Managing the school basketball team and working out twice a week at the New York Tennis & Squash Club kept him fit, as did a balanced regimen of high protein foods and vitamins.

Adjusting his clerical collar in the mirror of the closet door, Fr. Hamilton was an imposing figure, possessed of a face that was classically handsome. His hair, speckled with gray, brushed back over his ears, was long, even by Jesuitical standards but his cheerful grin, coupled with unmistakable charisma, went a long way toward disarming any straitlaced critics that might come along.

A blinking light on the wall phone caught his attention. He picked up the receiver.

"Sacristy. Father Hamilton speaking."

"Jimmy? It's Leslie. I have some bad news. It's about Annie Mulligan. There's been an accident. She's dead."

Fr. Hamilton listened in astonishment as his cousin outlined the grisly story of Annie's death. Though his closest ties were to Leslie and Richard, the priest, over the past two years, had grown fond of this honest, gentle woman whom he hoped Richard would eventually marry.

The senseless, sudden loss of a vibrant young person. This was always the most difficult kind of death to deal with, reflected Jimmy. Though he was a priest and had been trained to accept tragic events as part of a Divine plan, at times like this he never failed to think of his faith as being tested.

Yes, of course, he would say the Mass at Annie's funeral. As he gave Leslie his assent, his mind drifted back five years ago to a similar morning. The airplane crash that took the lives of Leslie's parents—Jimmy's Aunt Betty and Uncle Steve—had made front page headlines. They had been only in their late 40's, the prime of life. Jimmy was still a scholastic then, not yet ready to take his priestly vows, but he recalled the sorrowful funeral as if it were yesterday.

The funeral, the shared grieving, had brought Jimmy much closer to his cousins. Though they had grown up in neighboring towns in Vermont, their childhood meetings were confined mostly to holiday gatherings, birthdays and the like. Jimmy's vocation, which took him away to a pre-seminary academy, managed to separate them until the catastrophe of the jet crash brought them tragically back together.

Promising to meet Leslie that afternoon to make funeral arrangements, Jimmy hung up the phone. He stared out the sacristy window.

Dark clouds hovered overhead. Everything was still.

"The Lord is my shepherd, I shall not want; he makes me lie down in green pastures. He leads me beside still waters; he restores my soul . . ."

It was three days later, a balmy, sun-dappled morning, as Fr. James Hamilton intoned the words of the 23rd Psalm, standing in a cemetery, next to a flower-bedecked coffin, before a group of about 30 mourners who formed a semicircle around an open grave.

"He leads me in paths of righteousness for his name's sake. Even though I walk through the valley of the shadow of death, I fear no evil; for thou art with me; thy rod and thy staff, they comfort me . . ."

Fr. Hamilton paused, his eyes surveying the crowd, pinpointing Richard who was being supported on either side by Leslie and Jill. He's not holding up very well at all, thought the priest, noticing the young man's tears which were coursing freely down his face.

"Thou preparest a table before me in the presence of my enemies; thou anointest my head with oil, my cup overflows. Surely goodness and mercy shall follow me all the days of my life; and I shall dwell in the house of the Lord forever. Amen."

Taking a step forward to stand directly in front of the coffin, Jimmy sprinkled holy water on it. He made the sign of the cross.

"In the name of the Father and of the Son and of the Holy Ghost, Amen."

Several of the mourners echoed his "Amen." The priest closed his missal, signaling the end of the service. Several of Annie's friends and relatives began forming a single file, each throwing a flower into the open grave.

"Thanks, Jimmy," said Leslie, hugging the priest warmly.

"How's Richard?"

"Not too good, I'm afraid. He's still in shock."

Fr. Hamilton looked over toward the grave-site. There, head bowed, his feet planted firmly in the freshly turned dirt, Richard clutched a flower as though unwilling to part with the item which for him had become the last ceremonial vestige of Annie. After a moment, he dropped the flower and watched as it fluttered into the open grave. He turned away, taking Jill's arm, letting her lead him over to Leslie and the priest.

Fr. Hamilton put an arm around Richard's shoulder, feeling him grow tense immediately.

"I'm sorry, Jimmy," said Richard in a hoarse whisper. "I just want to get out of here."

"I understand."

Richard disengaged himself from the priest's grip and wandered off a few yards. He sat down on a large granite crypt and lit a cigarette.

"Do you think he'll be alright?" asked Leslie.

Jimmy nodded. "These things take time. But he's a good man from a good family. He's had to deal with sorrow before."

"That's true."

"He's going to need you. This is a time when the two of you can comfort each other." The priest turned to Jill. "He's going to need his friends too."

Jill extended her hand. "I wasn't sure you remembered me."

"Of course, Jill. Didn't we all go to the Joffrey Ballet that time?"

"Jill is in the show with me," offered Leslie.

"I haven't had a chance to see it yet," said Fr. Hamilton, "but I heard you were wonderful. Both of you."

"Thanks," replied Jill. "It's going to be rough going back there tonight and doing comedy."

Jimmy smiled encouragingly. "Sometimes work can be an answer. It helps take your mind off things."

Jill turned to Leslie. "Did you see Mr. Clark? He didn't even say a word to Richard. He just left the group as we were going by the grave."

"You mean the older man?" asked Jimmy. "I was wondering who that was."

"Annie's boss," explained Leslie. "I don't think he's a Catholic. Maybe he felt uncomfortable with the ceremony."

A cluster of mourners had formed, waiting for a parting word with Jimmy. As they pressed forward, Leslie took her cousin aside.

"Can you meet me for lunch tomorrow? I need to talk to you. It's important. It's about Richard."

"Richard?"

"Yes, Jimmy, there are a few things I haven't told you."

The priest studied her for a minute. "Yes, of course."

People were making their way across the grass to the flagstone path which led to the parking lot. Jill breathed in the warm Indian Summer air. The late morning sun glinted on the silver handles of Annie's coffin. It was hard to believe that her good friend was sealed up in that oppressive, impersonal container.

Poor, dear Richard, she thought. He looks so lost over there. And this is holy ground. He shouldn't be smoking cigarettes. But who's going to tell him to stop? I think it's time to go back to the car.

When she reached Richard's side, he gave no sign of noticing her. His attention was focused entirely on something across the gravesite.

"Richard. We're leaving."

There was no reply. Jill touched him gently on the shoulder. He moved away.

Following his gaze, an uneasy feeling welling up in the pit of her stomach, Jill looked out past the open grave, the casket, the mounds of dirt waiting to be filled in, to where a strangely familiar figure was standing.

It's a mistake, thought Jill, a trick of the light.

The Woman was the center of a small group

that included Mr. Clark. Yet somehow she seemed apart from them, as though occupying a special place all her own. Though her face was partially obscured, she radiated a powerful presence that was having a very clear effect on Richard.

He can't take his eyes off her, Jill realized. It's just like the other night with the woman in the limo.

But this couldn't be the same woman. That was impossible.

Instantly, The Woman's penetrating stare shifted from Richard to Jill.

Oh, God, thought Jill. She felt paralyzed. Why is she looking at me? And why can't I look away?

It couldn't be the same woman. Not looking so pure. So virginal. Not wearing the robes of a Roman Catholic nun.

CHAPTER EIGHT

"I'M WORRIED about Richard. He's been acting strangely for the past week—I mean even before Annie died."

Leslie toyed with her veal piccata, trying to keep her voice subdued in the close confines of the crowded family-style restaurant on Mulberry Street. Seated opposite Fr. Hamilton at a corner table near the front window, Leslie could observe the noontime congestion of shoppers, tourists, lunchgoers, scampering children—all on the narrow streets of Little Italy.

Jimmy poured some bardolino from a carafe into a pair of wine glasses. He extended a glass to Leslie and eyed her with concern.

"What do you mean, acting strangely?"

"Well, he and Annie had some terrible fights."

Jimmy twirled his spaghetti expertly. "That's not unusual. Couples quarrel."

"It was unusual for them. They almost never argued. Then recently something happened. Richard began picking on her for no reason. He'd start up with her about nothing and pretty soon it would escalate and he'd wind up storming out of the house."

Jimmy considered for a moment. "Perhaps Richard was growing tired of the relationship. Sometimes people pick fights when they're bored. Or to provoke the other person into calling it quits."

"That could be," Leslie conceded, "but Richard's always been the kind of guy to face a problem head on. He wouldn't play those games. Annie said he was behaving like a different person."

"Go on."

"I saw it myself. And for a while there, the police even suspected he had something to do with her death."

Jimmy took a sip of wine. "That's standard procedure. Detective Davis checked his alibi and there was no foundation for that."

"It's a good thing that bardender remembered."

Jimmy smiled. "Bartenders always do. What do you mean, you saw it yourself? What did Richard do?"

Leslie took a deep breath. "Okay. He's been telling outlandish lies. He said something to me the other day about Jill that was absolutely vile—and he never does that."

"You don't have to tell me," said Fr. Hamilton. "I can see you blushing already."

"Thanks. It was a pretty crude remark—something sexual. There's more. I went over to his house. He was running a fever but even so, there was no excuse for the way he was acting. He'd become obsessed with a bouquet of flowers that had been dead for three days. He'd arranged them in a circle on the floor with bits of garbage all over them. Then without even washing his hands, he started eating eclairs like a two year old, just stuffing them into his face. He even threw some custard on the wall. He frightened me. He called his students—those wonderful kids that he loves so much—'idiotic blind kids'!"

Jimmy's expression was thoughtful. "Do you think he's having some kind of a breakdown?"

"I'm not a doctor. It's hard to say. He's still functioning. He's still going to work."

"Does he go to a psychiatrist?"

"Not that I know of," replied Leslie. "Maybe he should. Maybe that's the answer. It's just that he doesn't seem like the same Richard I've known all my life."

"Do you want me to have a talk with him?"

"I think he'd listen to you. I tried. He threw me out of his apartment."

"I'll give him a ring. Maybe he'll come over for dinner. I'm not much of a cook but I can throw a couple of steaks on the fire."

"Thanks, Jimmy," said Leslie, pressing his hand. "I knew I could count on you."

"Well," said Fr. Hamilton, "after all, we are family. Now eat up. I've already finished my chicken and I'm starting to have sinful thoughts about the blueberry cheesecake over there."

Leslie relaxed. She felt better already. Talking about the situation had done her good. Jimmy was the person to convince Richard that he needed help. Leslie devoured the rest of her entree. She hadn't realized how hungry she was.

Over coffee, while Jimmy polished off the cheesecake, the conversation turned to lighter topics. Leslie filled him in on some of the backstage goings-on at "Straw Hat" and Jimmy surprised her by reporting that 77 year old great Aunt Gladys from back home in Vermont had phoned him asking if he could get her tickets.

Leslie opened her purse and searched for a cigarette. The sun, splashing through the front window of the restaurant, caught the shiny surface of something in Leslie's bag. Thinking it was her lighter, Leslie reached for it, only to feel a cold, round object that triggered her memory.

She lifted the gold medallion out of her purse. She hesitated, feeling a twinge of uneasiness. Oh, why not, she thought, I'm dying to know what this is.

"Jimmy? I want to show you something. I

don't mean to offend you, but I'm curious about this."

She handed the medal across the table. The priest examined it, looking at both sides. He frowned.

"Where did you get this?"

"It belonged to Annie."

"Did she tell you anything about it?"

"No, she was going to, but I didn't see her again."

"How did you happen to get a hold of it?"

"It was on a table in Annie's apartment. I don't even remember taking it."

Jimmy turned the coin over, weighing it in his hand. "Feels like solid gold. It's probably from the Middle Ages."

"How can you tell?"

"That happens to be my area of study. Particularly the fourteenth century. You know the Jesuits—they've got a man in every century."

"It looks sacrilegious. Do you know what it is?"

"I'm not sure," said Jimmy, holding the coin up to the light. "It could be some sort of occult artifact."

"Oh, dear, I hope I didn't upset you. It's just that there's something fascinating about it."

The priest's eyes met hers. "You mean the woman."

Leslie felt her face go red. "Yes," she admitted.

"Don't be embarrassed. I'm curious too. Do you mind if I hold onto it for a few days?"

"Sure. I'd just about forgotten that I even had it."

"My library has a shelf full of books on this period. I may be able to find out more about it."

Jimmy pocketed the coin. Almost instantly, he sensed that something was wrong. He shifted the medal to another pocket, away from his sacred rosary beads.

"Straw Hat" was an unqualified success. On the heels of the enthusiastic television and newspaper reviews came a wave of magazine notices which only served to lengthen the lines at the box office. The SRO sign was posted nightly and advance ticket sales were booming.

The atmosphere of a hit show pervaded the dressing room area. Congratulatory cards and telegrams decorated the makeup mirrors and what had once been bare, impersonal cubicles were, with the influx of personal items and gifts, taking on the ambience of home, signaling that the cast and crew were settling in for a long stay.

It was a few minutes before showtime, as Leslie and Jill sat before their mirrors, preparing for the evening's performance. The process of wig styling and the application of fake freckles had become rudimentary and the co-stars breezed through it with only the minimum of concentration.

"Leslie," said Jill, fastening one of her pigtails. "Do you remember that woman I told you about?"

"What woman?"

"The woman in the limousine that Richard was looking at the night he left me on the corner."

Leslie put down her eyebrow pencil and looked at her friend's reflection in the mirror. "Yeah?'

"Well, I think I saw her again, but you're not going to believe me when I tell you where."

"Where?"

"At Annie's funeral. I didn't want to say anything at the time."

"Which one was she?"

"You're gonna say I'm nuts, but I think she was the nun. Did you see the nun?"

Leslie resumed shading her eyebrows. "I remember a nun being there, but I didn't really look at her." She laughed nervously. "You're right—I think you're nuts. What would a nun be doing in a limousine?"

"I don't know," replied Jill defensively. "Ask Richard. He was staring at her. And he did the same thing at the cemetery."

"Are you sure it was the same woman?"

"No, I'm not sure at all. That's just it. Both times I only caught a quick glimpse. But each time she seemed to have this strange effect on Richard."

"Do you think she's really a nun?" asked Leslie, her voice betraying her apprehension.

"I don't know. Did Annie have a friend who was a nun?"

"She never mentioned any."

"Then who could it have been?"

Leslie stood up and adjusted her straw hat. "Maybe Jimmy would know."

A chilly wind was blowing as Jimmy left the city streets, passing through the gates of the cloistered grounds. Before him stood the clerical library, outlined against a bank of rolling cumulus clouds.

Jimmy was a familiar figure at the library. In fact, rarely did a night go by that he failed to put in an appearance there. Dressed in jeans and a turtleneck, he bounded up the front steps, opened the massive door and was greeted immediately by Mr. Lynch, the young scholastic who manned the central desk for the evening shift.

"Hi, Father, you're early tonight."

"I know. I've got a heavy work load."

"I'll blink the lights ten minutes before closing."

"Thanks," replied Jimmy.

Jimmy's mastery of the library system was such that he no longer had to consult the card catalogue to locate the books he required. Within minutes, he had found his favorite alcove, in a far corner of the third tier, and was diligently perusing several critiques of Thomas Aquinas for an essay he was working on, in hopes of submitting it to a religious journal.

Almost before he knew it, the library lights were flashing. Jimmy looked at his watch. He had been there two hours. He gathered up his notes and started downstairs. There was one more shelf he had to visit.

At the desk, Mr. Lynch raised an eyebrow, noticing the titles of the books Fr. Hamilton was checking out.

" 'Rituals of Devil Worship?' 'Cults Of The Middle Ages?' Father, I thought you were writing about the Angelic Doctor."

"Those aren't about Aquinas," Jimmy said with a laugh. "It's something else I've been asked to do some research on."

"I'm surprised we even have those books in here," said Mr. Lynch, handing them to the priest.

"It helps to know your enemy," Jimmy answered.

Back at his living quarters a short time later, Jimmy spread out the books on the long antique desk which served as his work space. His study was comfortable with a very lived-in quality; the walls were lined with book shelves. Relaxing into a large, overstuffed leather armchair, Jimmy took an address book from his desk drawer. He looked up Richard Bloch's telephone number, then dialed it.

The phone rang five times. Jimmy hung up.

Turning on a high intensity lamp, Fr. Hamilton examined the gold medal. Surely in one of these volumes, there would be some hint of what this fascinating coin represented.

He opened a book entitled "The Occult Revealed," hearing the binding crack. This one's been lying dormant for a few years, Jimmy surmised.

Once again, Jimmy drifted off into a world of research. Four volumes later, as his digital desk clock inched toward eleven o'clock, he was jolted out of his investigation by the ringing of the telephone.

"Hello?"

"Jimmy? It's Leslie. I'm at the theatre. We just got offstage a little while ago."

Jimmy glanced at the clock and chuckled. "I've got you to thank for the fact that I haven't done any work since I got home. That gold piece you gave me is making me nuts."

"Did you find anything out about it?"

"No, Leslie, I haven't gotten the answer yet, but it's been an interesting search."

"Well, I hope I'm not taking you away from your studies. I really appreciate what you're doing."

"Don't mention it. I love a good mystery."

"Good," said Leslie, "then I've got a question for you. Do you remember seeing a nun at Annie's funeral?"

"A nun? Yes, I did see a nun at the cemetery."

"Was she someone you knew?"

"No, I don't know who she was. I barely got a glimpse of her. I started to go over to her but she'd already left. Why?"

"Jill claims that this woman has come into Richard's life. According to her, she has a strange effect on him."

"What kind of effect?"

"I don't know. It could be that she's following him. I thought you ought to know because there could be some connection with the way he's been acting."

"Why would a nun be following Richard?" asked Jimmy.

"That's just it. We're not sure she is a nun."

"Has anyone talked to this woman?"

"No one's had the chance to," Leslie replied. "Jill and Richard are the only ones who have seen her. For any length of time anyway."

"Why do you think she's not a nun?"

Leslie hesitated. "Because Jill saw her last week in a limousine. She wasn't made up like any nun. She just stared at Richard like she was hypnotizing him. She did the same thing at the cemetery. Look, maybe you should talk to Jill. She can explain it better than I can. Is it too late for us to come over?"

"No, of course not. See you later."

"Thanks, Jimmy. Bye."

Well, thought Fr. Hamilton as he boiled some water for coffee, the sudden appearance of a bizarre woman in Richard's life could explain a lot of things. The arguments with Annie. His indifference to Leslie. Maybe I should call him again. No, it's too late.

Instead, he sat down at his desk, turning his attention to "Rituals of Devil Worship." He ran his finger down the table of contents only to pause in consternation at seeing the heading for chapter sixteen neatly scratched out. He turned to the end of chapter fifteen, at page 240. The next page was numbered 246.

An entire chapter was missing.

Grove Street was quiet. The lights from the last shop window had long since been extinguished. Only a few taxis roamed the area. The casual stroller, passing by the Forgotten Lore, would have had to press his ear to the store's service entrance to hear the sound of the strange, insistent chanting that was coming from the basement.

Downstairs, in the cellar, flickering candles sent shadows dancing wildly on the walls. The smell of incense permeated the air of the already dank room.

Mr. Clark's telephoning had produced results. Thirteen people were assembled in the basement, clad in loose-fitting black robes open to their waists. From each neck hung a gold medallion bearing the likeness of the beautiful woman.

At the center of the room, the focal point of the chanting, was an altar-like marble slab. On it stood a life-sized statue of the medallion figure, complete with serpent wrapped suggestively around her thigh, its tongue lapping anxiously upward.

"Ave Mater! Hosanna in excelsis! Ave Mater!"

The chant grew louder as the disciples swayed, moving to a rhythm from another age. Robes fell away. Hands reached out, caressing, groping. Several of the cult members slid to the floor, naked legs and arms entwined.

"Ave Mater! Hosanna in excelsis!"

Mr. Clark, his gray eyes lit with an unholy passion, bowed to the statue. Raising his hands, he addressed the gathering.

"Madonna walks among us again. Our strength is her life."

"What does this woman look like?"

Jimmy sat across from Leslie and Jill, stirring milk into his coffee.

"She's very beautiful," replied Jill. "Kind of exotic looking. She's got jet black hair, high cheekbones and these huge eyes."

Fr. Hamilton passed Jill the sugar. "I thought you didn't get a good look at her."

"I didn't. But it's not the kind of face you see every day."

"Tell him about what she did to Richard," prompted Leslie.

"Well," Jill went on, "when she looked at him, he kind of tuned out everything else around him. He just kept staring."

"Do you think Richard's having an affair with her?" asked Jimmy.

"I thought of that," answered Jill, "but why would she show up like that, in the limousine, at the cemetery? It's like she's taunting him."

"She even had the same effect on Jill," pointed out Leslie.

Jill blushed. "I found it hard to take my eyes away."

Jimmy took a sip of coffee. "You think she's following Richard?"

"I don't know," admitted Jill. "What was she doing dressed as a nun?"

"You're sure it was the same woman?" asked the priest.

"I think so."

Jimmy stood up. He'd always believed in hunches and Jill's description of the woman was really ringing a bell.

"Excuse me for a second. I just want to show you something."

He went over to the desk. The medal was still propped up against the high intensity lamp, yet it felt cold, almost icy to his touch. He handed the coin to Jill.

"Does she look anything like this?" asked Jimmy.

"Oh!" exclaimed Leslie, recognizing the medal.

Jill examined the coin carefully, turning it over in her palm. She placed it on the table.

"I'm not sure."

Leslie looked at Jimmy curiously. "You said this was from the Middle Ages. How could it be the same woman?"

"It can't," replied Jimmy, "but I've been looking at that coin all night and the description seemed to fit."

"It's got to be coincidence," suggested Leslie.

"Of course," said Jimmy with a nod. "I don't know why I did that."

It was after midnight when Leslie dropped Jill off at her Village apartment. Jill opened the door of the cab and put a consoling arm on Leslie's shoulder.

"Don't worry about Richard. I'm sure he'll be okay."

"I hope so," answered Leslie.

She waited until Jill was safely in her building before continuing on the few blocks to the brownstone where she lived. As she let herself in the front door of the building, she could already see a white, oblong box lying on the vestibule table. She collected her mail—two bills and a Publisher's Clearing House contest brochure—and smiled, noticing that the flower box was addressed to her.

Once inside her apartment, she unfastened the red ribbon and opened the box. Two bird of paradise flowers lay cushioned against a bed of greens and white tissue. Excitedly, Leslie tore open the accompanying envelope and read the hand-printed card:

"Thinking Of You, Michael."

So, she thought, today is ending on a hopeful note after all! Cradling the flowers in her arms, she hurried off to the kitchen to put them in fresh water. On the way, she flicked the "Playback" button on her phone answering machine. The first message was from Hal Weile.

"Hello, Leslie's machine. It's the next Edward Albee. When Leslie comes in, ask her to call me. Over and out."

Leslie ran the water, waiting for it to get colder. She could barely hear the second message, spoken in officious tones by a woman who seemed only vaguely familiar.

"This is Dr. Carmichael's office, confirming

your dental appointment for next Tuesday at eleven a.m."

"Oh, great," muttered Leslie. She turned off the water and arranged the flowers in a vase.

The third message began with loud, crackling static. As Leslie reentered the living room, she frowned at the machine. Suddenly she froze in her tracks.

From the speaker of the machine came the sound of a baby crying, in a pathetic sort of whimper. The cries were unnerving, as though the child were in pain. The static, brittle and intrusive, gave the tape an eerie, otherworldly effect.

The message ended. Her hand trembling, Leslie turned off the machine.

It must be a wrong number, reasoned Leslie. Some child playing with the telephone. When it heard my tape, it must have gotten scared and started to cry.

Leslie pressed "Rewind," then the "Playback" button. Again she heard the baby's mournful sobbing.

That child couldn't be more than an infant, Leslie concluded. There's no way it could have dialed a number.

Okay, said Leslie to herself as she sat down on the couch, there has to be a logical explanation for this. A wrong number. Some kind of practical joke.

The third possibility made Leslie wince: *someone is trying to frighten me.*

She dialed Jill's number. Her friend answered right away in a sleepy voice.

"Hello?"

"Jill? I want to play you something. Now don't get scared. It's a message that was on my machine."

"Okay," replied Jill.

Hearing the tape for the third time it seemed endless. Leslie clicked off the machine with relief. There was a moment of silence at the other end of the phone. When Jill spoke, she sounded fully awake.

"That *is* scary. Someone's got a weird fucking sense of humor."

"You think that's what it is?" asked Leslie anxiously. "A prank?"

"What else could it be?"

"I don't know. Who would play a trick like that on me?"

"You're not listed in the phone book, are you?" asked Jill.

"No," answered Leslie, "I haven't been for years. Not since I started acting."

"It could be a wrong number. Maybe the joke was meant for someone else."

"I thought of that, Jill. But who would do something like that with a crying baby? It sounds like it's in pain."

"You don't know it's a baby. It could be someone pretending."

"That's just as sick. What kind of person would do that?"

"Are you kidding? This is New York City. There's a lot of candidates for the funny farm out there."

"I suppose so," said Leslie, "but I can't help

thinking this was done deliberately—to make me feel afraid."

"Now take it easy," counseled Jill, "that's a big accusation. You don't have any enemies, not really. Who would want to frighten you like that?"

"I don't even want to guess."

"Are you alright, Leslie? Your voice sounds real shaky. Do you want me to come over?"

"No, I'm okay. It's just that I came home, I was feeling good, Michael sent me flowers—and then this tape . . ."

"I can understand," said Jill consolingly. "You want to know who did it."

"Yes, I want to know—but I'm afraid to find out."

"It is the east, and Juliet is the sun . . .
Two of the fairest stars in all the heaven,
Having some business, do entreat her eyes
To twinkle in their spheres till they return."

Donald Carter's deep, resonant voice filled the small classroom as he read from the Braille edition of "Romeo And Juliet." Late morning sun gave a cheerful glow to the four evenly-spaced rows of desks at which sat twenty students listening intently and following along on their own texts.

Richard sat at a large glass table near the door. Head down, he followed along in a standard Shakespeare. Tousled hair and a puffiness under the eyes testified to his recent ordeal but his innate good looks shone through, giving him a kind of rakish appeal.

The turmoil inside Richard's mind was a different matter entirely. He hadn't slept again last night. This was becoming a regular event—falling into bed exhausted in the early evening, only to toss and turn until dawn. Sleep seemed impossible, like some unattainable state that mocked him, just outside his reach. Even the strongest sleeping pill only lulled his body into a relaxed condition, while his brain raced ahead, sharp images flickering madly, at an increasingly accelerated pace.

In the morning he would try to recall the images that had tormented him. But they would disappear, withdrawing teasingly just as he was about to pinpoint them. Sometimes in the early hours there were voices too, quick, shrill and commanding, then gone before they could be understood.

Traveling to school had become a challenge. The crosstown bus ride, normally a humdrum affair, was fraught with anxiety. Sitting erect in the seat nearest the door, Richard would see things from the corner of his eye, dark clumps of matter scurrying crazily along the floor of the bus. He would turn his head quickly but nothing would be there.

The other passengers, once faceless forms in nondescript attire, now seemed to pose a constant threat. They whispered among themselves, casting sidelong glances in his direction. When he stared back at them, hoping to confront them on their own ground, they appeared to look away. Even when he buried his head in the Times, he felt them closing in.

When his stop finally came, Richard hastened out of the bus with relief.

Paranoia. The word itself made him laugh. Everyone talked about being paranoid in New York. It was a standard joke. But this was more than simple urban tension. Still, a part of Richard's mind knew that the voices weren't real, the fur-like shadows on the floor of the bus were imaginary, and his fellow riders cared as little about him as they did for the repetitious city landscape that rolled by the windows.

"Out of harm's way." Richard's pet phrase seemed to taunt him. It was hard to remember when he'd ever been "out of harm's way." And had he once dared to believe himself leading a charmed life?

"The brightness of her cheek would shame those stars,
As delight . . ."

Richard was jolted back into reality as he heard Donald's voice falter. He looked at his text. The phrase was a difficult one; Richard would have to help the boy through it.

" . . . doth a lamp," he prompted gently.

Richard raised his head. Donald smiled gratefully and resumed reading from his Braille edition. Richard's eyes traveled down the row of desks, taking in Sandy Phillips, who would be portraying Juliet; Johnny Green, his newly-chosen Mercutio; Angelo Torres, who would be playing Benvolio, Spanish accent and all . . .

Richard's blood turned to ice. He stared in disbelief.

At the end of the row, inconspicuous, demure in a conservative blue suit, watching attentively, was The Woman. She sat at the school desk, smiling slightly, hands folded before her, as if it were the most natural place in the world for her to be.

Oh, my God! thought Richard, catching his breath. How long has she been sitting there? The students can't see her. How long has she been observing me?

Richard opened his mouth. I have to speak to her this time, he knew. I can't let her get away. But what am I going to say? The students will hear me.

The Woman put a finger over her mouth to silence him. Richard obeyed. He looked into her eyes as Donald's recitation seemed to mock him.

"Her eyes in heaven
Would through the airy region
  stream so bright
That birds would sing and
  think it were not night."

Richard felt a stab of panic. The Woman was on her feet. She was heading for the door.

She can't leave, he said almost aloud. *I've got to stop her!*

He scrambled to his feet. His legs felt weighted. He kicked the chair back from his desk. His breathing was coming quickly now, in gasps. He started across the room just as The Woman closed the door behind her.

"Wait," he cried, stumbling in his haste. He crashed against the door. The room was suddenly hushed. The students' unseeing eyes were turned in his direction.

"Mr. Bloch?" asked Donald tentatively.

Richard tore open the door and raced into the corridor. He looked both ways.

The Woman was gone.

The football whizzed by Richard, narrowly missing his head.

"Hey, mister, get the ball," called out one of the neighborhood children.

Richard trudged along Riverside Drive, oblivious to the boy's demand. Seeing his apartment building at the corner, Richard's steps quickened. He had made it home safely one more time.

That had been a close call at school. What if the principal had walked in and seen that woman sitting there? How would he have explained it?

As it was, the students had sensed something was wrong. It had been all he could do to get through the rest of the period and dismiss the class, acting as if nothing had happened.

The Woman was getting closer. There was no pretending otherwise. Showing up at Annie's funeral in a nun's outfit had been a brazen, even defiant, act, but actually coming into the school, mingling with the pupils, this was an outrageous intrusion.

How did she know where to find me?

wondered Richard. That's ridiculous, he told himself, she knew where to find me those other times. The questions are: Who is she? And how did I let her get away?

Richard locked the door of his apartment. He took off his jacket and threw it over a chair. Going to the kitchen, he poured himself a Coke, sipping it distractedly. His brain was reeling from the day's events.

Richard felt tired. In the bathroom, he splashed cold water in his eyes. Toweling his face dry, he wandered into the bedroom. It would be good to get out of these clothes, into something more comfortable.

He opened the bedroom closet. On the inside of the door was a full-length mirror and Richard studied himself in it. I'm losing weight, he thought, running his hand along his jaw.

He took off his turtleneck and hung it in the closet. Doing so, he jarred the mirror slightly.

Nothing that had come before had prepared him for what was waiting.

Reflected in the glass, her dark hair framing her face, the blankets pulled up coquettishly under her chin, The Woman exuded an unspeakable radiance. Catching his eye, she smiled seductively, letting the covers fall away.

Her naked body, luscious and desirable, had haunted Richard ever since the day he spied her on the balcony. Now she was in his bed, moving the blanket teasingly downward, her eyes beckoning him to join her.

Or was she? Richard was afraid to turn around. At the moment, she was just an image in the mirror. If he spun around, she might not really be there.

"Who are you?" he heard himself ask in a choked, barely audible voice.

"I'm a woman who wants you."

Richard turned slowly. He could see that the image was real. This woman, whoever she might be, was there in his bed, fully uncovered now, her legs spread demandingly, waiting for him to move.

He eased down onto the bed. She took his hands and pulled him toward her.

"How did you get in here?" he asked helplessly.

She covered his mouth with a long, penetrating kiss. Her fingers loosened his belt and, in seconds, he was naked beside her. He buried his head in her shoulder, breathing in a perfume he'd never known before. Her fingernails raked his back, giving him a superb sensation of pain. She bit his lips, running her tongue along them thirstily. Richard moaned aloud with pleasure. Her hand reached between his legs, gently stroking him. She guided his fingers to her breast and moved them softly in a circular, caressing motion. Richard was totally under her control. Sweat poured freely from him, while she remained cool and aloof. The Woman moved him slowly down her body and Richard pressed his lips to her. She was moist and open. Richard explored her, savoring her warm pungency as she rocked rhythmically to his touch. Soon Richard felt her arms urgently encircling his shoulders. She kissed him hard and full on the mouth. Richard throbbed with desire, raising his body onto hers. Smiling, she maneuvered him onto his back and expertly mounted him. Richard thrust deeply into her. His eyes were closed, his head thrown back in ecstasy.

Detached, with a look of triumphant satisfaction, The Woman watched as Richard gave himself in abject surrender.

Later he lay like a baby at her breast. They were a study in contrast—he exhausted and drained of energy, she regal and untouched.

"Where are you from?" Richard asked softly.

"A place you've never dreamed of."

"No, tell me," insisted Richard. In his ear, he could hear her heartbeat. Or was it his own?

"Just rest," she said softly.

"You know, when I first saw you, I thought you were a dream."

The Woman's fingers played along the nape of his neck. "I am what dreams are made of," she said.

"That night when I saw you underneath the lamppost, in the rain, I felt like time had stopped."

"I remember."

"You felt it too?" he asked.

The Woman smiled. "Time is all some people have," she said, "but you have something more."

Richard was so drowsy. He loved the sound of The Woman's voice but the meaning of her words floated beyond him like an unreachable cloud. He strained to remain alert but it seemed hopeless.

"What do I have?"

The Woman smoothed his hair. "Rest now."

Richard tried to concentrate. Just to hold the most basic thought in his mind was an effort. Who was this woman who seemed to look right into his very soul? Richard felt as if today he had stepped off a cliff and was still falling. Just as in a dream, he thought.

But there was something that was supposed to happen to you, in a dream, when you finally landed. Richard couldn't remember what it was.

"What do you want with me?" But his eyes were already closing.

Richard never heard her answer. Seconds before he was asleep, he thought he heard, off in the distance of some unfathomable space, an infant crying.

CHAPTER NINE

The Evil reached out and touched The Woman, squirming and pulsating till it pushed its way into the depths of her body. It knew this body intimately. It had been here many times before, over many centuries. Through her eyes, it saw plague and famine. Through her hands, it felt pain and torture. It had experienced death, though it could not really die.

"WITH ALL these weird things going on, I really needed this," remarked Leslie as she turned off the phone message machine.

Fr. Hamilton sampled one of the stuffed mushrooms that his cousin had placed on the coffee table. Leslie removed the cassette from the machine and turned it over nervously in her hand.

"Could it be some sort of a practical joke?" asked Jimmy.

Leslie shook her head. "I've got some crazy friends but . . . no. Whoever made this call—I think they must be trying to frighten me."

"Well, it could have been a mixup. Maybe it was intended for somebody else."

"Yeah, maybe," replied Leslie, "that's what Jill said."

"What I can't figure out is the static," said the priest.

"I know. When it first came on, I thought it was an overseas call. It sounded like interference but after I heard it a few times, I began to get the feeling it was intentional."

"You know what? I've got a friend down at police headquarters who's an expert at sound analysis. Why don't I take the tape and play it for him?"

Leslie gazed out the window of her apartment. "To tell the truth, Jimmy, I was going to erase it. It's really starting to bother me—just knowing that it exists."

"I'm sure there's a logical explanation," said Jimmy. "Let me play it for Artie Wax down at the station."

Leslie pressed her hand to her throat. Her face was turning pale. The priest peered at her curiously. "What's wrong?" he asked.

"I feel nauseous. It's listening to that tape. The same thing happened last night."

His arm around her shoulder, the priest guided her to the sofa. He took the cassette from her hand.

"I'll take this now. You won't have to listen to it again."

Now as he drove his battered Volkswagen up Eighth Avenue, Jimmy could hear the sound of the infant crying in his head. No wonder Leslie had been scared, he thought to himself, the tape really stays with you. It's unnerving.

He stopped for a light at 43rd Street. On either side of the street, lights flashed from adult book stores, peep shows and triple X rated movie houses. Prostitutes lounged in doorways and nattily attired pimps paced about openly.

"Hell's Kitchen," said the priest aloud. The nickname for this, one of the city's oldest sections, had always intrigued him.

Driving through this part of town stirred ambivalent feelings in Jimmy. Though he was drawn to the scholarly, protected life he'd been assigned to, with its emphasis on history and tradition, he felt, upon looking at these sad, desperate street creatures, that perhaps he might better serve God by going among them, trying to help. After all, he pondered, hadn't Jesus shunned the academic world to walk among sinners?

The light changed and Jimmy proceeded uptown. Gradually the seamy streets of the West 40's receded, giving way to the more serene vistas of Central Park West. How quickly in this town, mused the priest, a person can go from squalor and deprivation to comfort and a sense of detachment.

Jimmy looked down at the cassette on the seat beside him. It would be nice to see Artie again. The priest's detective officer friend enjoyed a challenge and this tape seemed likely to give it to him.

Fr. Hamilton slowed his vehicle involuntarily as the castle-like contours of the Dakota loomed into view. As it always did when he drove by there, Jimmy's mind raced back to the December night John Lennon had been shot. There was madness afoot in these New York streets—no question about it.

Lately the madness seemed more pronounced. Or maybe, thought Jimmy, it's just touching me more directly. Annie's bizarre death. Richard's odd behavior. An elusive woman who seems to be haunting him. Now this disturbing message. Coincidence? Or were some of these events related?

Jimmy was still deliberating on these possibilities when he returned home to his apartment. He changed into his slippers and put a Rachmaninoff piano concerto on the phonograph. He sat back and closed his eyes, savoring the notes. In a world of craziness, there was always something soothing about classical music.

Jimmy opened his eyes. He reached for his telephone book. This would be a good time to catch Richard.

On the other side of town, the ringing telephone brought Richard out of a deep sleep. Dreamily he reached for the receiver. The Woman guided it into his hand.

"Hello?" Richard's voice was husky from sleep.

"Hello, Richard? This is Jimmy. I was wondering if you were free tomorrow night. I'd like you to come over and have some dinner with me."

Richard cleared his throat. "I don't know, Jimmy. Tomorrow night? It's kind of short notice."

"I realize that," replied the priest, "but I was hoping you'd be able to make it."

The Woman draped her leg seductively over Richard's thigh. She nuzzled him and ran her tongue along the folds of his ear.

"Go," she whispered commandingly.

"Leslie tells me you're doing 'Romeo And Juliet'," said Jimmy, pouring Richard an after dinner brandy.

The priest's dinner guest fidgeted in his armchair. On the table nearby, his meal had barely been touched.

"What else did she tell you?" Richard asked, a trace of scorn in his tone.

Jimmy studied his cousin. Richard was dressed in a suit but looked haggard and disheveled. The stubble of five o'clock shadow covered his face.

"Nothing," replied the priest. "She said she helped out during the auditions."

Richard smiled derisively. "She was only there one day."

Jimmy poured himself a brandy. He raised his glass sociably but Richard looked away. "How are the children enjoying Shakespeare?"

Richard shrugged. "They're getting through it."

"Leslie tells me you've really been working hard with them."

Richard's expression did little to conceal his annoyance. "Doesn't Leslie keep her mouth shut about anything?"

Jimmy paused. Richard's distracted, sarcastic manner was exactly as Leslie and Jill had portrayed it. The conversation during dinner had been forced with long periods of silence. If I hadn't initiated each topic, thought the priest, not a word would have been spoken. Now, with the evening almost over, Richard was turning distinctly hostile.

"Leslie also told me you'll be getting a few days off soon," said Jimmy, measuring his words carefully. "Maybe you should get away and relax for a little bit."

Richard eyed him with disdain. "Did Leslie also tell you to invite me over here for dinner?"

"As a matter of fact, she did," said Jimmy, meeting his gaze head on. "She's very worried about you, Richard."

"She's as bad as Annie," said Richard contemptuously. "Fucking cunts, both of them."

Jimmy sat up in his chair in shocked surprise. He hadn't expected this kind of outburst. His cousin was very sick indeed. He murmured a silent prayer. "Dear God, let it not be too late to help him."

Alison Bryant wanted to look older than her twenty-three years. But she needn't have bothered. Already she had a haunted, driven look in her sad brown eyes that was a dead giveaway to the kind of life she was living. The lack of laugh lines around her eyes was further testament to her unhappy existence.

During those rare times when she thought about it, Alison knew she pushed too hard and partied too long in her search to find contentment. Her parents had treated Alison with indifference as she was growing up, and the friends she had made—she could count them on one hand—were so wrapped up in their own lives that they didn't have time for Alison. Frantic self-indulgence seemed like a good answer.

So far in Alison's rather uneventful life, she couldn't remember even one day when she felt truly happy. But that was about to change tonight.

For weeks, Alison had a crush on Spark, a tall, brooding guy she had met at The Sphinx, a Lower East Side club inhabited by a punk crowd that she found exciting. She'd learned that Spark lived out on Long Island, about fifty miles away, and guessed that was the reason he hadn't asked her to spend the night. Alison hadn't been able to invite Spark back to the apartment she shared with her roommate, Janet. The flat was too small and Janet, the daughter of a Methodist minister, was a bit prudish. But Janet was away for a few days. Tonight Alison would make her move.

Alison had spent the day tidying up the apartment and most of the early evening relaxing in a bubble bath, bleaching her drab brown hair with blonde highlights and painting her uneven toenails a bright shade of magenta. Later, she stood in front of a full length mirror in the bedroom. She scrutinized her reflection. She wanted to look perfect tonight.

Alison's long shag hairstyle had been swept up with the aid of an entire can of hairspray to create points. Her eye makeup was heavy and she had applied lipstick so that her mouth had a strange pout. Alison ran her hands down her slim body. The black mini-skirt and off-white satin jacket looked great, she thought. Janet would be furious if she knew that Alison was borrowing that jacket for the evening. Fuck her, decided Alison.

She wiggled her small bottom and underdeveloped breasts in time to the Billy Idol record that was blasting on the stereo. She danced around the room, practicing each movement to make sure she looked as sexy as possible. Alison giggled out loud at the thought that Spark would be so horny for her tonight he'd be out of control.

She checked the contents of her purse. The gram of cocaine was tucked out of sight in her wallet. Alison couldn't afford to be spending money on drugs, not on the pay she earned as a secretary at a car rental agency. She had saved for weeks for this coke. Spark had better be worth it!

She turned off the stereo and gave the room a once-over. The place looked great; Spark would be impressed when they got back here. She had a half gallon of rose chilling in the fridge, she had drugs, and she would tell him she lived here by herself. Tonight belonged to Alison. The good feeling had been with her all day. Maybe my luck is changing, thought Alison. I'll splurge and take a cab to The Sphinx, she decided. After all, you only live once.

The ride downtown from the Upper East Side was bumper to bumper. Alison alighted from the taxi, giving the driver the finger. "Asshole!" Alison called out as the cab sped away from the curb. The driver had given her a hard time. Alison had told him to take Second Avenue but he'd insisted on the FDR Drive. The result was a $7.50 fare. Alison didn't tip him and he'd made some crude remark about her looking like a stupid whore with plastic hair.

The Sphinx was a converted warehouse. It had been gutted inside and a coat of black paint was its only decoration. Music blared from gigantic speakers in the dimly lit room. One of the club's chief attractions was that it had no special effect lighting at all.

Outside the Ladies Room, Alison pushed her way to the front of the line. "I'm gonna throw up," she warned, elbowing several women out of the way. She grinned. It always worked. Once inside the stall, Alison sniffed a few lines of cocaine, applied another coat of lipstick and sprayed cologne on her neck, her breasts and between her legs. She felt hot.

* * *

"Did I tell you I drove Jackie Onassis the other day?"

Michael grinned at Leslie, stirring his Scotch and soda as the Rolling Stones' "Emotional Rescue" blared from her speakers.

Leslie hummed along with Mick Jagger. "No, where'd you take her?"

"Would you believe Bloomingdales?"

Leslie waved a hand around her living room. "She's got good taste. I furnished half my apartment from Bloomingdales."

"It's lovely—very relaxing."

"Did she give you a good tip?"

"Jackie? Fifteen percent."

Michael moved closer to her on the sofa, drawing her toward him. Leslie eased out of his embrace gently.

"How was your audition?" she asked brightly.

Michael sat back. "Okay. I got a callback. It's a little theatre down in Soho that's doing a revival of 'Streetcar Named Desire.' Somehow I don't think they're gonna pick me for Stanley Kowalski."

Leslie reached for her white wine. Outside her range of vision for the briefest time, Michael's expression changed. His face grew harder. He looked at Leslie dispassionately.

She sipped her drink and leaned back, finding herself suddenly in his arms. His kiss was firm and insistent on her lips. Leslie responded eagerly but, after a moment, she pulled away.

"I'm sorry," she apologized. "It's not that I don't want to. It's just everything that's happened in the past few days. Annie's death, and I told you about my brother, Richard. I'm really worried. I just need a little time."

Michael cupped her face tenderly in his hands. "It's okay. I understand."

"Thanks."

Leslie felt a little foolish. She and Jill had often commiserated about the scarcity of available men in New York. Here she had one sitting on her couch, obviously attracted to her and she was turning him away. She hoped that Michael really did understand.

A few minutes later, as Michael was saying goodbye to her at the door, he looked at her earnestly.

"I'll call you tomorrow, Leslie, alright?"

"I'll look forward to it."

"You'll be okay," said Michael. "Things will work out for the best. You deserve it."

His kiss on her lips, brief but ardent, told Leslie she'd be hearing from him, just as he promised.

Richard's brandy glass remained exactly where Fr. Hamilton had placed it an hour earlier. A gloomy, almost surreal impasse had descended upon the room. A look of dull resignation was Richard's only expression. He can't wait to get out of here, thought Jimmy. If

I don't confront him now, he's going to be gone in two minutes.

"Richard, I'd like to ask you something," began the priest. "It's about this woman that you've been seeing."

Richard shifted in his chair, as though coming out of a deep reverie. "What woman? What are you talking about?"

"You know what I'm talking about. The woman in the limousine. The woman who came to Annie's funeral dressed as a nun."

"Oh, so Jill's been shooting her mouth off," replied Richard bitterly. "Another goddamn bitch."

Jimmy's face reddened angrily. "Let's leave God out of this."

"I'm sorry," Richard said softly, looking down at the carpet.

"Do you want to talk about this woman?" asked Jimmy, his tone inviting Richard to confide.

"There's nothing to talk about," said Richard evenly.

"Are you going out with her?"

"That's none of your business."

Jimmy considered for a moment. "You're right, it is none of my business, but your sister thinks there's a connection between this woman and the way you've been acting."

"The way I'm acting?" chuckled Richard sarcastically. "That's a good one. It's Leslie who's been hysterical. Spreading these stories about me. She exaggerates."

"I'm not so sure," said the priest. "She

thinks your health is deteriorating and I must say, looking at you, I'd be inclined to agree with her."

"What's that supposed to mean?" asked Richard defensively.

"You look tired. You're not eating." He pointed to the brandy. "That's Remy Martin. I've never known you to let a shot of good Remy just sit there like that."

"Well, I did lose Annie," snapped Richard, "or have you forgotten?"

The priest shook his head. "This was going on before Annie died."

"Oh, I see," rejoined Richard. "You people have been spying on me for awhile."

"No one's spying on you. We just can't help noticing what's going on."

"Spoken like a true meddler," said Richard icily.

Jimmy leaned forward. "This woman—I understand she's very beautiful."

"She's just a woman," replied Richard, shrugging his shoulders.

"What does she look like?"

"Will you stop with this woman?" Richard exploded. He slammed his hand down on the table. "I told you it's none of your business. You don't know her. You're never going to know her."

The priest got to his feet. It was time to play his long shot. "You're wrong, Richard. I think I may know her. I want to show you something."

He bounded out of the room, into his study.

Opening his desk drawer, he took out the gold medal. As before, it was unnaturally cold to his touch.

He returned to the living room. The front door stood wide open. Richard had fled.

The priest was becoming a bother, a regular pain in the ass, thought Richard, as he hurried down the street. It was bad enough when Jill and Leslie were giving me the third degree. Now I've got a holier-than-thou Jesuit sticking his nose into my affairs. He'd like to know what my lady friend looks like. I'll bet. He'd probably like to have her himself—forget about those vows of chastity! It's a fucking conspiracy—a trio of nitwits butting into my personal life. Well, this is all going to stop. I've answered my last prying question.

Richard continued to fume. But all the way home one thought was uppermost in his mind. Would The Woman be there in his apartment, waiting for him?

This afternoon had been devastating. Never had he felt so instantly turned on, so incredibly fulfilled. Whoever she was, The Woman was in his blood. He had to have her again. Over and over. No other woman would do.

He dreaded the thought of her not being there. What if she'd gone away while he was sitting there with that stupid priest? What if he never saw her again?

She had to be there. Hadn't she advised him to visit the priest in the first place? She wouldn't have sent me off like that if she hadn't intended to be there when I got back. Or would she? If she disappeared, I wouldn't know where to look for her. I don't even know her name.

Richard jumped from the taxi cab and raced into his apartment building. The elevator ride seemed endless. Richard was in a cold sweat by the time he reached his floor.

He inserted his key in the lock and opened his front door.

The lights were off but he could discern her in the slanting rays of the shuttered quarter moon. He breathed an audible sigh of relief. Naked, she held him spellbound from across the room.

Richard stood there motionless. He smiled gratefully. How could he ever have doubted she would be there?

Only when she held out her arms to him did he feel himself capable of moving. He rushed to the comforting circle of her embrace. He rested his head, childlike on her shoulder.

"Why did you tell me to go there?" he asked feebly. "It was horrible."

Her head back, staring off into the distance, The Woman caressed his neck consolingly.

"You must trust me," she whispered.

She kissed him on the mouth and began unbuttoning his shirt.

As Richard succumbed to her advances, a thought flashed through his mind: ever since that night he had seen her on the terrace, he had wanted to overwhelm her, to take her by force, to have her under his control.

But tonight, just as this afternoon, The Woman was completely in command.

Spark entered The Sphinx around eleven, as he always did. Alison's eyes picked him out as he moved toward the chrome bar. She smiled to herself. In a form fitting leather outfit, he looked delicious. Alison was at his side in an instant.

"I've been waiting for you," she said huskily as she took his arm. "I've got some coke."

Spark looked down at the girl. His face opened in a grin. "That's great, Ali. Let's have some."

Alison gave the packet to Spark and watched his tall, lithe body move across the dance floor toward the bathrooms. "I'll be waiting for you right here," said Alison.

She turned back to the bar and ordered herself another drink. Spark seemed really glad to see her, thought Alison. It was going to turn out alright tonight.

Someone tapped her on the shoulder. She looked up to see a young man sporting a bald head and five earrings in each ear. He asked her to dance. Alison waved him away. "Fucking turkey from New Jersey!" she mumbled under her breath.

In the Men's Room, Spark did two lines of Alison's cocaine, began to put the packet away, then changed his mind. He did almost half the amount before returning it to his pocket. The instant rush of the coke put him in a terrific mood. Alison wasn't too bad, he thought. A bit scrawny and, God, that makeup—but she would do. He knew she wanted him and, if nothing better turned up this evening, maybe he would let her sleep with him.

Spark stepped from the Men's Room into the dark, smoky club. At the other side of the room, lounging against the wall, untouched by the activities around her, dressed in black, with oversized dark glasses, The Woman seemed to blend into the surroundings. She went unnoticed by the manic crowd, but Spark saw her right away.

Even in the meagre light, Spark could tell The Woman was extraordinarily beautiful. So much so that he had to blink a few times to make sure she was real. He stared at The Woman and she smiled back. Spark felt privileged that she had picked him out. He shook off the slight feeling of fear he was experiencing and attributed it to cocaine paranoia. He walked toward where The Woman was standing but, as he got closer, she seemed to blend back into the shadows.

"Who are you looking for?" asked Alison as she peered up at Spark.

Spark nearly jumped at the sudden intrusion. He had been so taken in with The Woman that he had forgotten about Alison. Spark fought down an angry reply. "I'm looking for you," he lied.

"Good coke, huh?" said Alison eagerly. "I got some wine at home. Maybe you could come back to my place later on."

"Yeah, maybe." Spark passed the packet of

drugs back to Alison. "Listen, I gotta find someone. Some business I got to take care of. You wait at the bar, and I'll be back in a few minutes."

Alison's heart raced. Spark was going to come back to her apartment. She would finally have him to herself that night. "Sure," she said, trying to act nonchalant.

Spark barely heard Alison's answer. He was already heading in the direction where he had last seen The Woman. The loud music was beginning to get on his nerves. That's funny, he thought. Usually, the louder the better. His eyes searched for The Woman. *There.* He spotted her among some bikers. Oh, great, thought Spark. If they're trying to pick her up, I don't have a chance. If I put the make on her in front of them, they'll smash my head in.

The Woman turned. She said something to the bikers and they moved out of her way. She came up to Spark.

"Where did you go?" asked Spark.

The Woman took off her glasses. "I didn't want to make your girlfriend jealous," she said teasingly.

Spark stared at The Woman. For a second, it seemed as though her emerald eyes glowed with a luminous fury. Her scent, like a rainy forest, was making him grow dizzy. Almost at once, he felt his erection pressing against his tight trousers. It was not an unpleasant feeling. He had never forced himself on a woman before, but he could feel an overpowering impulse to push this woman against the wall and plunge into her right there, with all the people in the club standing around. At that thought, Spark turned to look—no one was paying the slightest bit of attention to them. It was like they were invisible, locked into another time, by themselves.

"Come here, Spark," The Woman invited. She stepped back into the corner and he followed. Her hand went to Spark's crotch, lightly stroking him there. Spark buried his face in The Woman's neck to stifle the moan of sheer pleasure that escaped from his mouth. Spark was aware that the music seemed to stop, even though the dancers were still moving wildly to it. It didn't matter. Nothing mattered but The Woman and what she was doing to him.

Spark started to make a feeble protest as The Woman unzipped his fly, but she silenced him with her lips. A moment later, she knelt before him, taking the length of him in her mouth. It was over quickly. The Woman licked at his seed as it came pouring from Spark. She rose and put her tongue in his mouth. He could taste himself on The Woman. He felt embarrassed that he had come in just seconds. That had never happened before. He reached to fondle The Woman but she pushed him away gently.

"I want you," pleaded Spark.

Suddenly, the music was back. Spark

grimaced as the sound assaulted his ears. The Woman was leaning against the wall, just as she had been before. She was wearing the dark glasses again, and just the whisper of a smile touched her face. Spark was disoriented. Could he have dreamed what had just happened? His hands went to the front of his pants. They were closed. He needed to ask The Woman what had happened, but his head throbbed with the rhythm of the blaring music. Just then, someone placed a hand on his back.

"Spark?" said Alison with concern, "are you alright?"

"Why the fuck did you sneak up on me like that?" demanded Spark.

Alison looked up at him in alarm. Spark seemed jumpy, downright scared. She eyed The Woman, who was moving away from them. "Let's get outta here," suggested Alison. "This place is for shits tonight."

Spark hesitated. He didn't want to leave The Woman, but something told him to go. "Yeah, okay. Let's get the fuck out of here," he agreed. He tried to sound casual, but his voice was pinched. He craned his neck, hoping for one last view of The Woman.

Alison took Spark by the arm and turned toward the exit. She couldn't resist tossing a triumphant look at The Woman. But when she sought her out in the crowd, what she saw made her blood freeze. The Woman had taken off her glasses and was staring at Alison. It seemed she was looking right into the core of

Alison's thoughts. A cold, hard gaze emanated from her. Though Alison had never confronted such a force, she knew without explanation that she was in the presence of pure Evil.

As Alison hurried outside, dragging Spark with her, she realized she had never been so frightened in her life. Or so sexually intrigued.

By the time they reached Alison's apartment, the dull pain in Spark's head that had started as soon as they left The Sphinx had turned into a pounding headache. Now, beginning to feel nauseous as well, he watched Alison darting about the small apartment, getting the wine, turning on the stereo, trying to make him feel comfortable. Spark wished he was somewhere else. He wished he hadn't left The Woman.

"Hey, Spark, you okay?" Alison's voice was in his ear. She sounded squeaky, like a little mouse, he thought. He laughed out loud.

"What's so funny?" Alison demanded. She sounded as if she had inhaled helium. That made Spark laugh louder.

Alison frowned. Spark hadn't said a word to her on the ride uptown and she was beginning to guess why. "Spark, did you want that woman? The one in black with the dark glasses?"

Spark looked away and smirked. "Oh, good fucking description, Ali. Half the chicks in the club looked like that."

Alison started to reply. Instead, she hesitated. She decided she wasn't going to do anything to ruin this night. If Spark was annoyed, she'd drop the questions and make her move. She knew how to put Spark in a good mood. She went over and sat next to him on the small loveseat.

"I can give you a good backrub," she offered. "Everyone says I have magic hands."

Alison began to knead the muscles around Spark's neck and shoulders. Her tiny hands felt like feathers on his back. He could feel the bile churning in his stomach. When his hands began to jitter as if he were a puppet being tugged by invisible strings, he shoved them deep into his pockets. Alison was starting to get on his nerves. Why is she talking non-stop? thought Spark. Why is she whining? From off in the distance, Spark could swear he heard a baby crying. But that was impossible. How could he hear anything over Alison's inane chatter?

"Alison, could you shut up for a fucking minute?" screamed Spark. He held his head in his hands.

Alison sat back on the couch as if she'd been physically struck. She watched Spark warily. "Spark, I haven't said a single word since I sat down."

Spark sat still under Alison's watchful eye. Okay, bucko, he thought, get a grip on yourself. Maybe the coke he had taken earlier was laced with something. No, that couldn't be. It was Alison's and she wouldn't have given him anything to fuck up his head this badly. Gotta pull yourself together, Spark thought.

"Sorry, Ali, I don't feel good."

Spark moved closer to the girl and put his arm around her. At least his hands had stopped shaking, he realized. He touched the thinness of Alison's shoulders. Suddenly, he felt brutishly strong. Like he could snap her skinny neck in one easy motion. Instead he moved his hand down to her breast. He began squeezing the tiny nipple through the sheer fabric of her blouse.

"Take off your clothes, Ali," he suggested in an oily voice that didn't sound anything like his own. Alison looked pleased. She stood, straightened her back and peeled off her clothing in just a few quick movements. Spark scarcely glanced at her. The throbbing in his head had eased but he felt disoriented. A thought nagged at he back of his brain. He tried to remember what it was he was supposed to do.

Alison was leading him into the bedroom now. He noticed her nudity for the first time. She moved in what she thought was an enticing manner but Spark could only look at her with detachment as if she were some kind of lab specimen.

He found himself sitting on her bed while she stood looking down at him, hands on hips, feet spread apart. Her skin was stretched over her bony frame. Spark could see her ribcage beneath her meagre breasts. Her hip bones jutted out angularly.

"Think I'm sexy?" Alison ran her tongue across her lips.

Spark made no reply. He pulled her roughly

onto the bed. Spark had an erection now, though he could not recall getting aroused. He began to undo his trousers. He spread Alison's legs apart, using his knee to make sure they stayed that way.

"Hey, not so fast, Spark," Alison protested, trying to take him in her arms. "We got all night."

Spark positioned himself and began to push into the warmth of Alison. He knew he was hurting her. It excited him. He drove harder.

"Stop it, you son of a bitch!" demanded Alison, attempting to twist out from under his body.

"Shut up, Alison. Isn't this what you wanted?" Spark couldn't stand the sound of Alison as she began to cry. Taking the pillow from behind her head, he placed it over her face. Her sobs became instantly muffled. There, that's much better, thought Spark.

His brain thundered in his skull. Conflicting emotions ricocheted through his mind. If he continued pressing down on this pillow, Alison would surely suffocate. But Spark was experiencing a rush of intense pleasure. He felt as though his excitement was perfectly aligned to the command of another being, an unseen voyeur whose image swam just beneath the surface of his consciousness. Spark bore down on the pillow with all his might.

Alison's spindly body thrashed like a wounded bird. Her shrieks of horror were reduced to a dull whimper. Her arms and legs flapped feebly as Spark threw his head back in a high pitch of orgasm. He exploded inside her and they both lay still.

After a moment, Spark stirred. He released the pressure on the pillow. There was no resistance. As though in someone else's dream, Spark moved the pillow aside and stared curiously at his handiwork.

Alison's eyes bulged. A thin trickle of blood ran down her chin. Her mouth was still open in a silent, accusing scream.

Alison Bryant had wanted to look older than her twenty-three years, but now she never would.

Spark eased himself out of her lifeless form. He got to his feet and stumbled off toward the bathroom. There, he vomited violently into the sink.

He looked at his reflection in the bathroom mirror. Tears were welled up in his eyes. He shook uncontrollably. A rage came upon him and he smashed his fist into the glass of the medicine cabinet.

"Oh, God help me!" he cried aloud.

Pain shot through his arm. He winced as he examined his bloody hand. Small splinters of glass were imbedded in his fingers. In the mirror, his face danced crazily, reflected in multiple shards of hanging glass.

With great care and selectivity, Spark decided upon the most vicious sliver in the mirror. Tenderly, he pried it loose from its moorings. It was long and triangular, perfect for what he had in his frenzied mind.

He ran his finger along the razor-thin edge,

admiring its sharpness. With a grunt of satisfaction, he loosened his collar. Then, with the grand sweeping motion of a symphony conductor, Spark brought the deadly triangle up to a point just behind his left ear. Deftly, he made an incision and smiled as blood spurted out onto the porcelain. Then, gripping the glass weapon tightly, he jabbed it deeper into the already open gash, puncturing the jugular vein. A torrent of blood gushed out like water from a faucet.

Methodically, Spark sliced downward along his neck, tracing a neat pattern from ear to ear. More blood sprayed from Spark's mouth, splashing against the bathroom fixtures. The skin of his neck hanging in tattered ribbons, his whole upper torso awash in blood, he slumped down to the tiles. The shard of glass slipped from his twitching fingers and slid harmlessly across the bathroom floor.

Within seconds, Spark's frantic convulsions ceased, while in another part of town, a chilled laughter rang out in victory, unheard in the silence of the night.

Leslie was in her pajamas watching Bette Davis in "Now, Voyager" when the telephone rang. She continued applying clear polish to her fingernails as Jimmy recounted the evening's conversation with Richard. When he had finished, Leslie tried to weigh the possibilities.

"Do you think maybe he's on drugs?" she asked anxiously.

"I wouldn't rule it out, but I don't think so,"

replied the priest. "And I don't think its grief over Annie either."

"And he didn't want to talk about the woman, huh?"

"He was very secretive, but somehow I think the woman may be the key to his problems."

"It's starting to look that way, isn't it?"

"Leslie," said the priest, "do you remember that coincidence we spoke about? Jill's description and the woman on the medal?"

"Yes," said Leslie uncertainly.

"Well, I went in the next room to show Richard the medal and he chose that moment to run out of my apartment."

"That's odd, isn't it? Did he know what you wanted him to look at?"

"Not really," said Jimmy, "but it almost seemed as if he did."

"How strange."

"Yes," the priest replied, "that's what I thought. Do you think perhaps you should give him a call?"

"I tried a few minutes ago. I think he has the phone off the hook."

"Well," said Jimmy, "at least he got home. Let's let it rest for tonight. I've still got a little bit of work to do before I go to sleep."

Remembering these words, five hours later, Jimmy smiled to himself. His "little bit of work" had turned into an almost obsessive research session as he pored over the volumes he had taken from the library.

With a half-eaten sandwich and a cup of coffee on his desk next to the gold medallion,

Jimmy had been patiently translating from German and Latin texts, making occasional notations on a legal-sized pad.

As his clock inched toward five a.m., Jimmy opened the book entitled "Satanic Cults." For a moment, he thumbed through the index, then turned to page 82. He skimmed over the page until something caught his eye at the bottom. He began reading:

"Little is known of the beautiful raven-haired woman depicted on the medal . . ."

The priest paused. He glanced at the gold coin.

" . . . but the Fathers of the Church believe that she is . . ."

Anxiously, Jimmy moved his hand up to the page on the right. Reading the first line, he frowned:

"the city of Frankfurt, located on the Main River . . ."

The priest stopped. It was numbered 87. Two full pages were missing from the text.

Jimmy made another note on the pad. This was the fourth time this had happened. In four separate volumes, key sections dealing with the gold medallion and the woman pictured on it, had been mysteriously deleted. It was as if someone were censoring details of her true identity.

Exasperated, Jimmy closed the book. He thought he knew who the censors were.

A ticker tape machine spewed out words into the darkness. He pressed closer, trying to get a look. The crowd closed ranks before him. He fought to get through but was knocked to the ground. A piece of the tape fluttered past him. He reached for it. He saw the words. German, Latin, French—with large spaces in between. The paper started to shred as if an invisible scissors were mutilating it. The pieces of ticker tape blew away. He struggled to his feet. The crowd was still watching the machine. He pushed his way through until he could see what they were looking at. The ticker tape had run out. Now the apparatus was spewing forth gold coins, like a frantic slot machine. The people surged forward, grabbing for the coins and hurling one another roughly out of the way. A coin flew into the air. Jimmy lunged wildly for it. He caught it and held it in his hand. From the surface of the coin, the woman's face challenged him and, as he looked at her resolutely, blood seeped from the metal and trickled down his arm. The woman's mocking laughter filled his ears, gradually modulating to the sound of his ringing alarm clock.

Jimmy sat up in bed. His hand trembling, he turned off the alarm. He felt his brow—it was wet with perspiration. He closed his eyes. He remembered the dream in vivid detail. That was strange, he thought, usually his dreams faded away the instant he woke up. He opened his eyes again. Jimmy had a feeling this dream would not go away.

An hour later, the priest was ascending the front steps of police headquarters, the gray municipal building that squatted amid the judicial and financial structures dominating the downtown area of Manhattan.

Detective Arthur Wax's office was on the third floor of the building. As a young policeman ushered Jimmy into the room, a thin, wiry man with glasses turned from a window which looked out on a brick wall and smiled a greeting.

"Well, Father Jimmy, what brings you down to this den of bureaucracy? Don't tell me you got a parking ticket."

The two men clasped hands. "No, Artie," laughed the priest, "but I had a close call the other day. I got back to my little VW just as a traffic cop was opening his ticket book. Fortunately I had my collar on and he was a good Catholic lad from Holy Cross."

"Say no more. I get the picture. We'll get you next time." He waved the priest to an aluminum folding chair nestled among banks of sound equipment. "What can I do for you?"

Jimmy took Leslie's cassette from his pocket. "I wonder if you'd listen to this, it's from my cousin's answering machine."

"What is it—an obscene caller?" asked Detective Wax.

"No," Jimmy shook his head. "Something a bit more puzzling."

The detective took the cassette from Jimmy and snapped it into the nearest recorder. He adjusted the sound as Hal Weile's message gave way to that of the dental secretary. After the second message clicked off, the priest nodded at Detective Wax.

"This is the one."

Wax turned up the volume. The two men waited. Ten seconds passed.

"That's funny," said the priest, "it was right there."

"Let me press 'Fast Forward.' Maybe it's a little further alone."

"No," replied Jimmy, "it was immediately following that woman from the dentist."

"I'll run it back," said the detective. "Could be the speaker gave out for a second."

Wax rewound the tape. Again they heard the first two messages. Again they listened in vain for a third.

The detective turned off the machine. "You must have erased it by accident."

Jimmy resisted the impulse to say "I doubt that—it erased itself," yet that thought was uppermost in his mind. This was crazy, he reasoned, a tape couldn't erase itself. Yet he and Leslie had heard the baby's crying and neither of them had touched the cassette since then. Perhaps someone else had. The tape had been in his apartment for a couple of days. Other people had been there—some priests, the housekeeper, Richard. It's conceivable someone could have played around with the cassette. But that's ridiculous—who would do something like that?

Who indeed? And how would he explain this to Leslie? Maybe it would be best not to mention it as long as she doesn't bring it up. Once things had calmed down a bit, he would give her the cassette and remark that it must have been erased accidentally.

The police art department was divided into three cubicles. Each boasted a drafting board and shelves which were overstuffed with art supplies. The first cubicle was empty and in the second Fr. Hamilton found his friend, Ray Price, a lean man, 35, meticulously handsome and, dressed in a Cerruti original, a bit too stylish in the drab civil service setting where he worked.

"Well, look who's here," he greeted the priest warmly.

"I was in the building, Ray, I hope I'm not disturbing you."

"I've always got time for you, Father. What's up?"

Jimmy took an envelope from his breast pocket and handed it to Ray. "First I've got a little present for you."

The other man opened the envelope. Inside were five postage stamps which had been torn from parcels. He smiled at the priest gratefully.

"You always remember," he said, examining the stamps. "Italy, Japan, Australia, Madagascar and Poland. Don't tell me—you're getting mail from Lech Walesa. Thanks, Father."

"Well, I know you collect them. I just saved them from being thrown out."

Ray replaced the stamps neatly in the envelope. "All the same, Jimmy, it's very thoughtful. I appreciate it."

"How's Ruth?" asked the priest.

"She's fine. She always asks about you. We have pictures of the baptism that you've never seen and Kevin is two years old already. You've got to come out to the house for an evening."

"I'd love to," replied the priest.

"Good," said Ray, "let's do that soon. I'll ask Ruth and we'll get back to you with a definite date, okay?"

"Fine." The priest paused. "Ray, I've got a favor to ask you."

"Sure, what can I do for you?"

Jimmy reached in his pocket for the gold medallion. He held it out to Ray. "Do you think you could do a sketch of this woman?"

Ray took the medal from him. He examined it carefully, scrutinizing both sides. "Where'd you get this—42nd Street?"

Jimmy chuckled. "Believe it or not, I think it's from the Middle Ages."

Ray crossed over to the window. "We don't get a lot of light in here considering it's an artist's room, but let me take a better look at this." After a moment, he turned to the priest. "Interesting face. Beautiful. Part of your research?"

"Yes," Jimmy nodded, "and it would help if I had a more lifelike picture of her."

"No problem."

Ray took a sketch pad from the shelf. He inserted a piece of carbon and began to draw the woman's face, his eyes darting back occasionally to the gold coin. Jimmy watched in admiration as a remarkable likeness took shape.

"Make her raven-haired," he prompted.

Ray deftly colored the woman's hair in black. He added some finishing touches and handed the completed drawing to the priest, who smiled at him in approval.

"You're amazing," said the priest enthusiastically.

"So is the face of this woman," replied Ray, handing Jimmy the original. The artist studied the carbon. "Where do I know her from?"

"She looks familiar?" asked Jimmy, sur-surprised.

"Vaguely, Father, you don't forget a face like that."

"I know," said Jimmy softly. "I know."

Jill peered at her reflection in the high-sheen polish of her coffee table. Satisfied with her cleaning effort, she recapped her can of Pledge and tossed it nonchalantly onto the sofa. Surveying her studio apartment, bright in the mid-afternoon sunlight, she considered her next chore. She turned off "The Doors Greatest Hits" and plugged in her vacuum cleaner. She clicked it on and the sudden whirring noise sent Kisser into a feline frenzy as he bounded up to the top ledge of the bookshelf.

Jill laughed at the cat's antics. "And stay up there," she commanded jovially, "or I'll Hoover you up, you little shit."

Jill adjusted the gauge control on the

machine to "light" and began vacuuming the sofa. Generally she found housework tedious but today she felt up to it. During the past week, the magazine drama critics had finally gotten around to "Straw Hat" and their words of praise for Jill's performance had been unanimous. This morning, she had seen *New York Magazine,* traditionally a bastion of faultfinding and critical nitpicking, and to her relief she had emerged unscathed. The critic had even described her as "winsome." It's almost enough to make me like cleaning, she thought.

The electrical hum of the vacuum blended with another sound. Jill listened, then dived for the phone.

"Hello? Let me turn off this damn thing."

She flicked the switch and heard Leslie's voice at the other end of the line.

"Hello?"

"Hi, Leslie."

"Jill, I've only got a second. What are you doing this afternoon?"

"Well, I *was* cleaning my apartment, but if you've got anything else in mind, just name it."

"I was thinking about going over to see Richard."

"Isn't he working?"

"No, I mean after school. I've got a commercial audition this afternoon."

"For what?" asked Jill curiously. "My agent didn't tell me anything."

"It's a suburban housewife, Jill," laughed

Leslie, "not your type at all. Some potato pancake mix. I thought I'd go directly to Richard's from there."

"Is Richard okay?"

"Well, Jimmy doesn't think so," Leslie replied soberly. "I thought it was just us but apparently Jimmy got a real performance the other night."

"What happened?"

"I'll tell you when I see you."

"Is it about the woman?" Jill asked.

"Yes," admitted Leslie. "Jimmy thinks she's the one that's making Richard act crazy."

"How can she do that?"

"I don't know," said Leslie. "That's what I'd like to find out."

Jill looked at her wall clock. "What time will you be at Richard's?"

"About three thirty."

"Good," said Jill decisively. "I'll meet you there."

As she hung up the receiver, Jill felt a twinge of guilt. It wouldn't hurt to be a little more understanding. Richard was obviously in need of some good friends right now. Besides, she'd had a taste of what that woman was all about.

She showered and dressed hurriedly, arriving at the bus stop nearest Richard's apartment at three fifteen. She stepped down from the bus onto the sidewalk, narrowly missing a broadly grinning, skateboarding youngster who was careening up Broadway, an oversized tape deck tucked under his arm.

Jill started down the street toward Richard's building. The sun, off the Hudson, gave a glare to the end of the block.

At first she didn't see them.

When she did, she was only a hundred feet away.

Richard slumped against the railing outside his front door. His jacket hung limply from his shoulders, his tie dangling from the side pocket. He twisted his hands nervously, jerking at the knuckles. Head thrown back almost lackadaisically, he stared westward toward the sun.

Beside him, her coolness contrasting with Richard's fevered intensity, The Woman gave off a majestic splendor that bathed the tawdry West Side street in an alien glow. Her white trenchcoat buttoned modestly up to her chin, she still communicated an eroticism that was undeniable.

Jill came to a dead stop.

My God, thought Jill in astonishment, she's absolutely gorgeous. No wonder Richard's been swept off his feet.

Who is she anyway? Well, this is the perfect time to find out.

She walked toward them. Instantly, The Woman turned. Her eyes found Jill's. She stared at her relentlessly. A faint smile crossed The Woman's face. Jill felt a sharp surge of pain, rising from her heart to her throat, then upward to her forehead. Her legs grew weak. Clutching her head, she leaned against a parked car.

The Woman's smile was one of exalted victory.

Taking Richard's arm commandingly, she steered him down the street in the opposite direction. His vacant stare hadn't left the sun —not even for a moment.

The couple disappeared around the corner.

Jill pressed her face against the roof of the car. A trickle of saliva escaped the corner of her mouth. The cold, metallic hardness of the roof was strangely soothing.

She was still there, her eyes shut tightly against the pain, five minutes later, when Leslie arrived in a cab.

"What's the matter?" she asked, taking Jill's head gently into her arms.

Jill hugged her in relief. "I'm so glad you're here. I saw Richard. He left with that woman. I don't think he saw me. But she did."

"Go on," Leslie prodded.

Jill gripped her throat. "I can't. I feel nauseous. That woman is beautiful, Leslie. Like no one you've ever seen. She looked at me and I couldn't move. My whole body started to hurt. I swear she never spoke to me or touched me. But I know she did this. She made me sick to my stomach."

"What are you saying?" Leslie asked, her voice trembling.

Jill looked her directly in the eye.

"She's evil. Richard doesn't have a chance."

CHAPTER TEN

It felt words forming in her mouth. It would be able to sing high praise to its Master once again. The Evil and The Woman were one now. They welcomed each other like sacred partners. The Evil could smell the scent of The Woman. It was animal. And sexual. It explored the inside of her womb. Knowing what once grew there, it became excited. The Woman's body was a holy temple. The Evil would worship her. It could feel The Woman breathing deeply as it nestled close to her heart. They spoke to each other using a kind of mad telepathy known only to beings who dwell in the sanctuary of the night.

JIMMY'S APPOINTMENT with Monsignor Hanrahan was for four p.m. that same afternoon. He arrived at the rectory at 3:45 and, seeing the time, laughed inwardly, reflecting that in ten years of knowing the Monsignor, he had never failed to show for an appointment early. I must be concerned about offending him by being late, he decided, and that's what comes of respect, but, after all these years, you'd think I would settle for just being on time.

The Monsignor's housekeeper, a white-haired matron with a pleasant but aloof manner, showed him to a chair in the waiting room and returned to her task of addressing manila envelopes.

"The Monsignor's on a conference call," she

explained, raising her voice to be heard over the clicking typewriter. "I'll buzz him when he's through."

"That's alright," said Jimmy. "I know I'm early."

The priest placed the three books he had brought on a nearby end table. He felt in his pocket for the legal sized pages he had torn from his notepad. Nothing's changed, he thought; even as a young seminarian, I was always anxious about being prepared.

Jimmy had first met Monsignor Hanrahan at a Jesuit retreat house in upstate New York. The older man had conducted a seminar on Pope John XXIII's reign and although Jimmy had disagreed with some of the Monsignor's conservative views, his conviction, his grasp of issues and his quiet, persuasive manner had impressed him.

Over the years they'd met periodically, their discussions sometimes taking on the air of a debate. As Jimmy cautiously advanced his progressive opinions, Monsignor Hanrahan deftly countered them, citing popes and theologians from every century. Despite their twenty year age difference and the older man's higher status, the conversations were invariably equitable, with each man listening thoughtfully to the other's point of view.

Still, considered Jimmy, as he sat patiently in the waiting room, he felt an overriding esteem for the Monsignor that often prevented him from pulling out all the stops in questioning some of the Church's traditional values.

He drummed his fingers on the library books. Today he wanted some answers. He couldn't let his admiration for the Monsignor get in the way of his obtaining them.

That's a bit strong, thought Jimmy, relaxing his fingers. Monsignor Hanrahan may know nothing about the missing pages. For that matter, they could have been cut out by some librarian or even by another researcher.

Somehow, Jimmy thought, there was more to it than that.

The light on the secretary's phone blinked off. The woman stopped typing and picked up the receiver.

"Fr. Hamilton to see you. He's a few minutes early."

Jimmy flushed as he got to his feet and started for the Monsignor's office. He had the uncomfortable feeling that this was not going to be easy.

The insistent blaring of an ambulance siren mingled with the blare of a police car as the two vehicles passed each other on 42nd Street and Broadway, going in the direction of two different emergencies. Nearby, the denizens of Times Square scarcely looked up from their sidewalk activities. Ambulances and cop cars were part of the area's routine and alarm noises that they emitted were as much a part of the neighborhood soundtrack as the anguished cries of junkies and the throbbing beat of highly amplified disco music. As pedestrians struggled to make their way through legions of loiterers and hawkers, the garishly-lit movie marquees promised feasts of sex, gore and kung fu violence, reducing even the most complex and artistic of Hollywood films to the common denominators that would lure the 42nd Street regulars into the dark, sadly deteriorated confines of what were once glorious Broadway showplaces.

Two drug dealers, propped up against the window of an all-night fast food restaurant, watched The Woman approach. The taller of the men whistled appreciatively through gleaming white teeth. He jabbed his companion roughly in the ribs.

"Look at that bitch. I bet she naked under that coat."

"She no hooker, man," his friend remarked. "I ain't never seen her on the street."

As The Woman drew nearer, her air was one of casual assurance. Hands tucked in the pockets of her trenchcoat, she seemed to clear a path through the sidewalk crowd as oncoming pedestrians and local "street people" moved instinctively out of her way. Her dark tresses glowed unnaturally in the surreal light of the overhead neon.

As she passed by, the taller man made sucking noises with his lips. He grabbed his crotch obscenely.

"I got some meat for you, momma. Right here. Make you feel real good."

His companion moved back into the protection of the restaurant doorway.

"Hey, don't mess with her, man," he advised. "She's trouble."

His warning went unheeded. The other man advanced on The Woman with a cocky swagger.

"Hey, bitch, I'm talkin' to you. I wanna fuck you. You hear that?"

His face was only inches from The Woman's when she turned calmly, giving him the briefest of glances. She smiled understandingly, but with a sharpness that stopped the man dead in his tracks. Without missing a stride, she continued on down the street.

The pusher stood riveted to the pavement. Seeing that The Woman had turned the corner, his friend scampered to his side.

"Hey, man, she look at you bad. You alright?"

"Yeah, I'm alright."

The smaller man pointed, laughing shrilly. "Then how come you just pissed in your pants?"

The other looked down in surprise. A stream of urine was running uncontrollably down his trousers onto the sidewalk.

Monsignor Hanrahan's study was spacious and airy, but a woodburning fireplace and richly ornamented oak furnishings gave it an intimate quality which was enhanced by the eighteenth century tapestries that hung from the walls.

The Monsignor, a slim, ascetic presence

whose aquiline nose threatened to obscure his thin-lipped sensitive mouth, squinted through bifocals in rapt attention as Jimmy, seated in a captain's chair opposite him, gestured emphatically at the open volumes before them on the table.

"They're all like this," said Jimmy. "Pages missing. Pictures scissored out. Sometimes they're replaced by other drawings."

The Monsignor nodded at the books. "These are from the clerical library, aren't they? These are Church books."

"Yes," said Jimmy forcefully. "That's what makes it so peculiar. It isn't as if just anybody could come in and tamper with them."

"What are you suggesting?"

Jimmy inhaled deeply. "I'm suggesting that somebody has systematically removed these pages."

"Somebody, meaning the Church?"

"I'm not saying that. Not necessarily. But I'm not ruling it out."

"Why would the Church do that?" asked the Monsignor.

"It wouldn't be the first time," said Jimmy gently. "The Church hasn't been above a certain amount of covering up in the past."

The Monsignor smiled indulgently. "This is the 1980's, Jimmy. We're not talking about the Inquisition."

"I know," said the priest, sitting back in his chair.

The Monsignor reexamined the texts, looking closely at the chapter headings and page numbers. Jimmy waited in silence. The Monsignor closed the books. He lit his pipe and puffed on it contemplatively.

"This research of yours—is it really important?"

"Yes," answered Jimmy, "otherwise I wouldn't be here."

The Monsignor passed the books back to the priest. "Well, I'm not familiar with any of this. Is there something you would like me to do?"

Jimmy's voice was firm. "I'd like you to speak to the Bishop."

The Monsignor blew smoke across the table. "Isn't that a bit extreme for a few missing pages?" he asked, his voice taking on a colder, more authoritative tone. "The Bishop is a busy man."

"I'd like to request it just the same," replied Fr. Hamilton, matching the Monsignor's measured cadence.

The older man paused. As he searched Jimmy's face, ten years of friendly debate seemed suddenly on the line.

"These missing passages—they all concern this woman?"

"Every one of them," replied Jimmy gravely.

"This woman—do you think perhaps she was a saint?"

"No," said Jimmy, the forcefulness of his answer surprising himself. "I think just the opposite."

After a wait that seemed interminable the Monsignor nodded his assent. "I'll set up an appointment with the Bishop."

"Thank you," said Jimmy with relief. He had cleared the first hurdle.

The hotel, a shabby five story building, teetered on the edge of decay at the corner of 43rd and Eighth. A blue, paint-flecked sign advertised rooms available for transients by day or night. Whores and winos slouched against the litter-strewn front steps which led to a dirt-encrusted glass labeled "Front Desk." Above, the narrow, rectangular windows, with their sooty, tattered curtains billowing inward, resembled mouths opened in silent screams of accusation and despair.

Room 501, at the top of a dimly-lit, dizzying flight of stairs, was a seedy masterpiece of claustrophobic gloom. Plaster hung in crazy patterns from the ceiling; the putrid yellow walls were caked with years of grime. The setting sun, its rays angrily diffused by clouds of industrial smoke and pollution from the factories of New Jersey, cast a strange, disorienting glow on the constricted interior.

The room seemed to tighten and exhale with every breath.

Next to the stained box spring mattress, wobbling on three legs, stood a broken-down night table, inscribed with initials and covered with a thin patina of filth. A desk calendar, courtesy of Murray's Tool & Dye, represented the room's only amenity.

The breathing grew more pronounced. Sighing was giving way to moans of passion.

On the mattress, her naked body writhing

with pleasure beneath the wildly thrusting man, her beautiful face soaked with ecstatic perspiration, The Woman gave herself completely. No longer the detached, controlled persona, she wrapped her legs eagerly around her lover, meeting each of his demands with the same uninhibited surrender. Like equally ardent combatants, they raged, kissing and biting, pawing each other's flesh, pushing each other teasingly toward ultimate release.

Moans of passion turned into cries of animal lust.

The sun's glow caught the icy fire in the eyes of The Woman. Her head thrown back in a delight of fulfillment, she shrieked madly, her body arched in a pose of savage pleading.

Above her, relentless in his loving assault, the man plunged deeper, roaring in bestial supremacy.

As her loins flooded in a spasm of yielding warmth, The Woman reached up gratefully to run her fingers through the thinning hair of her skillful and merciless lover, Mr. Clark.

As the evening performance of "Straw Hat" drew nearer, Jill entertained the thought of calling her understudy and asking if she would go on in her place. That "show must go on" crap was fine for summer stock, she decided, but whoever coined the phrase was probably never sick a day in his life. Besides, what happened this afternoon was no normal occurrence.

Leslie had been patient. Putting up with all

my talk about that woman being evil. Listening to me tell her that her own brother was doomed. She didn't buy it. Maybe if I hadn't been so hysterical. But I still think it's true.

She was a good friend. Practically lifting me into a cab, then taking me home and putting cold compresses on my head.

It didn't help. The pain and nausea went away as suddenly and mysteriously as they had come. Leslie had nothing to do with it.

Jill felt odd. It was as if that woman had willed her to be sick and then, after disappearing with Richard, had somehow restored her to health.

Was that irrational? Jill wondered. She'd read stories of people with the power to cast spells and will their victims into sick beds. And the papers were filled with reports of psychic healers who could cure from a distance. Could it be that this woman was gifted in that way?

But why would she do that to me, Jill asked herself. I don't even know her.

Maybe I should get to know her. If Richard really doesn't have a chance, she's got to be stopped. If she really is evil, then someone has to get Richard away from her.

But how? What if I see her again and she pulls that same stunt? I'd be too sick and too scared to ever find out who she was.

Too bad Leslie doesn't believe me, thought Jill. I could use an ally in this.

Jill reconsidered. Maybe she was being silly. That woman was mysterious all right but crediting her with supernatural powers was a bit farfetched. I've spent enough time thinking about her, she concluded, I'll be goddamned if she'll make me miss a performance.

Jill arrived at the theatre forty minutes early, pleased with her stamina and the ease with which she had transformed her mood. As she walked toward her dressing room, the stage manager looked up from his paperback.

"Can't keep you away from this place, huh?" he chortled.

"Show business must be in my blood," replied Jill, smiling broadly.

The stage manager groaned and returned to his Agatha Christie. Jill continued down the hallway. The silence was broken by a loudly ringing telephone. Only a few feet past the pay phone, Jill stopped.

"I'll get it," she called back to the stage manager. She picked up the receiver. "Backstage."

There was a pause. Instantly, Jill knew who was on the other end of the line.

The Woman's voice was throaty and persuasive. "I know you've been wondering about me, Jill. But I can explain everything."

Jill leaned against the brick wall, her surprise mixed with apprehension.

"How did you know my name?" she asked breathlessly.

"That's not important."

"Where did you get this number? How did you know I'd be here?"

"None of that matters. Will you wait for me

tonight after the show? At the theatre. Just the two of us. I want to talk to you alone."

"Who are you? Why did you look at me like that in the street today? What do you want with me?"

"So many questions," murmured The Woman. "Just meet me at the theatre. Nobody else must know. I want to tell *you* everything."

Jill felt the rough, exposed brick pressing into her back. She cast her eyes downward at the floor. In the cement, someone had carved the words "Snooky Was Here." Jill traced her toe along the letters and twirled the phone cord nervously.

"I'm not sure," she replied. "I don't like what happened this afternoon."

"Don't you want to know why I'm here?"

"Yes. And what you're doing to Richard."

"Then wait for me, Jill. We'll have a nice little talk."

Jill stepped away from the wall. She steadied herself.

"Yes, I'll wait."

There was a click at the other end of the line. Jill reached in her purse for her address book. She paged through it and took a quarter from her change purse. Jimmy answered on the first ring.

"Jimmy? It's Jill Martin. I'm so glad I got you."

"What is it?" asked the priest.

"I just got a call from that woman. The one Richard's been seeing. She wants me to meet her at the theatre after the show tonight. I'm not supposed to tell anyone, but I'd like it if you could be here."

"Have you told anyone else?"

"No."

"Good. I'll be there," promised Fr. Hamilton.

"He loves me . . . he loves me not . . . he loves me . . ."

The first act of "Straw Hat" had begun. Jill, downstage in front of a barnyard set, wearing her gingham dress, sat on a milking stool, plucking a prop chicken. Pulling out the feathers, she blew them playfully into the capacity audience, glancing quickly down the rows in hopes of spying the woman.

She spied her right away.

Resplendent in a red sheath evening gown, she occupied an aisle seat midway back in the house. Her hair was swept back under a turban, vamp style; a thin necklace of jewels glistened from her throat. Even in the dim light of the theatre, thought Jill, one couldn't escape her beauty.

Jill missed a beat. She could hardly remember her lines. The actor playing her father turned toward her.

"Daddy," she said, recovering, "I wish we could afford some flowers. I'm tired of working out my love life on a chicken's ass."

A hearty laugh rose from the audience. Jill shot a fast look at the woman. She was not smiling.

Jill felt a stirring. She crossed to stage left.

Even without looking, she knew that the woman's eyes had followed her.

Jill tried to relax. She had no speaking lines for the next two minutes. She could take a breather and . . . what was this sensation anyway?

She ventured another look. The woman regarded her intently, almost hungrily. Jill began to recognize the feeling that was fluttering inside her.

With an involuntary motion, Jill raised her hand. She caressed her neck tentatively. Once again she sought out the woman. She was mirroring her movements.

Jill took her hand away. So that's her game, she thought. She's trying to sexually arouse me from out there. And she succeeded. That's twice in one day she's controlled me. Well, I'm onto her now. She won't be able to do that again.

But Jill ran her hand lingeringly across her breast.

Jimmy had forgotten how difficult it was to find a parking spot in the Village. After driving around for half an hour, he felt exasperated and parked his VW across a driveway in front of Our Lady of Pompeii Church. He placed his "Clergyman On Call" card in the car's front window and escaped the premises guiltily before anyone could notice.

It was after ten p.m. when he reached the theatre. The ushers had left for the night and the lobby was deserted. The priest tiptoed inside and stood at the back of the house.

The final moments of "Straw Hat" were drawing appreciative laughs from the audience. Jimmy leaned on the back railing. He felt a trace of pride as he picked out Leslie onstage. She might look ridiculous in that country get-up he thought, but his cousin had come a long way.

"Looking for needles?" asked a shotgun-toting farmer.

Jill emerged from the upstage haystack, tugging a reluctant Burt Shulman in her wake. She brushed straw out of her hair and bounded sprightly downstage to confront the actor portraying her father.

"Daddy, it's not what you think!"

From the corner of her eye, Jill could see Burt looking a bit confused as he stood up in front of the haystack. Jill felt stupid. She had miscued a fellow actor, dragging him from the haystack before he was due to come out. Jill had been making tiny errors like this all night. It's that woman, she realized, just knowing she's in the audience has been throwing me off since Act I. Jill could only hope that her flawed performance had not been noticed by the rest of the people out front.

Well, she consoled herself, the show was almost over. She hadn't caused any major mishaps and, in a few more minutes, she would be offstage. What was she talking about, she asked herself in amazement. After the show she had to meet that woman. That was hardly something to look forward to.

Jill caught a slight movement at the rear of the house. Thank God, she breathed to herself, Jimmy had arrived. Surreptitiously, she'd been searching the theatre for him since intermission. It was a relief to know that he was here—she wouldn't have to face that woman by herself.

Jill was becoming aware of something. An extended silence had descended upon the stage. I forgot a line, she thought in panic. She concentrated. No, it was Burt's line. She turned. He was just standing there, dumbly holding his pitchfork instead of wielding it in self-defense.

He can't remember his line, Jill concluded. What the hell was it anyway? She struggled to recall it. She moved to the flat at stage left, hoping to hear the stage manager's prompting. Where was that jerk when you needed him, she thought in exasperation. Probably reading his damned mystery book.

Burt looked dazed and bewildered. He was staring downstage at a fixed point in the audience.

Oh, God, thought Jill, I know what's happening. A ringing tremor of fear shook her body. With mounting dread, she peered along the rows of seats, finding the face she wanted midway down the aisle.

She's controlling him, realized Jill, just as I thought. She's looking right at him.

At that very second, the woman turned

imperceptibly. Her penetrating gaze shifted from Burt to Jill. She smiled innocently.

Jill looked back at Burt. He blinked self-consciously, surprised at finding himself the center of attention. Belatedly, he assumed his character's stance of defiance.

Good, said Jill to herself, feeling as though she could cheer. Don't look at her. Don't let her control you.

Burt leaned forward. "I was just trying to sell," he stammered, " . . . trying to sell . . ."

Jill's heart sank. He was staring at that woman again. A rustle of audience impatience could be heard from out front.

"Liniment," prompted Jill, her voice several notches above a stage whisper.

"Sell her some liniment," blurted out Burt, his focus never leaving the woman.

Leslie moved to center stage. Good, thought Jill, she's trying to divert the audience's attention from Burt. Leslie crossed her arms angrily.

"Looks to me like you were giving her a free rubdown," she said, biting off the line.

The actor playing the farmer motioned to Burt with his shotgun. "Son, put down that pitchfork. We got us a wedding to discuss."

Burt Shulman seemed paralyzed. He cleared his throat but choked on his next line. Jill, Leslie and the other actors watched helplessly. There was an awkward pause.

The audience looked at Burt expectantly. The Woman looked at him with a certainty all her own.

From the semi-darkness of the house, she issued a silent command. Timeless, irresistible, it charted a course directly to his mind. Like a centuries-old intruder, it tore away the fabrics of conscience and morality, burrowing into the pure, primeval core, awakening sinister, barbaric impulses that would not rest until they could explode.

Burt raised his arm. With a bellow of ancient rage, he sent the pitchfork flying. It described a perfect arc to Jill's chest, piercing it, ripping deeply into her, driving her, with a sickening thud, onto the wall.

Impaled there, her torso a cavity of shredded flesh and gushing blood, Jill writhed in a seizure of convulsions, then was still.

The audience gasped as one. Burt's mouth dropped. He turned to the other actors in shattered dismay.

Leslie broke the stunned silence with a blood-curdling scream. She bolted across the stage to Jill's lifelessly hanging form and fell to her knees, sobbing uncontrollably.

The crowd was on its feet, surging toward the exit doors. Pandemonium was breaking out.

Jimmy had acted instantly, moving adroitly down the aisle, seconds after the pitchfork's prongs had embedded themselves in Jill's chest. He was almost to the stage when the alarmed mob rose from their seats, spilling into his way. Head ducked down, straightarming in his best varsity football style, he charged forward, casting disconcerted patrons roughly onto the floor. With a mighty push, he leaped onto the stage and raced to the hysterical Leslie.

"My God, call the police!" someone wailed.

Jimmy knelt down beside his cousin. He took her protectively in his arms.

A few feet away, a pair of burly stagehands had wrestled Burt Shulman to the floor. It wasn't necessary. The expression on his face showed that he would offer no resistance, that he would never register another emotion again.

Outside the theatre, The Woman stepped into the waiting shadows.

CHAPTER ELEVEN

"SHE TOUCHED audiences with her laughter and warmth. And for those of us who were fortunate enough to have known her and worked with her, she was a special friend. We loved her dearly. We'll miss her very much."

On the last sentence, Hal Weile's voice broke as he tried to hold back tears. He pulled up the collar of his overcoat against the raw October wind that whipped through the cemetery.

The playwright bowed his head reverently. The non-denominational service for Jill Martin was concluded. A crowd of mourners, many of them Jill's immediate family, filed past the bronze casket toward a row of waiting automobiles. Left behind was a circle of Jill's friends, among them Leslie, Fr. Hamilton and a curiously detached Richard.

Severely shaken, Leslie leaned on her cousin for support. Jimmy's firm-jawed visage strove for reassurance but was tinged with uncertainty.

Hal wordlessly embraced Leslie and Jimmy stepped aside. Spotting a familiar figure on the other side of the grave, the priest excused himself, placing Leslie in the playwright's care.

"I'll be right back."

Detective Davis grunted in recognition. Jimmy shook his hand.

"I've been dying for one of these," said Davis, cupping his hands to light a cigarette.

"Could I talk to you for a minute?" Jimmy asked.

"Of course, Father."

"How's Burt Shulman doing? Any change?"

The detective inhaled deeply. "No, he still hasn't spoken. He refuses to eat. They had to start feeding him intravenously. It's like he's in some kind of trance."

"Oh, that's interesting," replied Jimmy, glancing over at Richard.

"Yeah," continued Davis, "the people who were on stage said that something seemed to come over him right before it happened."

"It certainly seemed that way to me," Jimmy agreed.

Davis shook his head ruefully. "We get cases like this every now and then. Some ordinary guy just snaps, kills his wife and kids, whatever. People can be walking time bombs —you never know when they're gonna go off. This fellow, Shulman, though is a peculiar one. He acts without motivation, in front of a theatre full of witnesses and he doesn't snap back to reality. Usually they don't stay in a trance."

"You have no leads on why he did it?"

"Not really, Father. The backstage gossip was that he had a bit of a crush on the girl and she wanted nothing to do with him. But he was always coming on to women and they generally rejected him. Besides, that doesn't justify killing her—and in such a vicious, totally deranged way. No, this Shulman is unique. I've been on the force twenty years and I've never come up against a case quite like this one."

"Well, he could have just snapped, like you said," offered Jimmy.

"Oh, he snapped alright," replied the detective, "but I think there's more to it than that."

The priest digested Davis' remarks. "Would it be okay if I went to see him?"

The detective stubbed his cigarette out on the sole of his sturdy brown Oxford. "Could I ask why, Father?"

"I don't know. Just a hunch. Maybe I can help."

Davis paused to consider. "I don't suppose it could do any harm. I'll make arrangements."

Jimmy nodded gratefully. Seeing Burt was the next logical step. Though he was in a trance, he might be able to provide a slight response that would answer the question plaguing the priest's mind.

Jimmy had considered telling Davis about the woman's phone call to Jill but had decided not to. The case he was trying to build against this woman was so flimsy. What did he have anyway? A cousin who's been seeing her and acting strangely. A vague report about her dressing up as a nun. A farfetched coincidence that has her looking like someone on a gold medallion. And a phone call to Jill that wasn't even threatening, but conciliatory.

Davis wouldn't know what to make of any of that.

Neither do I, thought Jimmy, as he rejoined Leslie and Hal. Still, he was determined to follow through on his plan of attack. Somehow he felt that Richard's well-being might depend on it.

Hal was just saying goodbye to Leslie when Jimmy pressed her hand positively.

"We're going to miss you," said the playwright.

Leslie's eyes brimmed over with fresh tears. "I'll miss you too, Hal, but I could never go back to that theatre again."

Suddenly, her face blanched. She stiffened, drawing a breath in sharply.

"It's her," she said in a strangled whisper.

The two men looked in the direction she was indicating. Several rows of headstones away, the white-robed nun stood profiled against a blaze of autumn foliage. Her beautifully sculpted features were instantly reminiscent.

Leslie wrenched herself from Hal's embrace. She darted across the cemetery grass and hurled herself upon the unsuspecting woman, spinning her around violently.

"You filthy bitch!" she screamed fiercely.

The words were out before she could stop them. Leslie's knees buckled with embarrassment as she came face to face with the frightened and surprised Sister of Charity.

"Forgive me," Leslie gasped, "I thought you were someone else."

The nun regarded her in astonishment. Leslie backed off, feeling ridiculous and ashamed.

An hour later, Leslie had cornered Richard in his apartment.

"Enough is enough," she said vehemently. "I want to know who this woman is. Do you know that she called Jill the night that she died? Jimmy told me that. She wanted to meet Jill and 'explain everything.' Just what the hell does that mean, Richard? 'Explain everything.' Suppose you start to 'explain everything.' "

Richard nibbled at the cuticle of his right index finger. "I have nothing to say to you, Leslie."

"Oh, I think you do," his sister shot back. "Ever since your new 'ladyfriend' turned up, you've been deteriorating. Look at you, you're disgusting. Your hair is filthy. Look at your clothes. When was the last time you washed? This woman, whoever she is—the relationship —it's uhealthy."

Richard studied his hand indifferently. He bit off the fingernail and spat it casually onto the rug. "Are you finished?"

"No, goddamn it," Leslie stormed, "I'm not finished! This woman seems to have some kind of control over you. Not to mention the fact that since you met her, two people have died." Her voice softened. "Two people I loved very much."

"And I didn't love them," Richard replied caustically, "is that what you're saying?"

Leslie lowered her head. "That's not what I mean. It's just that her arrival in your life coincides with two very bizarre incidents."

"Annie's death was an accident," Richard said evenly. "Jill was murdered by some maniac in front of three hundred people. I think *you're* getting hysterical."

Leslie fought to regain her composure. "I'm not hysterical, Richard, I'm afraid."

"Oh, yeah?" Richard raised an eyebrow.

"I'm afraid you're going insane."

"Oh, is that your professional opinion?" asked Richard sarcastically.

"No, I'm not a doctor," Leslie replied wearily. Moving across the sofa, she touched Richard's arm lovingly. "Please let me help you. At least see a psychiatrist."

With a ferocious lurch, Richard pushed her away. Leslie fell backward onto the floor. She looked at her brother apprehensively.

Richard stood up and towered above her. "Why don't you mind your own fucking business? And stop shooting off your goddamn mouth to Jimmy."

"Jimmy wants to help you," she said, making an effort to keep her voice calm. "We both do. You've got to stop seeing this woman."

Richard smirked. "You don't even know her. You don't know what she means to me." He laughed cruelly. "She means more to me than you do, Leslie." His laughter accelerated. "More than you ever have or ever will."

Leslie surveyed him cooly. "More than Annie?"

Richard giggled. "That loser?"

Leslie gaped at her brother incredulously. "Oh, Annie was a loser?"

"She's dead, isn't she?" replied Richard icily.

Leslie rose slowly to her feet. This discussion was going nowhere, she decided. Richard was behaving like a five year old. It was impossible to get through to him. He's just challenging me, she realized, trying to shock me at every turn. He needed professional aid, that was all there was to it.

She steadied herself and faced Richard with conviction. "I can't stay here and listen to you talk like that. I can't stay here and watch you do this to yourself."

Richard grabbed her coat from the chair and jammed it roughly into her arms. "Good, I'll help you leave."

He began pushing her toward the door. She broke down, no longer able to refrain from crying.

"Oh, God, Richard," she sobbed imploringly.

Leslie crumpled to the floor but Richard lifted her immediately, seizing her by the arms. He yanked open the door and shoved her furiously into the hall. Nearly tripping over her coat, which had fallen in the scuffle, Richard swore. He rolled the garment into a ball and aimed it at her tear-stained face.

"You make me sick. You've always made me sick. You disgusting whore."

He slammed the door.

Leslie wrapped her arms around herself soothingly, rubbing the bruises that Richard had just inflicted. What had just happened was beyond the realm of credibility, she told herself. It was one thing for Richard to rave like a madman. It was quite another thing for him to exert physical force on his own sister. He had never done that before.

Leslie took a tissue from her purse and dabbed at her running mascara. I've got to get myself together, she resolved. I can't think straight standing here in the corridor. I'd better go home and see if I can put all this in perspective.

She was just about to start for the elevator when she heard the sound.

It was faint but unmistakable. And it was coming from behind Richard's door.

"Oh, dear God, please no," breathed Leslie, clutching her throat in fright.

The infant's pathetic cries were identical to the ones Leslie had heard on her answering machine. She pressed her ear to the door in horror. The child's whimpers grew louder.

Leslie put her hand to her mouth. She began to gag.

She whirled and ran head-down toward the elevator. The baby's wail followed her, transforming itself into a woman's mocking laughter.

Burt Shulman's room in the psychiatric ward was small and cheerless with iron bars on the windows. He lay propped up on the functional hospital bed, a network of tubes running in and out of his body. Next to the bed, machines recorded his vital signs. His brawny frame oddly dwarfed under the stark white sheets, he gave no indication of life, save for the slight rising and falling of his chest as he breathed noiselessly. He stared vacantly into space.

"He's been like that since he got here," remarked the nurse, an attractive, ebony-skinned woman who sat with Jimmy at the foot of the bed.

The priest searched Burt's face hopefully. "Do you think he can hear me?"

The nurse shrugged her shoulders. "We don't know. All his vital signs are normal. But he's not responding."

Fr. Hamilton nodded thoughtfully. He leaned forward, his face just inches away from Burt's.

"My name is Jimmy," he said kindly. "I'm

Leslie Bloch's cousin."

Jimmy waited optimistically. The patient gave no indication of hearing. His eyes remained riveted to the ceiling.

"I wonder if I could show you something," said the priest, undaunted. He reached into his breast pocket and unfolded the artist's sketch of the woman. As the nurse watched curiously, he held the drawing up in front of Burt's eyes.

"Burt, can you see this picture? Do you recognize this woman?"

Ten seconds passed. Jimmy was about to take the sketch away when Burt Shulman blinked. The priest waited anxiously, but Burt resumed his blank stare.

"Did you see that?" said Jimmy, turning excitedly to the nurse. "He blinked."

The nurse smiled sympathetically. "That doesn't mean anything. It could be just a nervous reaction."

"Of course," agreed Jimmy, "but I think he recognized the woman in this drawing."

"Who is she?"

"Someone who may have brought him to this very room."

For another quarter hour, Jimmy held up the sketch but there was no further response. His allotted visiting time over and, with the nurse beginning to regard him quizzically, Jimmy took his leave, forced to be content with that solitary blink.

All the way across town, in the snarl of lunch hour traffic, Jimmy had time to think about what had just occurred. Granted Burt's blink might have been just a nervous flicker as the nurse had suggested. But somehow it seemed to tie in with the way Burt had focused from the stage on someone in the "Straw Hat" audience seconds before throwing the pitch-fork into Jill. The priest tried to be logical. We know, he said to himself as he paused for yet another traffic light, that the woman called Jill the afternoon of her death. There is a strong possibility she attended the performance. And Burt was looking intently down the center aisle, almost as if waiting for instructions. She seems to have an extraordinary effect on people just by staring at them—is it too preposterous to think that she might have used some kind of mind control to make Burt do what he did?

And my cousin seems to be falling under her spell, he thought with a mixture of anger and fear.

Then there was the medallion. The books. The missing pages. Where does all that come in? Was there any connection between the woman on the coin and this strange figure who was popping up everywhere?

It could be just my overactive imagination, considered Jimmy, but there were a few too many coincidences to ignore.

Perhaps, he thought as he gunned his car engine, my next appointment will provide some answers.

"Fr. Hamilton, how long have you been a priest?"

Bishop Thomas Aloysius Walsh stirred his demitasse and peered across his desk at Jimmy, who shifted in his chair a bit uncomfortably.

Jimmy cleared his throat. "Seven years," he replied.

The Bishop, a stocky, impressive man with a shock of white hair, interlaced his fingers on his ample girth.

"And how long have you been engaged in scholastic study?" he inquired.

"Since college."

Bishop Walsh indicated the library volumes of Jimmy's that were spread out before him on the desk. He assumed an authoritative air.

"These books are old. Some of them date back to the Middle Ages. Why do you find it strange that there are missing pages? Isn't that to be expected? I have done a bit of research in my time—about fifty years' worth. And I have come across my share of missing pages, believe me."

"It's not the missing pages," Jimmy said haltingly. "It's the precision with which they've been removed."

The Bishop frowned. "Are you suggesting these books have been altered deliberately?"

Jimmy paused and took a sip of coffee. He searched for the right words. "Let me put it this way. There's little enough written about this mysterious woman, but whenever I get close to finding out specifics, the next page is missing or a picture has disappeared."

"I see," said the Bishop frostily.

"Someone seems to have gone to a great deal of trouble to cover up all references to this woman. I guess you could say that falls under the heading of deliberate."

The Bishop swiveled slightly in his desk chair and gazed out the ornately draped window onto the courtyard below. A light rain had begun to fall, crackling against the autumn leaves.

"This woman," he began, his back still turned to Jimmy, "you consider her some sort of seductress, am I correct?"

"Yes," Jimmy replied, "a seductress who appears to have diabolical powers."

The Bishop swung back in his chair to look at Jimmy sternly. "And also one who seems to be taking up much of your time these days. Am I right, Father?"

"I suppose so," admitted Jimmy, "but . . ."

The Bishop cut him off. "I believe you have other research that might be more constructive."

"She's not interfering with my other duties, if that's what you're getting at," the priest replied, his voice taking on a clipped tone.

"Of course not," rejoined the Bishop, closing the books and stacking them neatly in a pile. "Why don't you leave these with me and I will look into the matter?"

He got to his feet to indicate that the meeting was concluded. Jimmy rose too and regarded the older man with determination. "I'd like some answers as soon as possible," he asserted.

The Bishop's face flushed in annoyance. "You will get your answers in due time, Fr. Hamilton, and not before," he snapped.

Jimmy's reply was emphatic. "I'm afraid that's not good enough."

The Bishop raised an eyebrow disdainfully. "I beg your pardon."

"With all due respect," said Jimmy, softening his tone but maintaining his conviction, "I have reason to believe that people's lives may be at stake here."

The Bishop folded his arms disapprovingly. "I don't see the connection between people's lives and books that have been gathering dust for years. My advice to you, Fr. Hamilton, is to calm down. I think you're letting your imagination run wild."

Angrily Jimmy produced the gold medallion from his pocket. "Is this my imagination too?" he exploded.

Bishop Walsh took the coin from Jimmy's hand. He inspected it carefully.

"Where did you get this?" he asked finally.

"It was given to me by my cousin," Jimmy explained. "She was a friend of Annie and Jill—the two victims."

Bishop Walsh sighed. "The woman on this coin—is she the same as the woman you have been researching?"

"I have reason to think so," Jimmy acknowledged.

The Bishop walked silently to the window. He turned the coin over absently in his hand. Outside the rain was falling heavily. From somewhere in the distance, a car horn sounded persistently.

Jimmy waited expectantly. After what seemed like an eternity, the Bishop spoke.

"I am going to issue you a directive now which may be difficult for you to accept," he said gravely. "I want you to discontinue all further research on this subject. The Church will look into this matter. I believe you have entered into an area best left to Church hierarchy."

Jimmy stared at him in disbelief. "You're right," he exclaimed defiantly. "That is difficult to accept. And I don't accept it!"

Jimmy bolted across the room and tore the gold coin from the Bishop's grasp. Gathering the library books from the desk, the priest stalked to the door fiercely.

"I'm in too deep now," he blurted. "My own family is involved. I can't stand back and let anyone else die."

There was an uneasy hush. Only the rainfall intruded.

Jimmy opened the door. He looked at the Bishop plaintively. "I'm sorry," he said, his voice barely audible.

After he had gone, the Bishop sat in reflective thought for several minutes. He spooned sugar into his demitasse before realizing it had already gone cold. He closed his eyes wearily.

A moment later, he picked up the phone and buzzed Fr. Valenti, his secretary.

"Get me Cardinal Madori's office," he instructed.

* * *

At 3:15 the next afternoon, a freshly-painted yellow schoolbus made its way lazily up Madison Avenue. Inside, a regiment of second and third graders from an exclusive private school squealed delightedly at the prospect of a beautiful, sunny afternoon of playtime ahead.

In a seat near the door, Sean Peterson, a freckle-faced, mop-haired eight year old watched for his stop in anticipation. He hated the bus ride and longed to be out on the sidewalk trying out the brand new roller skates that had been given to him that very morning.

Today was Sean's birthday. His third grade class had celebrated with a party during recess, and Mrs. Demming, his teacher, had observed a school tradition by excusing him from homework that night. Sean would be able to skate till dinner time if he wanted to.

He rang the bell and waited by the door. The bus inched in toward the curb and came to a halt. Sean waved and shouted a goodbye to his classmates.

"Bye, Sean," they chorused. "Happy birthday!"

He leaped excitedly onto the pavement, wrinkling his eyes up at the brightness of the sun. He skipped blithely along, carefully avoiding the sidewalk cracks.

"Step on a crack, break your mother's back," he sang to himself.

Sean felt elated. Daddy had promised to leave his law firm early that day and Mom had given the housekeeper the recipe for his favorite dessert. It was going to be a wonderful birthday.

Sean knew every inch of this stretch of sidewalk. Two years of romping the short distance from the bus stop to his home had seen to that. He even knew the precise point at which to detour into the street to avoid the huge German Shepherd that lurked in the Gourmet Delicatessen.

Seeing a limousine in this part of town was not unusual for Sean. He paid the shiny black automobile scant attention, even as it drew up directly alongside him.

But when The Woman rolled down the car window, he couldn't look away.

He landed squarely on a crack of the sidewalk.

Sean gazed at the woman in wonderment. Dressed in billowy folds of white, she looked to him just like an angel.

She smiled radiantly. Sean drew back slightly. An often repeated warning flashed through his young mind.

Don't talk to strangers.

There was another one: Don't ever get in a car with someone you don't know.

The boy smiled back innocently. His parents' admonitions vanished. This was a magical lady. Like some princess in a fairy tale. She couldn't possibly mean him any harm.

The car door swung open invitingly. Sean stood there on the curb, awestruck. The Woman's smile broadened. Sean grinned.

She's a stranger, the boy thought, but how can I say no? I might never see her again.

Sean got into the limousine. The Woman closed the door. Gently she traced her fingers down the youthful contours of his face. She drew him tenderly into her embrace and kissed him hungrily on the mouth.

Sean felt as though he'd been plunged into a dream. So this was what it was like to be with an angel.

A few blocks away, his roller skates lay in their gift box. Sean would never have the need for them again.

It was another day for Burke's Lounge.

Richard sat broodingly on the barstool nearest the wall, idly skimming the foam off the top of his draft Schaefer. It was just after four p.m. and the lounge was nearly deserted. Just the way I like it, thought Richard to himself.

Overhead, the television was tuned to a game show. A man dressed up as an artichoke and a woman impersonating a squirrel were leaping about exuberantly, having just won a dream kitchen. The emcee stood aside as members of the winning couple's family raced on camera to congratulate them. The audience cheered enthusiastically.

"Look at those two, will ya," laughed the bartender.

Richard scowled at the TV. "Assholes," he muttered.

The bartender shot a quick glance at Richard, then moved off down the bar. Richard drummed his fingers on the counter impatiently.

As if in reply to his anxious gesture, the front door of the lounge swung open. A greasy, broad-shouldered man of about 30 shuffled in. His ferret-like face darted about warily, taking in every corner of the room. After a moment, he pulled up a barstool near Richard.

"That little item you ordered?" he said, leaning on the bar conspiratorially.

"Yeah?" replied Richard.

"It arrived."

The man opened his coat slightly. Richard could see a parcel which was wrapped in nondescript brown paper. He took a swallow of beer and nodded at the man meaningfully. He motioned to the bartender.

"Johnny, is it okay if we use your back room for a minute?" he asked.

The bartender hesitated. "Sure, go ahead."

Richard and the other man started for the rear of the bar. Johnny folded his arms and watched Richard with concern.

Richard opened the door to the storeroom. He flicked the light switch to reveal a small, congested area piled floor to ceiling with crates of liquor and beer. The man led Richard over to a corner of the room, out of sight from the bar. He took the parcel from his jacket and placed it on a case of Wild Turkey.

"I got you your money's worth on this one,"

he boasted, loosening an end of the wrapper.

"Good, Lenny, I knew I could count on you," replied Richard, his eyes glinting.

Lenny peeled back the wrapping paper, uncovering a sleek .357 Magnum. Richard took the revolver in his hand and fondled it.

"She's a real beauty, isn't she?" said Lenny admiringly.

Richard caught his breath. Maybe now, he thought, people will leave me alone.

CHAPTER TWELVE

The dream. Jimmy'd had it again last night. As he had tossed fitfully in bed, the maniacal ticker tape had reappeared in his mind, churning out words into a dark abyss. As before, he struggled to force his way through a crowd only to see the tape give way to a cascade of gold coins. Grabbing deliriously for one of them, he again saw blood ooze from the metal to drip down his arm. The woman's derisive laughter heralded the dream's newest touches of horror: the disembodied heads of Monsignor Hanrahan and Bishop Walsh that floated mistily in the air.

Hardly surprising that those two were now inhabiting his nightmare, thought Jimmy in the morning. After yesterday's stormy session at the Bishop's residence, it was a wonder he wasn't being haunted by the entire College of Cardinals.

All through nine o'clock Mass, Fr. Hamilton felt pangs of uneasiness and self-doubt. The Bishop had issued him a clear directive and Jimmy had thrown down the gauntlet, defying his superior openly. Not only was that a violation of Jimmy's vow of obedience, he recognized, but it might be a foolhardy, even impulsive act, of and by itself. The priest had always prided himself on being more level-headed than that.

After Mass, changing back into his street clothes in the sacristy, Jimmy was still tense. The departing altar boys tried to entice him into a Humphrey Bogart impression but Jimmy told them, not unkindly, that he wasn't in the mood for levity.

Returning to his study, the priest was greeted by a ringing telephone. He hurried across the room and picked up the receiver.

"Hello?"

"Father Jimmy?"

The priest recognized the voice of the police artist, Ray Price.

"Well, hello, Ray, how are you?"

"I'm fine," came the reply. "Listen, you know that sketch I did of that woman? Well, at the time, she looked familiar, but I couldn't place her. So I played a hunch. You ever play a hunch, Father?"

The priest smiled ironically. "All the time."

"I sent her out on the police wire," Ray continued. "It's a computer system that hooks into police departments in all the major cities. It only takes a few minutes and her picture is all over the country."

"I see," said Jimmy, feeling an odd anticipation.

"I just got an answer from Chicago," said Ray, pausing for effect. "They recognized the woman."

Jimmy sat down on the arm of the sofa. "Who is she?" he asked eagerly.

"You remember a case in Chicago about a year ago?" asked Ray, his excitement mounting. "This student named Stallmaster went berserk and murdered five stewardesses?"

"Yes, it was a big news story."

"Well, Detective Brown of the Chicago police recognized the woman in the sketch. Are you ready for this, Father? She used to date Stallmaster."

Jimmy's pulse quickened with an unfamiliar dread. "Was she implicated in the killings?"

"Detective Brown questioned her but she was never booked."

The priest pondered this for a moment. "Where is Stallmaster now?"

"He's in Chicago—in a padded cell. He's practically a vegetable."

Jimmy closed his eyes and breathed a silent prayer. The image of Burt Shulman, dazed and uncommunicative in his hospital bed, took on added meaning.

"Well, that's about it, Father." Ray's voice sounded far away. "I just thought you'd want to know."

"Thanks, Ray," said Jimmy mechanically. "I appreciate your help. Bye."

The priest hung up the phone. Another coincidence. This was almost too much to bear. Could it be that the woman on the coin was identical to the woman who seemed to be having this strange effect on everyone? And how could that be? More importantly, could a chain that began with Stallmaster, then moved to Burt Shulman be leading inevitably to Richard?

The answers had to be in the books, Jimmy reasoned. If only he could find out the identity of that woman from the past, he might have a clue as to who this present day person was. If she was a descendant, perhaps the volumes would explain her motivation for wanting to exercise mind control on innocent men.

Jimmy pounded his fist down on the table. Meanwhile, he fumed, my own Church is pulling out all the stops to cover the whole thing up!

Stallmaster. The name had a familiar ring. Ever since, moments before, Ray had said it, something had been tugging at the back of Jimmy's brain.

Stallmaster. He had remembered the name from the newspaper accounts but he had heard it somewhere else recently. Jimmy made an effort to concentrate.

Where had he heard that name?

Suddenly it hit him. He hadn't heard the name—he'd read it. And he knew exactly where.

He bounded across the study and rummaged through the library books on his desk. Finding the German text entitled "Deutschland, 1800-1850," he switched on the tensor light excitedly. He thumbed through the pages until he reached the chapter on the year 1820. Skimming the pages, he soon came to a paragraph featuring a list of names.

"Berger, Stern, Muller . . ."

The priest was having difficulty reading the fourth and fifth names, which were faded to the point of being virtually illegible. Impatiently, he skipped to the sixth name and spoke it aloud.

"Stahlmeister."

It was the German version of the name.

Jimmy was nearing the bottom of the page. With frenetic expectancy, the priest translated from the German:

"The six good Christian men crept into the room where the unholy creature was being worshipped. The raven-haired seductress was formidable but the faith of true believers . . ."

The priest moved his finger up to the top of the next page in anticipation. A look of anger crossed his face. The next paragraph, totally unrelated, was headed "1825."

Two entire pages were missing. The mysterious censors had done their work again.

Jimmy slammed the book in rage.

He needed more than the books to find the

answers, the priest concluded. If Richard is to survive, thought Jimmy, I must go to Chicago.

Kisser was curled up in a square of late afternoon light on the floor of Leslie's apartment. Sprawled nearby, after her daily exercise routine, Leslie stroked his fur playfully. The cat purred loudly.

For the first three days following Jill's death, Kisser had been anxious, frightened of being in new surroundings. Despite all Leslie's attempts to cajole him out, the cat had remained just out of reach in a hollowed out section of the wall in her bedroom closet. Finally, the enticement of fresh sardines had done the trick and though the animal seemed morose at times, evidently missing his mistress, he had warmed up enough for Leslie to believe that eventually they would become good friends. Still, seeing Kisser sometimes made Leslie ache with sad remembrances—the cat was a constant reminder of the person who had been taken suddenly and so brutally away.

Leslie flexed her leg. The exercise routine had succeeded in taking her mind off the awful events of the past several weeks—something Leslie was intent on doing to the fullest if she was ever to become clear-headed enough to figure out a solution to Richard's strange predicament.

The hours immediately after her last stormy visit with him had been muddled with apprehension and doubt. Returning that day to her apartment, she had not found the hoped for perspective, tormented instead by her brother's final vile remark.

"You make me sick. You've always made me sick. You disgusting whore!"

The words still resounded in her mind, bringing back every disagreement, however minor, that she and Richard had had, going back to childhood. At first, Leslie wondered. Was this true? Had Richard always hated her? Of course not, she concluded, after the tears had subsided. Richard had not meant what he said—his words had been the ravings of a seriously disturbed man.

Leslie's train of thought was interrupted by the ringing of the telephone. Kisser stirred and meowed, getting lazily to his feet and padding off toward his food dish. Leslie grinned and picked up the phone.

The receiver was still inches from her ear when she heard the crackling. Her body went taut; her skin prickled in fright. The baby's forlorn whimpers followed at once, nestling determinedly in her ear. Leslie shook with horror.

"Who is this?" she whispered desperately, but the child's sobbing was the only reply.

Leslie fought to stifle her panic. She listened intently. Maybe, she thought, I can hear something—a background noise that will tell me where this is coming from.

The cries continued, punctuated only by the piercing static.

"Who's there?" Leslie asked, striving to make her voice assertive.

Her question hung in the air. This is mad, thought Leslie, I can't listen to this. If I stay on the line, I'm playing right into the hands of whoever is doing this to me. Besides, there are no background noises. The static is drowning everything out.

With a resolute motion, Leslie hung up the phone. She sank down onto a hassock, her fear mingled with a certain satisfaction at the way she'd handled the situation. I was scared, she thought, but at least I remained calm.

She took her address book from the end table. Jimmy should know about this latest bit of craziness, she decided. Maybe by now that friend of his had analyzed the tape. They might have detected noises I couldn't hear.

Feeling a rush of self-assurance, Leslie picked up the receiver. Stunned, she dropped it at once onto the coffee table, shattering the glass.

She shrank from the phone in alarm.

The connection had never been broken. The crying would not go away.

"Feeling any better?" asked Jimmy sympathetically an hour later as Leslie sat propped up against pillows on the couch.

"Yes, much better," replied Leslie with a wan smile. "I'm glad you came over."

"I'm just sorry they weren't still on the line when I got here."

Leslie shook her head. "It's as if they knew I

was going to call you. As soon as they scared me the second time, they hung up."

"Too bad," Jimmy offered. "You could have taped it."

"Why? It was exactly the same as the tape we already have."

The priest took the answer machine cassette from his pocket and held it up meaningfully.

"Jimmy, don't play that," protested Leslie. "It's the last thing I want to hear."

"That's just it," said Jimmy. "The message is gone."

"Gone? I don't understand."

Jimmy shrugged. "We must have erased it. When I got to headquarters, there were only two messages on the tape."

Leslie looked at him keenly. "Why didn't you tell me this before?"

"I didn't want to upset you."

"Well, if it was just a matter of the tape being *accidentally* erased, why would that upset me?" Leslie paused to study her cousin pointedly. "You're trying to be casual, Jimmy. Do you think the tape just happened to get erased?"

Jimmy met her gaze directly. "Not really," he confessed, "but what other explanation could there be?"

"I wonder," replied Leslie absently. She cast a wary glance at the phone across the room. "I can't tell you how horrible it was to hear those baby's cries coming from the telephone. It was even worse than the tape. You know, I think I must be getting a little nuts—I'd swear I heard the same sounds coming from Richard's apartment."

"You mean the other day?" asked Jimmy.

"Yes," she nodded. "After I got out in the hallway. It sounded like there was a baby in there. Then it sounded like a woman laughing. Pretty weird, huh?"

"But not impossible," suggested the priest.

Leslie sat lost in thought for several moments. "You're not saying that Richard is hiding a woman and baby in his apartment and that they're calling me up trying to frighten me?"

"No," admitted Jimmy. "That's a little too incredible."

"Then do you think Richard is making those noises himself?"

"That's pretty farfetched too," said the priest, "but I'm not sure I could completely rule it out. I'm not sure we can rule *anything* out."

"I know what you mean," said Leslie soberly. "Jimmy, do you have any idea what the laws are in this state—to have someone committed?"

"You're talking about Richard?"

"If you had seen him the other day," Leslie began. "He was violent."

The priest weighed this consideration. "I don't think committing him is the answer," he said finally. "I think we've got to do something about this woman."

"It won't work," Leslie countered. "I

already tried it. He's incapable of discussing her rationally."

"I know," replied the priest. "But I've got a lead on the woman's identity. I'm going to Chicago in the morning. I think I can find out exactly who she is."

"Richard won't listen," Leslie objected. "It doesn't matter who she is."

"Trust me. I think it matters a lot."

Leslie watched from her window until Jimmy's VW disappeared around the corner. Slipping out of her clothes, she donned a terry-cloth robe and poured herself a glass of sherry. Kisser crawled out from the record cabinet and ambled over to her for some affection. She scratched his ears and he dug his paws into the cushion delightedly.

Leslie's eyes drifted drowsily around the room, coming to rest on the table where the tape cassette lay. Jimmy said there were two messages on there, she recalled. One of them was from Hal Weile. Who was the other one from?

She sipped her sherry and reached across to the telephone answering machine. She inserted the cassette and pushed the "Play-back" button.

Instantly, the room was alive with the infant's cries. The tape crackled tauntingly as Leslie fell back in terror. Kisser screeched and hissed at Leslie menacingly.

The Evil could not be erased.

* * *

Jimmy had been in Chicago only once before, fifteen years ago during his senior year at college. The occasion had been a national student government convention and the priest had been one of the keynote speakers.

How much my life has changed, he thought as he climbed the front steps of the small, compact hotel on the city's North side. I wasn't even a priest back then, he recalled, but immediately he was struck with an irony. I'm a priest now but I'm steering clear of the local seminary to check into a commercial hotel.

Jimmy had considered calling a friend, a priest at Loyola University, and asking to stay with him while he was in Chicago. But even though he trusted Fr. Lombardi, he'd have had to give him a minimal explanation of why he was in town and he felt reluctant to involve another person. Moreover, there was the risk that while on the campus of the University, he might encounter a Church official who could be in contact with Bishop Walsh.

Jimmy smiled to himself as he registered at the hotel's front desk. I'm like a fugitive out here, he thought, only Leslie knows my exact whereabouts. That romantic notion was dispelled by a twinge of guilt as Jimmy remembered the fib he had told his superior at St. Matthew's, asking for a day off to visit his sick aunt in Passaic. I'd better say some Hail Mary's for that one, he resolved, as the bellhop showed him to his room.

A few minutes later, in the cab on the way to

police headquarters, Jimmy watched as snow flurries were whisked about by the legendary Chicago winds. He thought about Leslie's midnight phone call the previous night, how she had played the answer machine tape for him over the phone. Those were babies' cries all right, coming from what he and Arthur Wax knew to be an erased tape. Whatever was happening—it had entered into the realm of the inexplicable, or perhaps even the supernatural.

Somebody was trying to frighten Leslie. Somebody with power that went beyond the natural order of things. But why? And where did Richard come in? Leslie had heard those same cries coming from his apartment. It was all getting incredibly complex but, at the center, there was always the woman.

Jimmy recollected the lines from the German text. Six good Christians had crept into a room where a raven-haired seductress was being worshipped. Was the woman on the gold medallion that seductress? Why did she so resemble this woman in Richard's life? One of the six Christian men was named Stahlmeister. The man Jimmy was going to see was named Stallmaster. The links between past and present were everywhere.

Detective Glendon Brown's office was a small but neatly furnished room at the end of the first floor hall marked Homicide Division. A round-faced, middle-aged man with a generous paunch, the detective welcomed Jimmy, making him feel instantly at ease. Ray Price must have given me a good recommendation, thought the priest.

The opening amenities dispensed with, Brown took the sketch of the woman and placed it in the center of his desk, where it contrasted eerily with the surrounding family photographs which depicted the detective, his wife and a brood of laughing children.

Brown rapped on the sketch with authority. "Her name is Laura Zimmer. We don't have a file on her because we never booked her. But I remember her clearly. May I ask why you're interested?"

"She looks like a woman who's been going out with my cousin," replied Jimmy.

Brown looked at him skeptically. "There's got to be more to it than that, Father."

Jimmy nodded. "I have reason to believe she's influencing him."

"Influencing? How do you mean, Father?"

"I'm not really sure," admitted Jimmy. "I think she may be exercising some kind of mind control over him."

Detective Brown contemplated the drawing. "Have you met her?" he inquired significantly.

"No," replied Jimmy.

"I didn't think so," said the detective.

"I'm not even positive it's the same woman."

Brown leaned back in his chair. His face took on a haunted, reminiscent look. "Well, I've met Laura Zimmer," he began, "and I know what you mean about control. She's a very strong lady. Very magnetic. If you want to know the truth, Father, she gave me the creeps. We had no evidence against her but I questioned her for several hours. It was the strangest thing, Father. We were alone in a a room—just me and her—and five minutes after she came in, the place was like an icebox. It's like she could look right through me. And when I looked at her, there was no depth to her eyes. I couldn't wait to get out of there."

Jimmy sat there thoughtfully, letting the detective's account sink in. "I understand she went out with Stallmaster. Is that correct?"

"She just appeared in his life a short time before the murders. None of his friends or relatives ever met her but they all seemed to know that they were dating. No one really knew very much about her."

"But you questioned her? Who was she? What was her background?"

"Well," said the detective, "we found her address in Stallmaster's wallet. We went there. She came down to headquarters willingly enough. She seemed surprised that Stallmaster had committed a crime. I questioned her primarily about him. We really didn't delve into her background at all."

"Why not?" asked Jimmy. "You said she was strange."

Detective Brown sighed. "That was only my personal impression. She scared me, but, as far as the law is concerned, she was just a citizen volunteering information. She was miles away with an airtight alibi when the killings took place. She was never even a suspect as an accessory or anything. There was absolutely no reason for us to dig into her past. And you can't detain a person just because *you* think they're strange."

"No, of course not," said Jimmy. "But you sat in a room with her. Do you think she was capable of commanding a person and making them go out and kill?"

Brown thought for several moments. "If anybody could do that, she could," he said decisively.

"Let me get this straight," said the priest. "If someone orders a murder, even if that person is far away when it takes place—aren't they subject to prosecution?"

Detective Brown smiled wryly. "Not if the only witness is a vegetable, Father."

Once again, the image of the hospitalized Burt Shulman crossed the priest's mind.

"Stallmaster was no help at all?"

"When we found the dead girls, he was just sitting there smiling. He hasn't said anything coherent since that night."

Jimmy nodded sadly. "What would you say the woman's total effect was on Stallmaster?"

The detective glanced down at the sketch. "He worshipped her."

The altar had been fashioned from makeshift cardboard boxes. A white linen cloth was spread across the top and hung down on either side. In the center of the cloth, leaning precariously against the wall, was a crude, oval portrait done in red crayon, of a woman that

Jimmy recognized the minute he entered the padded cell.

In the center of the room was a thick white mattress; on it lay a man, curled up in the fetal position. Horribly emaciated with gaunt cheeks and sunken eyes, he lay there motionless as the attendant carefully closed the heavy iron door behind him.

"It won't do any good, Father," the attendant advised. "This one's really gone."

Jimmy's eyes returned to the makeshift shrine. He leaned closer to inspect the oval portrait. The figure on the mattress stirred.

"Careful, Father, don't touch anything over there. It's the only thing that makes him violent."

Jimmy drew back. The patient grew still. The priest turned to the attendant.

"It looks like an altar," Jimmy observed. "Isn't that a bit unusual—letting him have something like that in here?"

The attendant, a strapping, light-skinned Jamaican, smiled philosophically. "It keeps him calm. When we tried taking it away from him, he got out of control."

Jimmy nodded understandingly. The attendant went on, warming up to the subject.

"He made that altar himself. It's the only thing he's done in eleven months. The doctors thought it was good therapy. I hear he had another altar—a lot more elaborate—where he lived."

"That's interesting," commented the priest.

"What does he do at this altar? Anything?"

"No," replied the attendant, "but he keeps a close eye on it. When we clean the cell down, we have to go *around* it. Otherwise, he gets wild. All hell breaks loose." He looked at the priest sheepishly. "Sorry, Father."

Jimmy knelt down beside Stallmaster, who seemed to focus on him for the first time.

"Hello Charles," said the priest gently. "I'm Jimmy. I'm your friend."

Stallmaster grinned foolishly and gurgled. Jimmy pointed to the crude portrait by the wall. The patient's grin widened.

"Is she your girlfriend?" asked Jimmy. "She's very beautiful."

Stallmaster giggled crazily and rolled his eyes.

"That's about all you'll get from him," remarked the attendant coldly.

Jimmy pointed again to the altar drawing. The patient tittered and flapped his arms. The priest waited for a moment, then reached into his pocket. He took out the police sketch of Laura Zimmer.

"I have a picture of her too," said the priest. "See?"

He held the sketch directly in front of Charles Stallmaster's face.

The giggling ceased. A few seconds passed. Jimmy held his breath. Something was beginning to register on the patient's face.

"It's the same woman, Charles," prompted the priest. "You know it is."

Stallmaster's eyes glinted for what seemed

to be one lucid moment. He looked at Jimmy and nodded in briefest agreement.

Thank God, thought the priest excitedly, at least he can wrench himself out of her control. Maybe there's hope for him after all.

As if in mocking answer to his thought, Stallmaster collapsed back onto the mattress, curling back protectively into his fetal state. He whimpered helplessly, like an infant in distress.

Jimmy shuddered, remembering Leslie's tape. The Woman knows I'm here, he thought. She's still controlling him. She'll never let him go.

Dear God, what is she?

After the door to the padded cell swung closed, Stallmaster waited, counting slowly to seven in his feverish mind.

"One. Iggledy-Piggledy. Two. Iggledy-Piggledy. Three. Iggledy-Piggledy. . . ."

He uncoiled his skeletal body, his bones creaking as he sat up on the bed. His whines had ceased as quickly as they had started. Now his eyes flashed wildly around the tiny room.

"Four. Iggledy-Piggledy. Five. Iggledy-Piggledy."

Stallmaster knew from experience that if he could count to seven without an intrusion, that he could then begin clearing the area. But sometimes when he started to say "Iggledy-Piggledy," he'd get confused and "Wiggledy-Jiggledy" would come out instead. Then he would have to start *all* over . . .

"Six. Iggledy-Piggledy."

He put his bare feet down onto the soft surface beneath his cot. He screwed up his face and grasped his bony knees in concentration.

"Seven . . ."

He took a deep breath. What came next? He wasn't sure. But he had to say something or the other numbers would be wasted.

"Iggledy-Piggledy!" The words burst in his head. He had done it! Now the ritual could begin.

Standing up wearily, he shuffled over to the cardboard altar. Nothing had been touched by the God-Man. Still, it was necessary to remove the air boogers that the priest had left behind. Doggedly, Stallmaster circled the makeshift shrine, flailing the air with his arms like a manic pterodactyl. Rushing through his inflamed mind was the required refrain:

"The eentsy-weentsy spider
Crept up the water spout.
Down came the rain
And washed the spider out.
Out came the sun
And dried up all the rain.
And the eentsy-weentsy spider
Went up the spout again."

Stallmaster had completed the circle. The area was cleansed. He sank down onto his haunches, gazing up devoutly at the red crayoned likeness of The Woman.

Images of That Day stabbed his brain in quick, lucid flashes.

He and The Woman tangled in bed sheets, her mouth hard against his . . . Stalking the

Japanese girl, the blue of her uniform tossed by the blustery winds off Lake Michigan . . . Trapping her alone in her apartment, her eyes pleading for mercy . . . The imprint of his fingers on her lifeless throat . . . Finding the butcher knife and surprising the other girls down the hall . . . The blonde who tried to scratch him as his teeth ripped into the soft flesh of her neck . . . The dumpy one who went for the phone; how he twisted the wire around her throat until she was still . . . The redhead in the bathrobe whose eyes had to be put out . . . The one in the glasses that he disemboweled—her insides got all over his good loafers . . . Sitting in the deathly room, waiting for The Woman. She had promised to return after the killing was done. She never came.

The images stopped. Humbly, Stallmaster lowered his head. He had no idea how much time had passed since then. But time was all he had now. Some day The Woman would be back for him. She had given her word. He didn't mind waiting. He had his altar. He would keep it nice until she returned. Together, he and The Woman would go to heaven. They would have eternal life. They would come to judge the living and the dead. And of their kingdom there would be no end.

Iggledy-Piggledy.

So why was he crying?

"Call Ray, Police HQ, New York, Urgent."

The message was waiting for Jimmy when he returned, still a bit shaken, to his hotel.

What now, he wondered anxiously, as he rode upstairs in the elevator; please, God, let this not be another victory for that woman.

Once inside his room, Jimmy went immediately to the phone. He dialed the number on the message slip.

Back in New York, at police headquarters, Ray Price was just finishing a pastrami sandwich. He washed it down with a quick swallow of coffee and picked up the receiver.

"Price."

"Ray, it's Jimmy. I got your message. How did you track me down?"

"Glen Brown told me where you were staying. I got some news for you. Better sit down for this one. I got two more replies on that woman's sketch—Laura Zimmer."

Jimmy steeled himself for the worst. Price went on.

"Remember that guy who went nuts in Florida—shot three people from a tower?"

The priest leaned against the hotel room wall. His face grew ashen.

"Berger, wasn't it?" he asked.

"Right," Price replied. "George Berger. He used to date Laura Zimmer."

"Dear God," murmured the priest. "Are you sure?"

"Positive. But that's not all. There was that case in New Orleans last month. Young up and coming executive—Roger Stern—guns down four secretaries in his office. Laura Zimmer was his girlfriend."

Jimmy stared out the window in dismay.

The snow was beginning to stick, covering the downtown streets with a patina of pure white.

"Are you there, Father?" Ray asked anxiously.

"Yes," replied Jimmy in a thin voice. "Thanks for your help, Ray."

Before Price could answer, the phone clicked off. That must have hit him like a ton of bricks, thought the policeman. I wonder if he's all right. If he's mixed up with this woman, he might be getting in over his head. Well, Jimmy knew what he was doing, he'd always been able to take care of himself.

A buzzer sounded on Ray's desk. He switched on the intercom.

"Ray," said a voice, "the chief of detectives can see you now."

"Fine. I'll be right down."

This ought to be fun, he thought wryly. Talk about circumstantial evidence.

He tucked the sketch of the woman under his arm, then gathered up the Telexes from Chicago, Florida and New Orleans. He left the room.

The dim afternoon sun peeked through the small casement window above the artist's desk, sending a hazy shaft of light onto the wall, where a charcoal drawing was pinned. On the sheet of paper, under the heading, "Missing Child," the face of eight-year-old Sean Peterson stared out helplessly.

CHAPTER THIRTEEN

The Woman laughed as the Evil reminded her of what the two would be capable of doing to The Ones Who Came After. The humans. The Evil grew smaller and shrank back as The Woman reminded it that She did not need the power. She was the revered one. She was of The Old One himself. She was the life fluid of The Master. Together they prayed a centuries old prayer, praising the impenetrable darkness that was The Master's House.

"O SERPENT heart, hid with a flowering face..."

Sandy Phillips, the fourteen year old blonde-haired Juliet, read with fervor from the Braille edition of the play. A pretty, petite girl with an upturned nose and sparkling smile, she kept the other blind students enthralled with her spirited yet precise reading.

"Did ever dragon keep so fair a cave?
Beautiful tyrant! Fiend angelical!
Dove-feather'd raven! Wolvish-ravening lamb!
Despised substance of divinest show!"

Donald Carter, enjoying a respite during a scene in which Romeo did not appear, sat at a desk near the front of the classroom, listening appreciatively. But his admiration for Sandy's reading seemed shadowed by a vague uneasiness somehow connected to the man who was overseeing the entire group.

Richard Bloch's arms were folded on the front desk and his head rested wearily upon them. Shirt sleeves rolled up, tie askew, he rocked his head back and forth childishly, his eyes darting maniacally about the room.

"Just opposite to what thou justly seem'st;
A damned saint, an honourable villain!"

Richard lifted his right arm slightly. He nudged the .357 Magnum forward on the desk. Smiling playfully at the unsuspecting blind children, he fingered the revolver's long metal barrel. He straightened up in his chair and giggled sadistically.

Look at those blind bastards, thought Richard, his mind careening wildly. They're just sitting there as if nothing could hurt them. They have no idea of my power. All I have to do is aim this little baby at any one of them, squeeze off a round, and I can splatter a head all over the wall.

Richard raised the revolver. He squinted down the gun sight at Juliet who continued reciting in a clear voice, unaware of her teacher's fevered concentration.

"O nature! What hadst thou to do in hell
When thou didst bower the spirit of a fiend
In mortal paradise of such sweet flesh?"

Sweet flesh, scoffed Richard to himself, caressing the gun's trigger. She's never even seen flesh. I could tell her a few things about sweet flesh. I could tell her about the woman with the sweetesh flesh I've ever known.

Just thinking about The Woman, Richard felt flushed. He remembered the day she had appeared in his classroom, sitting among the unseeing children. Growing hard with desire, Richard fantasized—if she came in now, we could fuck right here in the front of the room and those asshole kids would go right on reading Shakespeare.

Richard moved the revolver to the left, training it on Carol Marsh, his ponytailed Lady Capulet. She mispronounced "Verona" the other day, he thought angrily. Called it "Veronia." I should blow her brains out just for that.

"Was ever book containing such vile matter
So fairly bound?"

No, reasoned Richard, the Marsh girl isn't worth the price of a bullet. I've got a much better idea—why not eliminate my leading man?

He pointed the gun directly at Donald Carter's head. Okay, Romeo, he said to himself, it's time for you to bite the dust. If I pumped a bullet into your thick skull, who would really miss you? They say that you're my prize student. Suppose I honor you with my first shot?

As if he could sense what was churning in Richard's mind, Donald shifted slightly in his chair. Richard adjusted the gun accordingly. Aiming squarely between the boy's eyes,

Richard tightened his hold on the trigger.

He began to squeeze.

"O! That deceit should dwell
In such a gorgeous palace."

He pulled the trigger.

The gun clicked harmlessly. Donald looked up, puzzled. Smiling at the gun's empty chamber, Richard chuckled softly.

Next time, he swore, it would be loaded.

Vincent Mallory walked down the street with the swagger of a successful young businessman. He paused before the plate glass window of a dingy dry goods store to adjust his silk tie. Even in a poverty stricken neighborhood like this, Vincent was a man who cared about his appearance. People had told Vince that with his Continental good looks he could have been a model, or maybe an actor, but Vince thought that was for sissies. Vince's line of business allowed him to have many hours of free time, and it was lucrative. Vince needed the time and money to pursue his two favorite hobbies—pampering himself and scoring pussy.

At twenty-five, Vince had set himself up as a small-time heroin dealer. It wasn't a big operation. This way, Vince didn't have to answer to the mob who controlled drug trafficking. Vince's enterprise consisted of himself and his three employees. Vince never actually dealt the drug to the public. He just sold it to the three punks working for him who in turn would go out on the streets of Manhattan and deal to their clientele. No, Vince was smart. He thought of himself as a wholesaler—and he never took the drug either. Doing heroin was for losers, and Vincent Mallory was no loser.

It was just before noon as Vince approached the small coffee shop on Rivington Street where he was meeting his three workers. A nasty gleam came to his eye. Jack, Washington and Freddy—three heroin addicts who would never amount to anything. For a few bucks a night and a free fix, the trio hustled their asses off for him. The few times they'd tried to rip him off, Vince had showed them who was boss. Freddy still wore the scar under his left eye where Vince had stuck the knife. Washington had received a broken nose for holding back twenty-five dollars from Vince. Jack had always been honest with Vince, but he'd roughed him up also—as a warning. Besides, Jack was a faggot. He deserved to get his head smashed a few times.

Respect, thought Vince. That's what good business relations were built on. Goddamn fuckin' junkies.

Vince entered the restaurant. The smell of bacon grease, grime and age assaulted his senses. He wrinkled his nose in disgust. Fuckin' joint, he thought. But it was a good place to take care of last night's business. No one paid any attention to you in here. He felt the packages of heroin in his pocket. Three large ones for selling—the three smaller as payment for yesterday's work. The transaction wouldn't take long. Then Vince would be free until tomorrow when he would come here again. Anytime he wanted to change the meeting place, he'd call Washington and he would get in touch with the others. None of the three had Vince's phone number—they didn't even know where he lived.

Vince slipped into his corner booth. The overweight, blonde woman came to take his order. As usual, he asked for a diet soda in a bottle. Vince didn't trust the glasses in this dump. The waitress brought back his order and waddled off. Vince took a few swallows of the soda and thought about last night. He'd been with Cara. The tall redhead was his favorite piece of ass these days. He could still feel her long, muscular legs wrapped tightly around his back. His shoulder was slightly sore where she had bit him in her passion.

Vince had screwed hundreds of women in his short life. They were always falling all over him. Sometimes he would have as many as three or four different chicks in one night. Usually, these quick hops in the sack meant nothing to him. Once in a while, if he was interested in a girl, he'd see her again. But it was just a matter of time before Vince got violent with them and many was the morning that a bruised young woman would be seen leaving Vince's Gramercy Park apartment building wearing her shame and hurt like a brand in the early sun.

Vince smiled. Cara was one he liked. They'd been out three times and he hadn't beat her once. Cara reminded him of his mother.

Vince's mother had once been a dancer and she had red hair too, though it was dyed. Vince had loved his mother when he was a little boy. But she was a nag. That was the problem with chicks. They were nags. When Vince was a kid, his mother kept after Vince, Sr. to get a better job so they could move out of the slum they were living in. One night, Vince's father had heard enough and dragged his screaming wife over to the stove. Holding her hands over the flame, he burned them so badly Vince could smell the scorched flesh. It took several months for her hands to heal, but Vince's mother had never nagged her husband again.

One morning, Vince got up to go to school and his mother wasn't there. Sometime in the night, Margaret Mallory had crept quietly out of the apartment, away from her husband and small son, never to return again. Vince had felt frightened and cried a lot for the next few days. But he got over his mother's abandonment and began to enjoy the freedom he had without her around looking after him. Vince's father acted like nothing had happened. Later, he took up with another woman. By then, Vince was on his own, finding solace in his independence.

The closing of the coffee shop door brought Vince back to the present. He eyed the three men as they came toward his table. They moved with nervous energy and had the pallor of longtime junk users. They were his breadwinners but Vince could feel his skin crawl as they sat down next to him. He looked them over. They passed inspection—barely. Vince had warned them they could scratch and nod out and do all the things junkies did but not at his table. He would get this over as soon as possible. They all looked hungry for a fix and he had better things to do then sit around with a bunch of weaklings that were slaves to a drug. Vince had nothing but contempt for these three low-lifes. He'd smoked pot for kicks as a teenager but outgrew it. He liked an occasional toot of coke or maybe some poppers to keep him going. But how someone could be so desperate for a high that they'd stick a needle in their arm—well, that was a mystery to him. They were pathetic losers, that's all there was to it.

Vince entered the squalid bathroom with a wad of bills in his hand. Quickly, he counted up his take in a dirty stall. It was about what it should be. Fine. He was not in the mood for hassles today. He was washing his hands in the cracked porcelain sink when there was a knock at the restroom door.

"Just a minute," he called out.

Another knock. This one much louder.

"Jesus Christ," said Vince angrily. "What the fuck's the matter with you?" He turned off the faucet. Probably one of those goddamn junkies who couldn't wait to shoot up. He tore open the door and jumped back in surprise. He swallowed the curse that was on his lips. In the narrow passageway separating the bathroom from the steamy kitchen where there was barely room for a person to stand, her body instantly pressed against his, was the most beautiful creature he'd ever laid eyes on. He scarcely had time to take in her full ripe breasts straining against the thin fabric of her low-cut dress. He caught only a glimpse of her perfectly shaped thighs as she shoved him backward into the airless cubicle of the bathroom. Kicking the door shut behind her, she was on top of Vince, pushing him onto the sink. Her lips tasted silky and demanding. Her teeth ground against his in an animal frenzy. Vince was overpowered.

"What the hell?" he managed to stammer.

The Woman leaned forward. He could see the nipples of her breasts. Her legs were apart. With a swift motion, she hiked up the hem of her skirt. Vince caught his breath. She wore nothing underneath.

Just as Vince was beginning to recover from his initial shock, The Woman stepped back. Excited now, Vince reached for her but, deftly, she maneuvered the door open and, without so much as a backward glance, was gone. Vince steadied himself against the sink. He shook his head. After a moment, he had to laugh. What the fuck was that all about, he wondered.

Vince straightened his tie. That bitch had been a knockout. Another minute and he would have been down on the floor with her. But who was she? He was certain he didn't know her. Maybe one of his friends was playing a joke on him. Maybe she was some whore and they paid her to do that. But that couldn't be. None of Vince's buddies even knew he was down here. Alarmed, Vince shoved his hands in his pockets. The money was still there. So she wasn't a pickpocket either. Vince couldn't figure it out. But he knew one thing. He wanted to see that chick again so he could finish what she started.

Vince left the tiny bathroom. The quicker he paid off his flunkies and got rid of them, the sooner he could try to find that woman. He didn't have to look very far. Perched on a stool at the counter, shapely legs crossed almost modestly, a cup in her delicate hand, she sat waiting for him. Good, thought Vince, the cunt must really want me! Let her wait a little longer.

He rejoined the three men back at his booth. He paid his dealers off hurriedly and divvied up the heroin. A packet of the white powder slipped through his fingers.

"Hey, man, watch what the fuck you doin'," warned Washington. "Someone will see that shit."

Vince retrieved the dope from the floor. He ignored Washington's tone of voice. If Vince weren't so hot for that woman, he would have slammed the black man's face in for talking to him like that.

Washington noticed that Vince was preoccupied and turned to look in the direction of the counter. Even with heroin still running through his veins, making his perception cloudy, Washington became uncomfortable. Suddenly, he needed a fix. He needed it bad. Jack and Freddy had also begun to fidget, as if sensing their friend's anxiety. The three rose as one and quickly left the restaurant.

Jack and Freddy wandered off down Rivington Street. It was Washington who began to run. It was something he had seen back there in the coffee shop. As he had looked at the woman sitting at the counter, she had turned, right before his eyes, into a huge, scaly beast. In place of her mouth was a gaping hole with protruding fangs that dripped deadly saliva. And while Washington ran, he kept repeating that things like that didn't happen. Washington didn't stop sprinting until he was safe in his dirty little apartment, a dead bolt shot into place on the battered door. As he deftly slipped the needle into his vein and felt the immediate rush of the heroin, he began to pray. But seconds later, the drug kicked in and praying wasn't necessary anymore. Washington slid into a welcomed stupor, the last few minutes already just a foggy memory in his mind.

A few blocks away, Vince and The Woman were leaving the restaurant. As soon as the three men had departed from Vince's booth, The Woman had come over and looked down at him. It was enough of an invitation for Vince. He walked outside with her and she began leading him East on Rivington. She seemed to have a destination in mind, so Vince didn't say anything. He still couldn't figure out what her game was. Probably some kinky rich bitch who came slumming for kicks. Just pick up some guy, no questions asked, no names given. When it was over, she probably changed into decent clothes and went home to her rich husband, the sucker.

Vince glanced over at her. Inside the coffee shop she'd looked like a whore, but out here, the sun brought sparkle to her jet black hair and her green eyes were the color of fresh grass. Vince could see now that though her clothes were gaudy, they must've cost a bundle. Yeah, thought Vince, this chick was definitely out of her league down here. This neighborhood was Reality. Vince knew the ropes here. Vince almost laughed aloud at the thought of what he would do to her once they were alone. She'd better like it rough, 'cause that's the way it was going to be. Well, I'm one quick fuck she won't forget, thought Vince excitedly.

The Woman led him down a side street. There were only a few tenements here. The neighborhood was being knocked down to make way for a housing development. The building that they stopped in front of made Vince stare in disbelief. Most of the windows had been boarded up. There couldn't be more than two families occupying the structure. Vince was becoming nervous. What the hell was a chick like this doing here? Hesitantly, he followed her through the dark, narrow hallway to the last apartment on the right.

The Woman was turning the key in the lock. Inside, the apartment was bleak and shabby. The three rooms ran together. The only furniture in the kitchen was a beat-up table and some chairs. In the second room, an enormous bed took up most of the space. Vince was relieved to see the clean satin sheets and fluffy pillows. She must bring all her pick-ups here, Vince thought, but she'll have her hands full with me.

Vince walked through to the last room. His heart lurched. The cunt had fooled him. On a tiny table in the corner were all the components of a heroin fix. The white powder itself was loose, piled neatly in a mound. The chick was a junkie. Vince felt cheated.

His first reaction was to leave. This whole thing could be a set-up. Then Vince shook his head. No, that didn't figure. If she was a cop, she could have nabbed him back in the greasy spoon. He went over to the table. He took a small amount of the powder on his finger and tasted it. Pure. This wasn't street shit. It was high quality dope.

He felt her eyes on his back. She was staring at him in the doorway of the room. "Have some," she said gently. "It's the finest there is."

Vince turned. "Are you a dealer?" he asked suspiciously.

The Woman smiled. She shook her head. "We can have a wonderful afternoon together, Vincent."

That was it then, he thought. She *was* a goddamn junkie. Fuck it, he decided. Let her get stoned. She was a piece of ass and if she was high, he'd be able to get real rough with her. Fuckin' junkie wouldn't even feel it.

"Have some," she said again.

"No, thanks, lady," he answered. "I don't mess with that shit."

Slowly, The Woman began undoing her top. She had revealed most of her breasts before but, seeing her naked to the waist now, Vince had to catch his breath. She was flawless. Her perfection seemed to block out the desolation of the apartment. Her hand went to her skirt. In one motion, the garment was on the floor and she was completely naked.

Catlike, she walked toward him. She ran herself up and down Vince's still clothed body. She began helping Vince out of his clothes. Vince was transfixed. It wasn't like him to let a woman act this way. Usually, he took the lead—but he was helpless. He waited for her to finish, his erection growing full and hard. Soon he was naked too, and ready for her.

Vince felt a surge of masculine power. He'd taken over now. Roughly, he grabbed The Woman by the hair and tried to force her to her knees. But she was strong. She smiled at him slyly.

Vince grinned back at her. "So you *do* like to play rough. I knew it."

He put his hand around her lovely throat and brought her face to his, mouths touching. Then The Woman pulled back.

"Not yet, Vincent. First this." She walked over to the table containing the heroin.

Vince came up behind her. Grasping her around the waist, he spun her off balance.

"You don't need that now. You can shoot up that garbage when I leave."

But The Woman ignored him. She began heating the heroin.

"No," Vincent shouted. "I said later."

The Woman looked him squarely in the eye. "Not later, Vincent, now."

Vince clenched his fist. This had gone far enough. There was no use arguing with a junkie. What this bitch needed was a punch in her pretty face to forget about her fix so she could spread her legs in the goddamn bed where she belonged. Vince started to swing but something in her cold green eyes made him put his hand down.

Vince stood motionless as The Woman drew the clear liquid up into the syringe. She held the needle out to him invitingly. "The first one's for you, Vincent," she whispered.

The Woman took a long piece of black silk from the table and tied it tightly around Vince's bicep. He felt the material dig into his arm. This was nuts, he told himself. This chick was getting him ready for a fix—the one thing he swore he'd never do—and he was just standing there. He despised junkies. They were degenerate low-lifes. How could he let her do this to him? He should stop her right now and knock her teeth right out of her mouth. Still, there was something appealing, seductive, about the way she was taking care of him. The Woman offered him the needle.

"I told you no," said Vince quietly.

As though unconnected to his body, Vince's arm reached out. His fingers wrapped around the syringe. He could feel the heat of the drug through the thin glass. An inexplicable craving had been lit inside his body.

"Go on," she said encouragingly.

Vince tightened his hold on the needle. His stomach cramped up and his mouth was beginning to feel very dry. His hand trembled in anticipation. He looked at the vein that was bulging in his arm. The craving was getting stronger.

"Go on," The Woman repeated.

Obediently, Vince brought the tip of the needle up against the pulsating vein. It pierced his flesh and he felt a brief stab of pain as he plunged the first drops of heroin into his bloodstream. Vince watched with wonder as his blood mingled with the drug in the syringe. He paused.

"It's over now," The Woman said sweetly.

Vince nodded. With a quick stab, he shot the remainder of the drug into his arm. His whole body stiffened. Vince's heart had stopped beating before he hit the floor. The needle still embedded in his vein, he lay lifeless in a rectangle of afternoon sun that poured through the window.

The Woman stepped over Vincent Mallory's corpse, her wintry laughter echoing in the cheerless room.

Jimmy had only been gone a day but he was glad to be home. The flight back to Chicago had been a bumpy one and there had even been a possibility of the plane being diverted to Philadelphia. But after circling LaGuardia for the better part of an hour, the aircraft had landed, much to the priest's relief.

Now in the seclusion of his study, a bracing tea with brandy within easy reach, he was about to confirm what he already fearfully suspected.

Opening "Deutschland, 1800-1850," he searched for the passage containing the names of the six Christian men. Listed just above "Stahlmeister," he saw "Berger, Stern, Muller" and the two faded spaces.

Berger, he verified, just like the man in Florida. Stern, the executive in New Orleans.

More links with the past. Three of the names from 1820 matched the names of mass murderers from the present. And all three killers went out with Laura Zimmer, who looks just like the woman on the gold coin.

Muller. Had there been any deranged assailant recently named Muller? The priest concentrated. Not that he could recall.

He took a magnifying glass from the drawer and examined the two faded names. Holding the pages up to the light, he was able to discern two letters, separated from each other by several spaces, in one of the names.

"B and C," he said aloud, with a gasp of realization, just as the telephone rang.

"Hello?" he answered a bit breathlessly.

The caller was cordial but to the point. "This is Father Valenti from Bishop Walsh's office.

His Excellency would like to see you tomorrow morning at nine o'clock. Here at the Residence."

Jimmy felt a twinge of worry. Could it be that his trip to Chicago had been reported? "Do you know what it's in reference to?" he asked warily.

"I haven't the slightest idea," said Father Valenti in a clipped tone. "I'm sure you'll find out tomorrow."

"Of course," said Jimmy. "Thank you, Father. I'll be there."

The clock in Father Valenti's office was just chiming nine when Jimmy strode through the door, looking no worse for wear from the sleepless night that he had just spent.

The Bishop's secretary looked up from the sheaf of morning mail. "Father Hamilton?"

Jimmy nodded politely and squared his shoulders.

"His Excellency just called," Father Valenti continued. "He'll be a few minutes late. You can wait in the study. Make yourself comfortable."

"Thank you," replied Jimmy.

Entering the study, Jimmy felt momentarily relieved. He'd have some time to get his thoughts together and prepare for the Bishop's onslaught. This was almost certain to be a very serious dressing down, designed to halt Jimmy's investigations before he could get at the core of truth that had so far evaded him. Even if the Bishop doesn't know about Chicago, Jimmy reasoned, he's got to be burned up about the way I walked out of here the other day.

Jimmy sat down in an armchair and paged through a copy of *Commonweal Magazine* distractedly. After a moment, he put the magazine down and paced impatiently. I've got to be ready for him, he resolved. Whatever he says, I can't lose sight of what this woman has done. And what she might be planning for Richard. I know too much to stop now—and this is too heavy to ignore.

Jimmy's eyes wandered about the room. The heavily brocaded curtains were still drawn and little light came in from the courtyard. Guess I'm the first appointment for the day, reflected Jimmy grimly. The Biship probably wants to read me the riot act right away so he can get on to more important things.

Jimmy found himself standing by the window. He opened the drapes, admitting the morning sunshine into the study. On his way back to the armchair, he glanced casually at the Bishop's desk.

What he saw on the notepad made his head spin.

Written in the Bishop's meticulous hand were the words: "Stahlmeister. Berger. Germany, 1820."

He's onto it, thought Jimmy excitedly. He knows.

Abandoning all caution, the priest rifled through the other papers on the desk. What else does he know, Jimmy wondered anxiously. There must be something else here.

Moving some business letters aside, he noticed a dusty, dilapidated text with a leather bookmark protruding from between its pages. The volume was in Latin and Jimmy opened to the bookmarked page.

The drawings were side by side, carefully detailed, embellished with a border of swirling curlicues, presenting with astonishing clarity the close-up portrait and the full-figured depiction of The Woman, in exactly the same poses as on the gold medallion.

Jimmy's pulse pounded. A knot was forming in his stomach. His hands grew clammy.

With trepidation, he began translating from the Latin. His voice shook as he spoke the words aloud.

"She is called Madonna. Her beauty has enchanted mankind through the centuries—for nearly 2000 years. She is believed to be the supreme seductress who entices her victims into committing unspeakable acts of violence. She feeds on the worship of her evil cult and when their perverted faith becomes strong enough, then and only then can she walk the earth. In 1820, Madonna's evil surfaced in Germany when she set off a string of brutal killings. A band of six men—true Christian believers all—ended her reign of terror there and plunged her back to the pits of hell, shrieking promises of bloody revenge on the descendants of those brave Christian men. She is believed to be the anti-Blessed Virgin, the antithesis of Christ's mother. There is every reason to believe that Madonna is, in fact, the mother of Satan himself."

"Oh, God. Oh, dear Jesus," whispered Jimmy, appalled. He sank down onto the Bishop's chair, feeling his skin creep. He took a deep breath, not wanting to read on. Finally, he resumed translating.

"Her Vulnerability—Her One Basic Flaw," he read the paragraph heading. "As the Blessed Virgin is pure, Madonna is a foul creature with an insatiable appetite for the most vile pleasures of the flesh. But her lustful hunger can transport her back to the Devil's Kingdom. Christian men have discovered the way to return her to hell through her weakness—her one basic flaw . . ."

Breathlessly, almost afraid of what he might find, Jimmy turned the page. What he saw overwhelmed him with fury and exasperation.

The next page was gone.

Beaten again, the priest dejectedly closed the book. He rested his head in his hands.

From the doorway, the Bishop had been watching him. His sympathetic voice interrupted Jimmy's reverie.

"I looked for it too, Fr. Hamilton, but it is not there."

"Leslie, it's about Richard. I think he's in serious danger."

Leslie took Jimmy's coat and showed him into her apartment. The priest wasted no time in getting directly to the point.

"This woman he's been seeing—I have reason to believe she's been connected with three mass murders. There may even be more, but I can't say right now."

Leslie put the priest's coat down on a chair awkwardly. Her eyes widened with fear.

"Oh, my God, what do you mean?" she stammered.

It took Jimmy the better part of twenty minutes to fill his cousin in on the trip to Chicago, the conversation with Detective Brown, the strange visit with Charles Stallmaster and the startling revelations from Ray Price.

On the way over to Leslie's, Jimmy had carefully planned what he would tell her. There was enough evidence from present day events to convince his cousin that Richard was in grave trouble without making mention of this woman's apparent ties to the past. Much of what he had unearthed from the library books was, after all, Church business and if, God forbid, the allegation that the woman was the mother of Satan were true, the priest could well understand the Church's wanting to cover the matter up. Whether it was true or not, Leslie was frightened enough—there was no reason to add to her alarm. Besides, Bishop Walsh had assured him he would take the entire matter up with higher authorities.

So, as Leslie listened with rapt attention, Jimmy stressed the enormity of Richard's danger, while leaving out all references to the legendary seductress and the Church's efforts to deal with her.

When Jimmy finished his account, there was a long silence. Leslie sat lost in contemplation. The priest's heart went out to her. She looked so confused and shattered. No wonder, he thought. What he had just told her was an awful lot to absorb.

"We have to go to Richard's. The two of us. Right now." Her tone was one of sudden determination.

Jimmy nodded. "I was hoping you'd say that."

A half hour later, they were outside Richard's apartment, ringing the doorbell. A lock clicked and the door opened slowly.

Richard came eerily into view. With his hollow cheeks and lifeless eyes, he had deteriorated markedly since they had last seen him. His clothing, dirty and rumpled, hung unnaturally on his still muscular frame. Leslie could not suppress a gasp at seeing her brother's shockingly neglected condition.

"Richard," began the priest.

A groan of irritation interrupted him. "Oh, shit, give me a break," muttered Richard, starting to close the door on them.

The priest was too fast for him. He wedged his foot into the doorway, pushing Richard roughly back into the apartment.

Jimmy stepped inside. Leslie followed, closing the door behind her and leaning against it guardedly.

Richard retreated further into the litter-strewn room. He squared his jaw aggressively.

"What do you want from me?" he asked angrily. "I don't want to see you."

Jimmy grabbed him by his wrinkled shirt, nearly lifting him from the floor.

"Well, I want to see *you!*" shot back the priest fiercely.

With a powerful urgency, Jimmy steered Richard across the room, planting him unceremoniously on the sofa. Puffs of dust billowed from the couch cushions in protest as Richard looked around uncomprehendingly.

"You can't come barging in here, shoving me around," Richard growled. "I could have you arrested."

"You're not going to have anyone arrested," said the priest emphatically. "You're going to sit there until I'm finished with what I have to say."

Richard ran a hand sulkily through his hair. His eyes traveled to the coffee table and his face took on a mooning expression.

Leslie and Jimmy followed his line of vision and found themselves staring at a framed pen and ink likeness of Laura Zimmer.

"It's the same woman," said Jimmy, turning to Leslie meaningfully. "The one that's on the police sketch."

"Oh, God," murmured Leslie.

Jimmy was on his feet, jabbing a finger into Richard's chest.

"Richard, I'm going to tell you something,"

he said through clenched teeth, "and I want you to listen. You can no longer see this woman."

Richard burst into shrill laughter. His feet kicked childishly in the air.

"Stop that!" warned the priest.

Richard held his sides with hysterical delight. The priest smacked him firmly across the face.

"You can no longer see this woman!" Jimmy bellowed.

Richard's laughter ceased at once. He smirked at the priest with a superior air.

"What do you know about seeing women, Father?" Richard asked caustically.

"I know about this woman," snapped Jimmy, grabbing the framed drawing.

Richard was instantly enraged and on his feet. He lunged at the priest, desperately trying to wrest the portrait from his hand. Effortlessly, his adrenalin racing, Jimmy flung him back onto the couch.

Her eyes brimming with tears, Leslie intervened.

"Richard, I know you're sick," she cried pleadingly, "but for God's sake, listen! He's trying to save your life!"

Richard giggled foolishly, then looked to the priest, who was holding the framed sketch behind his back.

"You going to save my soul too?" he asked mockingly.

"I only hope it's not too late," replied the

priest gravely. He waved the portrait in the air. "Let me tell you about her—this Laura Zimmer. Charles Stallmaster, Chicago, dated Laura Zimmer. George Berger, Miami, dated Laura Zimmer. Roger Stern, New Orleans, dated Laura Zimmer. These were normal men until they dated Laura Zimmer. But then they changed—into killers. Each one went berserk and committed mass murder." The priest paused and stared deeply into Richard's eyes. "Now *you* are dating Laura Zimmer."

"And look what she's done to you, Richard," added Leslie, her voice rising imploringly.

"She's made me happy," said Richard quietly but with conviction.

Jimmy fought to control his temper. "What about those killers? Did she make *them* happy too?"

"Killers?" asked Richard innocently. "I don't believe any of that. You made that up. You're liars."

"Richard, please," protested Leslie.

Jimmy cut her off. "Richard, I'm not a liar," he said, fixing the other man with a look of icy self-restraint. "What I told you was the truth. I went to Chicago. I met Charles Stallmaster. I saw what that woman did to him. He's a patient in an institution for the criminally insane, locked up in a padded cell, worshipping at a pathetic altar that he built for this woman."

"You're lying," said Richard calmly.

"If you think so," countered the priest, "why don't you ask her yourself?"

Richard crashed his hand down onto the coffee table and leaped to his feet.

"I don't have to ask her anything," he roared. Crossing the room with bold, purposeful strides, he opened the front door. "I want you both to get out of here," he said in a measured voice. "Get out now! This is my home. You have no right to be here."

"Richard, how can you?" began Leslie tearfully.

Jimmy touched her arm gently and turned to Richard. "No, we have no right to be here," he said wearily. "But we care about you, Richard. We love you."

Richard sneered at him. "How nice," he said sarcastically. "Now will you get the fuck out?"

Jimmy guided Leslie to the door. Richard sniggered and made a sweeping motion with his hand as though to usher them grandly out of the apartment. As Leslie stood in the hallway, the priest confronted Richard one last time.

"I can't force you to listen to reason," he said softly. "That woman is obviously stronger than I thought. But that could change."

"Get out," said Richard harshly.

"Ask her about those killers," Jimmy advised, "if you're not afraid."

"Just leave, okay?"

Leslie stepped inside and touched her brother's face gently. "Why won't you let us help you?" she entreated.

For the first time since Annie's death, a tear came to Richard's eye.

"Because you can't," he said solemnly.

Outside Richard's apartment building, Leslie stopped to light a cigarette.

"I'm scared, Jimmy," she confessed. "Do you think we should leave him alone like that?"

The priest was consoling. "We don't have a choice—for now."

"But he's getting worse. It's like he's going over the edge."

"I know," said Jimmy.

"If only there was a way to keep him from seeing this woman," said Leslie.

"He's obsessed with her," said the priest. "She's got her hooks into him. But I think there's a way to beat her at her own game."

"Do you really think so?" asked Leslie hopefully.

The priest took her arm and they started off down the street. "With the help of God, she can be stopped," he told her. "I'm certain of it."

Arm in arm, intent on their hopes for Richard, the priest and Leslie failed to notice the sleek black coupe parked at the corner of the block.

In the front seat, next to the anonymous driver, The Woman watched them with a knowing smile.

"And what did the priest tell you?" asked The Woman, running her tongue languorously along the nape of Richard's neck.

Lounging on the sofa, dressed in a one piece,

white leather jumpsuit, she toyed with a lock of his hair, curling it counter-clockwise around her finger.

"He made up a story about you and some killers," replied Richard dreamily.

"And did you believe him?" she cooed.

"No."

She massaged the muscles of his shoulders as he leaned his head back into her lap.

"They don't understand about us," she breathed in his ear.

"No," replied Richard automatically.

"Tell me what you did in school," she coaxed.

Richard smiled wistfully. "I played with my gun."

"This one?" she asked teasingly, indicating the .357 Magnum he held in his hand.

She caressed the side of his face. Under her skillful touch, Richard seemed to glow with a new vitality.

"You bet," Richard answered boyishly. "This beauty here." He ran the barrel of the gun suggestively along the length of her shapely leg.

"I like when you play in school," she said approvingly. "How did that feel?"

"It was exciting," Richard acknowledged, his eyes gleaming. "I had the power of life and death."

Seductively, slowly, The Woman began unzipping her jumpsuit.

"That *is* exciting," she agreed.

* * *

Midnight blanketed Grove Street with a protective shadow. The Forgotten Lore Book Shop, nestled between a boutique and a Chinese laundry, both of them long darkened, throbbed with an inner light.

The deserted ground floor shone in the innocent order of carefully arranged books, unremembered in the moonlight. A cash register proclaiming "No Sale" stood idly by the door.

One flight down, in the gloomy basement, a worship service was in progress. Mr. Clark's crusade had blossomed—more than three dozen people thronged the room.

The smell of brightly burning votive lights mingled with that of incense as the black-robed cult members raised their arms in exaltation. The gold medallions, shining with captured fire, glistened from their necks.

Howard Clark, his lined face alight with fervor, beamed down at the joyful crowd from his position of eminence on a raised platform at the front of the room.

"Ave, Mater! Hosanna in excelsis," he exhorted, his voice booming magnetically.

"Ave, Mater," the congregation responded eagerly.

Mr. Clark bowed his head respectfully. "We thank our Lord God, Satan," he proclaimed, "for answering our pleas. He has sent us his most revered Mother, Queen of Darkness. Our clan has grown. Our strength has increased, giving her the power to walk among us again. arly two hundred years have passed since she last appeared to her devoted followers—now it is our deepest hope that she will never leave! *Ave, Mater! Hosanna in excelsis!"*

"Ave, Mater," answered the disciples.

Dark robes slipped to the floor as the worshippers enfolded one another. The gentle fondling of flesh brought a renewed chanting which grew in urgency.

"Ave, Mater! Ave, Mater!"

Suddenly, a devout hush enveloped the dank cellar. The followers, as one, fell to their knees in awe.

The Woman had come into the room. Regal in a robe of vermilion, she glided through her adoring legion to assume her rightful place on the altar-like slab.

"We welcome you," cried Mr. Clark. "We rejoice at your return."

The Woman raised her head in authoritative splendor. She reached out to her genuflecting multitude with a sweeping gesture of benediction.

"My faithful children," she intoned lovingly.

As though by signal, the assemblage rose to their feet. The Woman unclasped her robe and let it slide to the floor, leaving her magnificently naked.

The lid of a wicker basket was quietly lifted. A serpent's head rose into view, its tongue extended in fiendish anticipation.

The snake squirmed toward the altar. The Woman smiled to it summoningly.

The serpent began its sensuous ascent, entwining its demanding bulk at first around her ankle, then easing up her calf, tongue darting avidly to nuzzle at her thigh.

"*Ave, Mater!*" chanted the gathering.

The snake moved higher, encircling the bare flesh of The Woman's desirous naked thigh.

A look of blissful serenity on her face, The Woman stood poised to receive the full hardness of the serpent chosen for this—the most diabolic of rites.

The snake's tongue shot upward thirstily. The Woman sighed with an ancient longing.

The flickering candlelight caught the image on the gold medallions which was mirrored by the ceremony on the altar.

The ritual, thwarted in Bad Hoffberg, Germany, in 1820 was about to be consummated.

Madonna had returned.

CHAPTER FOURTEEN

JIMMY HAD never met the Cardinal. The closest he had come was sitting three rows away from him at Pope John Paul II's mass at Yankee Stadium, back in the late 70's.

Now he was riding in a chauffeur-driven limousine, along with Bishop Walsh, to Cardinal Madori's private chambers.

As the driver maneuvered the automobile through Park Avenue traffic, Jimmy regarded the Bishop with admiration. It had taken courage for him to set up this appointment. Even though the evidence of the censored pages was clear-cut, the Bishop, just by calling attention to it, was going way out on a limb.

He's taking a chance on me, thought Jimmy

appreciatively, and I'd better not let him down.

Soon after, the limousine pulled up in front of an old, majestic and very dignified building. Jimmy and Bishop Walsh alighted from the limo and entered the sanctuary of Anthony Cardinal Madori.

A robust, sensitive looking man in his late sixties, Cardinal Madori welcomed the two men into his large, high-ceilinged suite.

Introductions over, Jimmy managed to turn his eyes away from the original El Grecos that adorned the wall to accept the Cardinal's challenge.

"Let's get right to it, Fr. Hamilton," said Cardinal Madori. "Let me see the medal."

Jimmy took the gold coin from his pocket. He handed it to the Cardinal, who inspected both sides of it intently.

Jimmy watched anxiously as the Cardinal's eyes welled up with tears of recognition.

"I was hoping she couldn't come back," the Cardinal said dispiritedly. "Her cult must have been growing all these years. Do you know where she is?"

Fr. Hamilton felt torn between elation and despair. The Cardinal was not only acknowledging the woman's existence but hinting undeniably at her power.

"I'm afraid she's right here in New York," the priest answered.

"Have you seen her?" inquired the Cardinal.

Jimmy let a few seconds go by. "No, but my cousin has become involved with her."

The Cardinal's tone was offhand but his question was pointed. "What is your cousin's name?"

"Richard. Richard Bloch."

Cardinal Madori bowed his head. "God help him!"

Jimmy observed the Cardinal as he got to his feet and paced the length of the room. The Cardinal's visage grew stern and decisive.

"What I am about to tell you," he instructed, "will not leave this room. I must impose on you a strict vow of secrecy. Is that agreed?"

The question hung in the air. Jimmy was the first to nod, then Bishop Walsh followed.

"I believe that both of you have read the books," Cardinal Madori continued.

"That's correct," Bishop Walsh concurred.

The Cardinal's voice was weighted with the grief of centuries.

"You know that this woman is reputed to be the mother of Satan. The Church has known of her existence for ages but has not publicly confirmed it. The Vatican position is that to admit her existence is to run the risk of setting off world-wide hysteria and despondence. The Church has hoped each time she has been sent back to hell, she would remain there. But it has not been the case. She always returns."

Jimmy let all of that sink in. "Then it was the Church that tampered with the books?" he asked not unkindly.

"Under orders from the highest authority," replied the Cardinal.

Jimmy marveled as the Bishop spoke up.

"One of the omissions was particularly maddening. It was about to describe this woman's weak point—the way to send her back to Hell."

The Cardinal deliberated. From the street outside, a truck backfired noisily.

Cardinal Madori looked at the two men evenly. "I have that information."

He crossed the room to a mahogany cabinet near the window. He opened the cabinet to reveal a small metal safe which was secured with a combination lock. Deftly he twirled the numbered knob and a moment later the safe clicked open.

Cardinal Madori reached inside for a red velvet pouch tied with black cord. His hands trembled slightly as he untied the ribbon, taking out a yellowed, time-worn sheet of paper.

"The missing page!" said Jimmy, catching his breath.

"Exactly," nodded the Cardinal. "Now, Father, do you recall the last sentence—from the previous page of the book?"

Jimmy recited from memory: "Christian men have discovered the way to return her to hell through her weakness—her one basic flaw."

"Good," noted the Cardinal. He handed Jimmy the page. "Now translate this."

Jimmy's heartbeat quickened as he held the ancient paper up to the light. The Latin words seemed to sear the very essence of Jimmy's soul as he converted them expertly into English.

"She must be stabbed in the heart with a blessed and sharpened crucifix while she is . . ."

The priest paused and looked at the two older men uncomfortably.

"Go ahead, Father," prompted the Cardinal.

Jimmy resumed translating. " . . . while she is at the peak of sexual excitement."

"God have mercy," breathed Bishop Walsh in astonishment. "Is there no other way?"

The Cardinal shook his head resignedly. "No, I'm afraid there isn't. She draws her strength in two ways. Through the worship of her cult and through sexual congress. It is only in the latter that she abandons herself to the point where she can be vanquished."

Jimmy handed back the page. "What is the Church's position on this ritual? Who can perform it?"

"The book says simply: 'A true believer in Christ Our Lord and the Blessed Mother, Mary.' "

"In that case," said Jimmy firmly, "I'd like to volunteer."

The Cardinal returned the page to its velvet holder. He studied the young priest thoughtfully.

"That is commendable, Father," he said. "but keep in mind: in 1820, *six* men were required. This may be too much for *one* man."

"Just the same, I'd like to try," replied Jimmy resolutely.

The Cardinal shuffled some papers on his massive, lion-pawed oak desk. He arranged them neatly, placing them beneath a frosted crystal paperweight.

"You realize, of course, Fr. Hamilton," he said, "that we will have to contact Rome before proceeding any further."

"That could take a long time," protested Jimmy, his voice rising angrily. "I'm afraid my cousin is too far gone."

"Please, Fr. Hamilton," cautioned Bishop Walsh, "remember where you are. Listen to his Eminence."

"I'm sorry," said Jimmy, making an effort to maintain his composure. "It's just that I know how to find this woman. My cousin Richard can lead me to her. If we don't act soon, more people could die and she might even disappear."

"I realize that, Father," said the Cardinal sympathetically.

Jimmy paused, bracing himself. From the wall, the faces of El Greco martyrs, tortured and fanatical, looked down on him pityingly.

The priest cleared his throat. "Suppose I were to try it on my own, what would *your* position be?"

The Cardinal's answer was as Jimmy had expected. "I would be forced to deny any knowledge of your actions."

"I'm willing to take that chance," Jimmy offered.

"Yes, I believe you are," replied the Cardinal. "You would be entirely on your own." His eyes took in the Bishop. "We would deny that this meeting even took place."

"I understand," said Jimmy.

"Then you will need this," said Cardinal Madori, reaching into the velvet pouch.

He handed Jimmy a sharpened crucifix.

"We will pray for you."

"Leslie, it's Jimmy. I need the keys to Richard's apartment. Do you have them?"

On the other end of the phone, Leslie thought for a moment. "There may be a set around someplace. Why do you need them?"

Jimmy eyed the sharpened crucifix which rested on his desk.

"I can't say right now," he told her, "but I think everything is going to be all right."

"You're being very mysterious."

"I'm aware of that. But I think I can help Richard. You'll have to trust me."

"Of course, I trust you, Jimmy," said Leslie sincerely.

"I'll need those keys as soon as possible."

"I'll drop them off," Leslie promised.

"Thanks, I'll talk to you later."

Jimmy hung up the receiver, thankful that his cousin had not pressed for further information. She really does trust me, thought the priest. He hoped he'd be worthy of that trust.

If she had even an inkling of what I'm preparing to do, he mused, she'd probably do anything to stop me. As it is, the Cardinal and the Bishop think I'm acting hastily—taking on more than I can handle. I'm only one man, and six were needed back in 1820, but with God's help, I can prevail.

I have to prevail or Richard is doomed. Not to mention the other innocent people who may fall victim to this woman's evil power.

Jimmy ran his finger along the razor-sharp edge of the crucifix. The mere touch of the blade's steely surface was enough to draw a droplet of blood. He hefted the foot-long crucifix in his hand, admiring the precision of its craftsmanship and its smoothly sculpted lines that tapered to a deadly point. Carefully, he wrapped it in a sanctified cloth and locked it in the bottom drawer of his desk.

Thoughts of 1820 filled his mind. It was a cross such as this one, he considered, that those six Christian men had used to send her back to Hell. If only she had remained there!

Jimmy opened "Deutschland, 1800-1850" for perhaps the hundredth time. Automatically, he turned to the passage listing the six names. Again he noted the names: Berger, Stern, Muller, Stahlmeister along with the faded spaces, in one of which he had darkened in the letters "B" and "C."

A feeling of dread closed over him.

A fragment of dialogue from this afternoon's meeting at the Cardinal's chambers pounded in his brain.

"What is your cousin's name?" the Cardinal had asked.

"Richard. Richard Bloch," Jimmy had responded.

"God help him!"

Somehow he had known all along, but Jimmy shuddered in repulsion as he penciled in the remaining letters to form the name of yet another of the six Christian men.

Bloch.

"Mr. Bloch?"

Richard looked up from his desk to see a hesitant Donald Carter standing in the classroom doorway.

Richard cursed inwardly. Donald was becoming a goddamned nuisance, he fumed. Class was dismissed ten minutes ago and that blind idiot is still hanging around!

He continued doodling on a sketch pad, drawing a likeness of The Woman. Maybe if I'm very quiet, he reasoned, Donald won't know I'm in here and he'll go away.

"Mr. Bloch?" the student persisted, taking a step forward with the aid of his cane.

Richard sighed. He knows I'm here, all right. Glassy-eyed, he regarded the young man.

"Yes, what is it?" he snapped.

Donald shifted uncertainly. "I was just wondering something," he said tentatively. "Classes have been a little strange lately. Is anything the matter?"

Richard drummed his fingers on the desk in annoyance. Terrific, he muttered to himself. This is all I need. It's bad enough Leslie and Jimmy are on my case—now I've got to put up with this jerk!

"Donald, I'm very busy," he said sharply. "Don't bother me now."

"I'm sorry, sir," said the boy diffidently, "it's just that something seems to be wrong."

"There's nothing wrong, Donald," the teacher said coldly. "Now would you mind leaving? School's over for the day."

"But, sir . . ." Donald began.

"But nothing," Richard interrupted. "School is over for the day!"

Head down, with a look of dejection, Donald retreated from the classroom. Richard watched through the open door as the boy tapped with his cane on the familiar walk down the long corridor toward the elevator.

Richard chuckled. Good, I've hurt his feelings, he thought with satisfaction. Yes, Donald, classes *have* been a little strange lately, he agreed silently, as the student progressed down the hallway. The other day I had a gun pointed right at your head. I could have drilled a bullet into you, just snuffed out your life, and you wouldn't have even known what hit you.

The boy had reached the end of the corridor. He felt the wall, searching for the elevator button. Finding it, he pressed "Down."

A few seconds later, the elevator door opened. Richard gaped in amazement at what he saw.

There was no elevator car, only an empty shaft.

Isn't that interesting, thought Richard matter-of-factly. The door isn't supposed to open when the elevator isn't there. Wonder where the elevator is? Maybe it got stuck in the basement.

Donald took a step forward toward the empty shaft.

Isn't he in for a surprise, tittered Richard. He's going to be downstairs in record time!

The boy stood poised at the edge of the yawning abyss. His foot inched forward.

A piercing scream rang out.

"Stop!"

A round-shouldered school janitor, coming up the stairs with his mop and pail, had taken in the situation.

"Get back," he shouted.

Bewildered but with lightning fast reflexes, Donald jumped back, falling to the safety of the corridor floor. The janitor dropped his cleaning utensils and hurried to the boy's aid.

Aw, shit! Richard complained to himself. That old fucker came along and spoiled everything!

The janitor helped Donald to his feet. As he steadied the boy, he glanced down to the end of the hallway, spying Richard who was taking everything in, arms folded casually, a benign grin on his face.

"You saw that!" the janitor said accusingly. "Why didn't you try and stop him?"

Richard shrugged. He made no reply.

Donald, perceiving at last what had happened, began to weep silently.

Night shrouded the city. An Indian Summer warmth had kissed the air with a sultry finesse. Heat lightning flickered in the skies over the Hudson. The darkness was charged with expectancy. It was the kind of night dreams were made of and in which nightmares came true.

Kneeling before a statue of Christ and one of the Blessed Virgin, Jimmy bowed his head in solemn prayer. Behind him on the desk of his study, the library books were stacked neatly; coffee cups, sandwich wrappers and other remnants of the priest's frenzied research had been cleared away. The study was tidy, returned to its customary order.

As he prayed, Jimmy's handsome face appeared calm but fired with a driving determination. In the hours since he'd confirmed Bloch as one of the six Christian men, he'd been feeling his confidence grow, strengthened by the grace he believed to be flowing from Almighty God.

He knew what had to be done. Even at this very moment, Richard might be in that woman's arms.

There was a soft knock at the door.

Jimmy blinked. He looked up, puzzled. Getting to his feet, he glanced at his watch. That's odd, he thought, I'm not expecting anyone.

He went to the door and opened it.

He gasped in startled dismay.

Jimmy had lived with that face for weeks—on the gold coin, then on the police sketch. Next, Stallmaster's crude drawing. The book in Bishop Walsh's office. Richard's framed portrait. Her face had even invaded his dreams. But none of that had prepared him for the Vision that stood majestically on his threshold.

Her emerald eyes, almond shaped and radiant, glistened appraisingly from a countenance that was a model of perfection. From her full, pouting mouth, the pinkness of her tongue could be seen as she moistened her lips. Her raven hair, hanging loosely, gave her a defined aura in contrast to the simple white scarf and trenchcoat she was wearing.

"Hello, Jimmy," she breathed. "I'm here for your soul."

Involuntarily, Jimmy took a step backward. He made the sign of the cross.

Effortlessly, The Woman slipped into the room.

Jimmy felt faint. He was gripped by confusion. Years of study in the priesthood had convinced him that evil could take on any form. But how, he asked himself, could someone so vile look so magnificent?

Enveloped by her presence, the priest felt his confidence ebb. As though she could discern his thoughts, The Woman moved closer, a smile beginning to form.

Jimmy shuddered. Was he imagining it or had the room grown suddenly chilled? He exhaled. Oh, my God, he thought, I can see my breath.

There was a clattering noise. On a nearby shelf, books and a vase began to shake violently.

Enticingly, The Woman undid her scarf and opened the top button of her coat, staring intently at Jimmy, who withdrew further into the room.

A potted plant toppled from the window ledge, its porcelain shattering loudly on the floor. The clock on Jimmy's wall chimed crazily as its hands began to spin in frantic revolutions.

Jimmy turned away. He fell on his knees before the statues of Jesus and the Virgin.

"Don't look at them," The Woman ordered, "look at me. Look what I can give you."

She opened another button on her coat, hinting at the nakedness that waited beneath.

The priest summoned up all his faith. With a concentration of will, he began to pray, his voice resounding forcefully in the room.

"Hail, Mary, full of grace, the Lord is with thee . . ."

The Woman stepped between Jimmy and the statues. Her smile a luscious invitation, she opened another button. Jimmy averted his eyes.

The Woman indicated the statues disparagingly. "They're not real," she said. "Look at me. I'm flesh and blood. I'm warm. I'm warm for you, Jimmy."

" . . . blessed art thou among women and blessed is the fruit of thy womb, Jesus. Holy Mary, Mother of God . . ."

The woman glared at him angrily. Jimmy trembled as the air around him grew icy.

"You're shivering, Jimmy," she observed. "Are you cold? I can warm you."

" . . . pray for us sinners now and at the hour of our death, Amen."

The Woman unclasped the final button. She opened her coat completely, letting it slide from her shoulders to stand nude and tantalizing before him.

"Look at me, priest!" she demanded.

Jimmy, eyes shut tightly, was in turmoil. The Woman was so beautiful, so desirable. He longed to open his eyes and feast them upon her.

"Oh, God, give me strength," he prayed inwardly, both his hands closing into fists. He heard more items crashing about the room.

"Look at me!" she commanded. Her voice lowered to a suggestive plea. "You've never had a woman, have you?"

Jimmy opened his eyes.

On his knees, only inches from her voluptuous body, he looked at her achingly. A sweet smile of victory on her lips, she parted her legs alluringly.

"Come and fuck me, priest!" she commanded. "Come and fuck me!"

The Madonna, thought Jimmy. She's my salvation.

Abruptly, with entreating hands, he reached forward. His fingers closed around the statue of the Blessed Virgin, clutching it to his breast.

"Mother of God," he prayed aloud, "I am a true believer in Christ Our Lord and you, the Blessed Virgin. This woman is your evil counterpart. Oh, Mary, help me to resist her foul advances! Help me to be strong. Give me the power to fight her as long as there is life in my body!"

The Woman laughed contemptuously. "Pray, Jimmy," she scoffed. "Pray to your graven images. It won't do you any good. They aren't a match for me."

Gazing fiercely at the Virgin's statue that Jimmy clung to desperately, The Woman let a low, primitive growl come from her throat.

The statue exploded in Jimmy's hand.

Jolted by the impact, feeling an incisive stab of pain, the priest fell back heavily to the floor, where he lay for a moment in shocked semi-consciousness. More explosions rang out and there were repeated rumblings as articles of furniture careened around the room.

Later on, he calculated that he had only blacked out for about a minute. When he came to, he noticed at once that the room had lost its chill and a pervasive quiet had settled upon it.

He also noticed that The Woman was gone.

Jimmy rose unsteadily to his feet. The study was in shambles, with broken plaster and glass everywhere. On the floor, the statue of Jesus was smashed irreparably.

Beside it, near the desk, the shattered face of the Blessed Virgin bore an expression of infinite sadness.

Emerging from his daze, Jimmy stared at his hand. Miraculously, there wasn't a scratch on it.

CHAPTER FIFTEEN

LESLIE HAD spent the entire day hovering dangerously close to a deep depression. She had risen early after a fitful night's sleep, lacking the energy to do her morning exercises. With no appetite to eat her customary hearty breakfast, she'd gone for what she thought would be a bracing walk down to Soho but had gotten no further south than Bleecker Street before deciding to return home, feeling listless.

The phone call from Jimmy hadn't helped, but had rather added to her confusion. Though she'd meant it when she'd expressed her trust in him, his request for Richard's apartment keys had made her feel vaguely left out, wondering from a distance what course of action Jimmy was planning to take on his own.

Leslie was worried for the priest's welfare. If Jimmy lets himself into Richard's apartment, for whatever reason, she thought logically, and Richard should happen to find him there, things could really get out of hand. In the state Richard's in, he's liable to attack him, or at the very least press charges against him.

Leslie had found the keys quickly enough in the drawer of her night table. But if a mere walk to Washington Square Park had tired her out, she reasoned, there was no way she was going to get uptown to drop them off at Jimmy's as promised. She'd called a messenger service and sent them over in a plain manila envelope.

The afternoon had droned on. She'd spent most of it slumped on the sofa, mulling over all the monstrous events that had happened since the "Straw Hat" premiere. By evening, she felt absolutely drained.

Sitting here like this isn't doing me a damned bit of good, she concluded.

Being depressed is just negative energy, she thought, jumping to her feet. I've got to turn this around. If Jimmy can be strong and positive, I have to be the same.

She viewed herself critically in the full-length mirror. Wow, she thought, I don't exactly look terrific.

It was time to shape up, to do all the things that invariably pulled her out of a blue funk. That meant some toning up calisthenics, a facial, a henna treatment, an oil bath, and, she thought with a giggle, I'll paint my toenails blushing pink.

Tomorrow would not be a repeat of today, she vowed. I'll get a good night's sleep, call my agent first thing in the morning, take a few dance classes and go out on some interviews.

And, she decided with a renewed faith, I'll stop off at St. Patrick's and say a prayer for Jimmy.

Uptown that evening, Jimmy was doing some praying of his own. At a side altar of the virtually deserted St. Matthew's Church, he raised his hands in supplication to a large statue of Our Lady Of Mercy.

From nearby, a mahogany cross bearing the likeness of the crucified Jesus cast a shadow on the young priest's visage, the lines of which reflected his revitalized conviction.

A few minutes later, Jimmy was behind the wheel of his Volkswagen, heading down Riverside Drive. The dashboard clock read ten to nine as he turned off onto the street where Richard lived.

Thunder crackled ominously overhead as the priest steered the car in to the curb next to a fire hydrant, directly across from Richard's apartment building.

Jimmy looked up at Richard's third floor window. The shutters were open and the light was on. He watched for a minute, but there was no sign of activity in the apartment.

Jimmy reached down to a leather bag on the seat next to him. He took out a set of keys, a vial of holy water and a prayer book. Glancing around cautiously to make sure there were no passersby who might observe him, he extracted the sharpened crucifix.

Again he tested the sharpness of the steel blade—its murderous point sent a twinge of revulsion through his body.

His eyes returned to Richard's window. Someone was moving up there. He leaned forward, trying to make out who it was.

It was Richard.

Though the apartment light was dim, Jimmy could see his face clearly. His hair hung down in his eyes and he appeared to be draped in a terrycloth bathrobe.

The priest waited, wondering if The Woman were upstairs too. Richard continued pacing about but no one else could be seen. After a moment, he disappeared from sight.

Jimmy sighed, gathered up his implements and got out of the car.

Adjusting the priest's stole around his neck, he crossed the street, letting himself into Richard's apartment building. Seeing no one in the lobby, he hurried to the elevator.

A glance upward stopped him in his tracks.

The arrow on the bronze art deco arch that served as the floor indicator was poised on three.

Someone was getting on or off the elevator at Richard's floor.

Acting with quick reflexes, the priest dashed over to the stairwell door. Tugging on its heavy bulk, he opened it clumsily and stepped onto the narrow, darkened landing.

Moving rapidly up the fire stairs, Jimmy approached the second floor.

Suddenly, a bright shaft of light illuminated him. The second floor door had flown open. Two shots rang out.

Clutching his heart, Jimmy fell back against the wall.

He stood there baffled as two small children, brandishing cap pistols, ran past him, whooping joyfully, down to the first floor.

Jimmy felt for his heartbeat with relief. Well, he told himself, if that didn't take five years off my life, nothing will!

He resumed his climb and exited the stairwell on the third floor.

The hallway was empty. He moved stealthily down to the door of Richard's apartment.

He stopped. No sound came from within. He put his ear to the door and listened diligently.

No conversation, he noted. No indication that she's with him. Not yet anyway.

After five minutes, still hearing nothing from inside the apartment, the priest tiptoed away.

Back downstairs, he went straight to his car. He settled in the front seat for his vigil as the first heavy drops of rain splattered the windshield.

He would wait for her, no matter how long it took.

The Checker cab cut through the sudden downpour to come to a halt in front of Leslie's brownstone. Leaving the taxi double-parked, the young man alighted from the driver's seat and peered up through the sheet of rain at Leslie's brightened window. For the briefest of moments, he stood bathed in the light of a lamppost's beam. Then, tucking up the collar of his suede jacket, he raced through the raindrops to the shelter of Leslie's vestibule.

Leslie was lounging in panties and a sweatshirt, reading a Lanford Wilson play, when she heard the buzz of the intercom.

She looked up, surprised. Should I answer that? she asked herself. It's probably Mrs. Bigelow on the top floor, she's always locking herself out.

Maybe it's Jimmy, she thought anxiously. No, that's ridiculous—he would have called.

The buzzer rang again. Oh, what the hell, she sighed to herself, trudging over to the intercom.

"Who is it?" she asked, pressing the button.

"Hi, it's Michael," came the crackling reply. "I just dropped off my last fare and I was a block away. Okay if I come up?"

Help, thought Leslie comically as she hesitated. What do I do now? I don't hear from the guy for ages and then he just shows up. But I really do like him and it *is* pouring out there...

She buzzed back. "Sure," she agreed, "come on up—but take your time."

"Are you sure it's alright?"

"Absolutely," she responded.

Flicking off the button, she sprinted into the

bedroom to dive into a pair of designer jeans. She peeled off her sweatshirt, changing into a delicate floral blouse she had bought the month before at Lord & Taylor.

As the doorbell rang, she gave herself the once-over in the mirror. She smiled at her reflection. I'm glad I pampered myself earlier, she thought; now at least I look presentable. In fact, maybe even a little better than presentable. It would be nice to see Michael again.

Opening the door, she greeted him. "This is a surprise."

"Is it okay?" he asked, giving her a kiss on the cheek as she admitted him to the apartment. "Were you in the middle of something?"

"Well, I did have an anxiety attack for most of the day, but I feel better now."

"Well," he said, appraising her, "you look wonderful."

"Thanks," she said, hanging up his jacket.

"I heard about Jill. I'm sorry. I was going to call you a few times but . . ."

"It was terrible, Michael. I really wasn't talking to very many people."

"I'm sure," he said sincerely. "But I was thinking about you."

"That's nice," she said, taking his hand and leading him over to the couch. "Can I get you something?"

"Maybe a gin and tonic. Sit there. I'll fix it."

Grinning cheerfully, Michael ambled into the kitchen. Leslie settled contentedly on the sofa.

God, he's cute, she thought, and such a sweetheart. And last time I almost scared him away.

"Should I make that two gin and tonics?" he called from the kitchen.

"Yes, please," she answered, "but make mine heavy on the tonic, okay?"

Michael stood at the sink and popped ice cubes from a tray into some frosted tumblers. From the slightly ajar utility closet, a pair of emerald eyes watched him in silence.

"Did you ever get the part in 'Streetcar?' " asked Leslie from the living room.

Michael put a lime down on the counter. He slid open the silverware drawer and contemplated Leslie's assortment of kitchen knives.

"What?"

"You know, Stanley Kowalski?"

"Oh, that," he said matter-of-factly. "No, I wasn't the type."

He selected the sharpest of the knives and tested its serrated edge. The utility closet door opened further and Kisser, the pupils of his green eyes dilated, stared at him accusingly.

Michael brought the knife down expertly on the lime. With an angry hiss, the cat bolted, screeching, from the kitchen.

In the next room, Leslie jumped. "Kisser," she exclaimed, "you really scared me!"

But Kisser had already scurried into the bedroom, retreating fearfully into a corner.

"What was that?" asked Michael in the

kitchen doorway, the sharp knife still in his hand.

"The cat," Leslie replied. "You must have frightened him."

The dashboard clock showed nine-forty. Jimmy sat up in the front seat, massaging his cramped legs. He fought against impatience.

Outside the car, the downpour had dwindled to a persistent drizzle. The air had cooled slightly with the summer-like storm but the priest felt warm and uncomfortable.

He rubbed his eyes, longing for a cup of coffee. Briefly, he considered a quick trip to the luncheonette on Broadway to pick one up. No, he decided, I can't chance missing The Woman. Besides, coffee's out. I'll need steady nerves for what I have to do.

Checking to make sure Richard was not by the window, Jimmy got out of the car. Fresh air, however wet, would be the next best thing.

He stretched his arms over his head and loosened his neck muscles. Feeling better at once, he essayed a few impromptu knee bends.

"Shouldn't you be doing those exercises inside, Father?"

Jimmy turned to face a little, old, white-haired lady. In one tiny hand she held an "I Love New York" umbrella, in the other a dog leash attached to a lugubrious, waddling bulldog.

"Yes, ma'am," he said, unable to suppress a smile.

"You'll catch your death out here, Father," she said, tugging at the leash as she passed by. She nodded at the bulldog. "I wouldn't venture out myself if it weren't for Petunia."

"Thanks for the advice. Enjoy your evening, ma'am."

The woman and her dog continued on toward West End Avenue.

Jimmy shook his head. Nothing like being inconspicuous, he said to himself wryly. I'd better get back in the car.

At the corner, the old lady turned and looked back. She clucked her tongue reprovingly.

"Crazy Catholics!"

"It's ten p.m. Do you know where your children are?"

On Leslie's television, the announcer's voice, officious and patronizing, asked its nightly question. Across the room, Leslie and Michael were hardly paying attention.

They were kissing, nuzzled in each other's arms. Michael's tongue explored her mouth expertly with a gentle circular motion. His tapered fingers softly stroked her hair, her face, the back of her neck as his body pressed against her breasts with increasing demand.

Help, thought Leslie, for the second time that night. He knows just how to touch me. We're just fooling around on the couch, we've still got all our clothes on and I'm really aroused. I've got a pretty good idea where this is going to end up.

Michael's hand slid beneath the sheer fabric of her blouse, cupping her breast.

A sigh escaped her lips. He licked the contours of her ear.

Leslie gripped his shoulders tightly, feeling a need that had been denied too long. Her kisses covered his face as she caressed the firm lines of his back. Her mouth sought his hungrily, tongue probing him with an urgency she found surprising.

Seconds later, she was pushing him away.

"I'm sorry," she began in a halting voice. "I know I did this last time. I've just been so upset . . . with Annie . . . and Jill . . . my brother . . ."

"Shhh." He put a reassuring finger to her lips. She kissed it gratefully.

Michael reached across her to the gin bottle on the table. He poured out two jiggers and offered one to her.

"Here, drink this," he said compassionately, drawing her head back onto his shoulder.

She took a small swallow of gin. Michael drained his glass in one gulp and his eyes took on a faraway cast. He petted her, drawing a lazy pattern in the downy hair of her forearm.

"How is your brother?" he asked. "Richard, isn't it?"

On the TV set, the anchorman introduced a report from the Middle East. Rain blew in sudden gusts against the window. Leslie leaned into Michael's protective embrace.

"You don't want to hear about it," she protested. "It's so horrible."

"Oh, but I would like to hear about it," he said as he began to massage her shoulder.

"Richard's gotten much worse," she sighed. "I think he's on the verge of a serious collapse. His life might even be in danger."

"Well, Leslie," he said, "when you think about it, we're all in danger."

"What?"

"You heard me."

"What do you mean?"

"All of us live on the edge of the unknown," he said. "That danger of never quite knowing what will happen next—it's what makes life exciting. Today I was driving the cab and I almost had a collision. I swerved at the last minute to avoid hitting a bus. For the next couple of hours, I felt exhilarated. That's just it. One second you're alive and the next second you could be dead."

Leslie shuddered. Michael's fingers dug deeper into her shoulders.

"I wish you wouldn't talk like that," said Leslie. "What's happening to Richard isn't exhilarating. It's scary."

"Maybe it's exhilarating for Richard," Michael observed.

"He seems obsessed with this woman," said Leslie. "It's as if she's controlling him."

She heard Michael laugh in a knowing way, just behind her right ear.

"Control? You're a woman, Leslie. Haven't you ever wanted to control a man?"

"No. Absolutely not!"

"Oh, I think you'd like to try. Surely you've

wanted to have control, say, in a relationship."

"What Richard has with this woman isn't a relationship," said Leslie emphatically. "The police think she's been mixed up with mass murderers."

"You mean she dated them?"

"Yes—like she's dating Richard."

"His life *must* be exciting," said Michael softly.

"I really wish you'd stop talking like that," said Leslie evenly. "It frightens me."

Michael laid his hand upon her breast and fondled her hardened nipple. "No, it doesn't, Leslie, it makes you hot."

Leslie flushed. Michael covered her mouth with his. She felt her body go limp; all her previous resistance seemed to melt away. A blaze of desire ignited her loins. Her blouse was open now. Michael's teasing mouth traveled downward, licking her neck, her breasts, her stomach. Responding to him, Leslie arched her body in eager submission.

"Oh, Michael, yes, I want you," she found herself saying.

His eyes burned into hers; she felt mesmerized as she led him the few short steps to the bedroom. The dimly lit room, dominated by the large, quilt covered double bed, welcomed them.

As they began to undress, Kisser, his long hair bristling, crept furtively from beneath the bed. Crouched low to the ground, his eyes watchful, he slinked toward the doorway.

Her heart pounding with unaccustomed

anticipation, Leslie slipped out of her blouse. Turning from Michael with a shyness that had never left her since adolescence, she unzipped her jeans and pulled them down. Michael's t-shirt sailed casually past her onto the bed.

Hooking her fingers into the elastic waist-band of her bikini panties, she eased them down her legs. From the corner of her eye, she saw Michael's trousers fall to the floor.

Stepping out of her panties, nude, Leslie shivered with a sudden chill. Expectantly, she turned. Her eyes widened.

Naked, smiling, arms outstretched, the figure that was there only resembled Michael.

Leslie staggered back in shock.

"Michael?" she called out fearfully.

Even as she spoke, the firm skin of Michael's body was changing, softening into the supple exterior of a beautiful woman. As Leslie stared in horror, waves of raven hair bloomed, tumbling down in folds to suddenly ripening breasts. Michael's finely-sculpted face grew even more delicate as his blue eyes changed to emerald. He stepped into a shard of light and Leslie could see that the transformation was complete.

The Woman stood before her.

Her breath catching in her throat, Leslie took another step backward. The Woman smiled to her endearingly.

"Don't be frightened," she whispered like wind rustling through autumn leaves. "Your brother wants me. Annie wanted me. Jill wanted me. I know you, Leslie Bloch. You want me too."

The Woman moved toward her. Leslie felt powerless to retreat.

The last sane thought Leslie had, as The Woman took her lovingly in her arms, guiding her toward the bed was: *Yes, I do want her. I want her more than life itself!*

The rain had tapered off, cooling the night air. Dark clouds were dispersing, drifting off toward Long Island, giving intermittent glimpses of a sliver of October moon.

Rivulets of water rushed along the curb of Grove Street, uprooting debris and sweeping it along toward the sewer drain at the corner where it swirled in dizzying eddies. On the roof of a produce warehouse, a line of pigeons sat watchfully, waiting for dawn and the first vegetable deliveries.

Downstairs in the crowded, clammy cellar of the Forgotten Lore Book Shop, a quiet chant rent the silence. The Woman's cult had expanded, swelling to more than sixty devotees, who packed the basement, occupying every conceivable space, their eyes riveted to the candle encircled statue at the front of the room.

Mr. Clark, a flickering flame distorting his aged face, cast a worshipful eye on the life-sized marble figure of The Woman. His voice low but commanding, he launched into his unholy incantation as the assemblage pressed forward, attentive to his every word, enraptured by the gospel-like passion of his testimony.

"Hail, Mother of Satan," he invoked, "great one from the darkness. See the dimensions of our gathering! See how our forces have grown! Wondrous Madonna, it is written that you will intercede for us with your son, Master of the Nether World, Granter of Wishes, Keeper of Souls, Lord of Darkness."

"Ave, Mater!" the multitude responded, their voices like the hum of a finely-tuned engine.

Mr. Clark's eyes flashed. With inspired control, he raised his voice to the next gradation.

"Hail, Madonna, Mother of Satan, you walk among us again as we give you life!"

Its face was bestial, bloodless, with deep gaping pits for eyes. Its flared nostrils seemed to sniff the air for danger. Below them, distended lips were bared to reveal a gash of a mouth, snarling with canine ferocity.

The gargoyle, a stone sentinel on the cornice of Richard's apartment building, looked down at Jimmy with a pitying relentlessness.

In the front seat of the car, contorted into a position of relative comfort, with his left leg draped over the floor shift, the priest regarded the mythical figure thoughtfully.

Those gargoyles are watchers, he reminded himself, sculpted to look menacing and stationed on a building to ward off evil. It's an enchanting thought, Jimmy admitted, but obviously just a fairy tale. Nothing had been able to keep the evil out of that building.

Suddenly, he sat straight up in his seat.

Someone had come around the corner—someone very familiar.

The mere sight of the white trenchcoat sent a tremor of unwanted excitement through his body. Looking to neither side, her dark hair still retaining moist vestiges of the evening's storm that gleamed pearl-like, she strode willfully toward the front entrance of Richard's apartment building.

The gargoyles stared ahead helplessly as she went inside.

Jimmy fingered his rosary beads. A quick prayer restored his composure. He checked the time: 11:45.

As midnight approached, the fever on Grove Street was reaching a higher level. Mr. Clark led the congregation jubilantly as gold medallions radiated an unearthly glow. The Madonna statue smiled approvingly as black robes were discarded into a ceremonial heap at her feet. The aroma of incense mixed with candle wax gave way to the overpowering scent of ecstatic naked bodies, entwined around one another just as the snake had wrapped its sinewy form around The Woman's leg.

"Oh, Satan," cried Mr. Clark from the raised platform, his voice becoming more pronounced, "Master of us all, we worship your mother, seductress of the flesh. As our flesh becomes one, we honor her, Angel of Darkness!"

Jimmy's eyes were glued to Richard's window. When the light went out, he knew it would be time to move.

Three hours in the cramped confines of the Volkswagen had put a fine edge on Jimmy's determination. His eyes traveling the length of the sharpened crucifix beside him on the upholstered seat, he tried to direct all his energy to the task at hand.

Cardinal Madori's warning intruded on his efforts to concentrate.

"Keep in mind," the old prelate had advised, "in 1820, six men were required. This may be too much for *one* man."

Jimmy shook his head vehemently. He had to dispel all traces of self-doubt if he was to have any chance of success. He bolstered himself. The element of surprise is with me. The woman will never suspect that I've recovered this quickly from what she did to me earlier this evening.

Remembering the tremor he had felt upon seeing her turn the corner, Jimmy wondered: *had* he recovered?

The light in Richard's apartment was extinguished.

A last silent prayer and Jimmy was out on the pavement. Leather bag in hand, he approached Richard's building. From the rapidly clearing skies, the narrow moon seemed to wink down its compliance.

The priest's stealthy footsteps echoed with a ghost-like clatter as he crossed the tiled black and white squares of the desolate lobby. The tarnished brass sconces with their faded lamps and the cracked leather armchairs that lined the wall were silent spectators to his midnight mission.

Jimmy headed directly for the fire stairs. At this time of night, he reasoned, the elevator was out of the question. Too noisy. Richard and the woman might hear it stopping at their floor.

He resisted the impulse to take the stairs two at a time. That will just make me out of breath, he told himself. Better to go slowly. Still, as he ascended to the third floor, he could feel his heart thumping.

He opened the third floor door, wincing at the heavy metallic sound it made. He looked down the corridor and gave a start. His reflection, peering at him from the gold trimmed mirror at the far end of the hall, was the only sign of life.

Cradling the bag under his arm, Jimmy made his way to the door of Richard's apartment. Thank God, he said to himself, there aren't any noises coming from the other apartments. At a time like this, I don't need any distractions.

Listening for a moment at Richard's door, the priest heard nothing. With baited breath, he inserted Leslie's key in the lock. As he exerted the gentlest of pressure, he felt the tumbler begin to give way. He twisted a bit more and the lock clicked open.

Jimmy had a sudden thought. What if Richard had put the chain on the door? He turned the knob. The door opened slowly. He sighed with relief. Nothing was in the way.

He eased the door open a few more inches. He felt a sudden pang of alarm. The door creaked noticeably, groaning on its hinges loudly enough for anyone inside the apartment to hear.

No, thought Jimmy, that's just my own paranoia. If they're in the bedroom—God, let them be in the bedroom!—they couldn't hear a little noise like that from so far away.

He nudged the door further open, thankful that the creak had subsided. The living room shutters were closed, blocking out all light from outside. The priest paused, his shoulder wedged in the doorway, waiting until his eyes became accustomed to the darkness.

In the cellar on Grove Street, the chant of the assemblage had begun. "Hail, Mother, Hosanna in the highest!"

Jimmy looked around the room intently, searching for any sign of Richard or The Woman. With the aid of the slight illumination from the hallway, his eyes roamed the floor, the length of the sofa, finding nothing.

Good, he thought, they must be in the bedroom. He closed the door carefully behind him.

Setting his leather bag down gingerly on the cushion of a wicker chair, he removed the holy water and sharpened crucifix. He stepped further into the room.

He could now see the bedroom door, which was slightly ajar. A bar of light came from within. He moved toward it.

Halfway across the living room, Jimmy halted. He could hear moans and the squeak of a box spring coming from the bedroom.

They were in there making love, he knew, his pulse beginning to hammer in his ears.

The chant was growing in pitch: "Hail Madonna, we draw our strength from you and return it tenfold. Lucifer is with thee. We bow before you as we give you life!"

His fingers gripping the crucifix with white-knuckled urgency, Jimmy continued toward the bedroom.

This is it, he told himself as the moaning intensified. God give me the strength to end this woman's evil and send her back to Hell!

Something moved, just outside his line of vision. A second later, it was coming toward him, threatening to knock him to the floor. He whirled just in time to grasp the heavy brass rod of the floorlamp that was wavering dangerously, only inches away from a horrendous crash.

He froze, holding the lamp at a crazy angle to the floor. Listening desperately, he heard no cessation of the sounds from the bedroom. He set the lamp upright again, taking care not to rock the base against the hardwood floor. He disentangled his foot from the electrical wire that had tripped him.

That was a close one, Jimmy thought, as perspiration coursed down his face. He mopped himself with a handkerchief and reached for the bedroom door. He pressed on it lightly with his fingers and it began to swing open.

He could see onto the bed immediately. Lit only by the streetlight and the slim sliver of a moon, Richard and The Woman lay naked on top of the blankets.

Jimmy blessed himself, murmuring a silent prayer. He could tell at a glance that Richard, mounted on the gently sighing woman, was already inside her.

The words from the Latin text seemed to march across his brain: "She must be stabbed in the heart with a blessed and sharpened crucifix while she is at the peak of sexual excitement."

Jimmy raised the crucifix and stepped into the bedroom.

On Grove Street, the cult members' chants blended with their cries of heightening pleasure as their nude forms squirmed in contorted wildness on the dank cement floor.

"Yes, children," Mr. Clark encouraged, looking down approvingly. "Join your bodies to-

gether. Abandon all restraint. Madonna needs you tonight!"

In answer to his exhortation, the writhing figures let out a collective moan, approaching a mutual point of excitement.

"Madonna! Madonna!" they cried, shrieking in the throes of release.

The Woman's lithe, beautiful body rocked with excitement as Jimmy stood poised at the foot of the bed, ready to drive the crucifix into her heart.

"Oh, yes, yes, my darling Richard," she coaxed as her lover, his face bathed with the glow of a conqueror's power, thrust into her with faster and faster strokes.

"Oh, yes, yes," The Woman screamed. *"Now!"*

Jimmy sprang foward. With one hand he doused the bed with holy water, letting the vial fall to the carpet. Grabbing Richard violently by the shoulder, he wrenched him backward, pulling him entirely off The Woman. The priest threw him roughly to the floor.

Madonna fixed him with her raging eyes as she rose slowly, deliberately from the bed. The priest brought the sharp blade of the crucifix down toward her chest.

His arm froze in mid-air.

Madonna's emerald eyes gleamed with a quiet command. In response, Richard, dazed and deliriously obedient, rose from the side of the bed.

Howling like a man possessed, he hurled

himself onto the point of the sharpened crucifix. Its blade ripped into his naked chest, penetrating his heart. With a cry of agony, he fell back on the bed, blood pumping furiously into the air.

After one mighty convulsion, Richard was dead.

Horrified, his throat gagging, Jimmy stumbled backward, away from the bed. He clutched at the air, which had grown instantly frigid.

Madonna's mocking laughter roared through the room. As the priest watched in open-eyed astonishment, her body levitated from the bed, raven tresses streaming down luxuriously.

Icy breath came in gusts from The Woman's mouth, sending tables and chairs swirling as though caught in a tornado's spin. The holy water vial shot dramatically into the air and shattered on the ceiling to shower the bewildered priest with its contents.

Jimmy sank to his knees, weeping in defeat. The Woman hovered over him fiercely.

"Pig priest!" she spat. "Do you think *he* could arouse me?" She laughed scornfully at Richard's corpse.

Jimmy drew back, cowering in a corner.

"I saw you," she hissed. "I knew where you were all night. I could have stopped you before. In your room. The minute I saw you wanted me. You call yourself a priest, but you're just a man, like all the others. You should have listened to your Cardinal, Jimmy.

You shouldn't have tried to stop me by yourself. Did you really think you could send me back? This time I'm here to stay!"

Madonna threw back her head in victory. Jimmy buried his face in his hands as the room shook to the sound of a baby's whimpers, punctuated by bursts of The Woman's demonic laughter.

In the Grove Street basement, a hush had fallen. Sprawled figures on the concrete floor smiled in satiated contentment. Mr. Clark's weathered face was suffused with triumph.

"It is done," he said solemnly.

CHAPTER SIXTEEN

THE BLOOD of Erich Josef Bloch, printer and partime blacksmith, who lived in Bad Hoffberg, Germany from 1790 until his death in 1853, flowed through the veins of Leslie Bloch, who strolled along Lexington Avenue, in the shadow of the Chrysler Building, on the bright, chilly autumn morning.

With her innate beauty shining through, she walked undaunted by the occasional curious glances that questioned the slightly off-center aspect of her makeup. Few on the street even noticed her clownlike mascara and the smudged thickness of her raspberry red lipstick.

Leslie looked in the window of a jewelry shop and noted the time: eight-thirty. She nodded, pleased, patting the Louis Vuitton bag that hung from her shoulder. She was right on time. It wouldn't do to be late for the commuter rush hour.

Hurrying to the office buildings, the crowd surged by her as Leslie walked unhurriedly along 42nd Street. Passing a newsstand, she looked quizzically at a tabloid headline that read: "Death Ritual: Teacher Found Slain." She continued on, her expression unchanged.

"Excuse me," said the bearded young executive sarcastically, "you don't have to run me over."

Leslie looked right through him and he backed away, his attitude changing.

"Are you okay, Miss?" he asked with concern.

Leslie ignored him, turning the corner onto Vanderbilt Avenue. She smiled, taking in the gilded doorway, her favorite entrance to Grand Central Station.

Pressing against the onrush of exiting people, Leslie stood her ground, forcing the crowd to disperse around her. Despite a few annoyed curses and grumbles from outgoing commuters, she soon found her pathway clear into the station.

She stood on the elevated landing, with an overhead view of the terminal lobby. This was the place to be, she knew, where she could get a good look at everybody.

Placing the shoulder bag on the marble ledge before her, Leslie looked out at the thousands of railroad passengers who were scurrying about the station.

Don't they look like rats, she asked herself. Unhappy little unimportant rats. I'll be doing them a big favor.

A thin film of perspiration had formed on her forehead. Her eyes misted over dreamily.

She reached into her bag and withdrew the .357 Magnum revolver. She gripped the pistol in her hand, stroking the metal barrel appreciatively.

Leslie closed her eyes in sweet recollection. It had been so thoughtful of The Woman to present her with such a lovely gift. And the gun had originally been intended for someone else. How nice of her to give it to me instead.

She unclicked the safety and blew a train conductor halfway across the floor of the station. His lifeless body landed in a heap unnoticed, alongside some sagging mailbags.

Many of the commuters looked up casually at the sound of the shot, which reverberated through the domed enclosure like a crackle from the p.a. system which went on, blithely announcing outgoing trains.

"Train to Brewster, leaving at 9:05, from track 115 on the lower level."

Leslie bared her teeth in a feral grimace, staring down the barrel of the gun.

"This is fun," she congratulated herself. "I was born to play this part."

The second bullet claimed the life of Lisa Winston, eleven years old, on her way to a piano lesson in White Plains.

The child fell to the marble floor, her intestines spilling out from the gaping wound that had rent her stomach. Her mother screamed hysterically, falling to her knees, pulling at her hair, and shielding her already dead daughter from further gunshots.

Leslie laughed, surveying the chaos that was breaking out before her amused eyes. A gigantic Kodak blowup of Rocky Mountain serenity looked down in calm contrast to the panic-stricken stampede that sent people diving blindly behind the information booth and racing in a headlong frenzy for the departure gates.

The resulting madness, to Leslie, was immensely gratifying. She smiled gleefully as an aged woman on crutches was mashed to the ground by a charging horde. An elderly man collapsed beneath the feet of an oncoming mob.

"O Romeo, Romeo! Wherefore art thou, Romeo?" Leslie projected, her arms raising dramatically in the air.

How perfect, Leslie thought to herself, I'm even on a balcony. My best performance!

Where is my Romeo? she wondered. She searched the lobby for a likely candidate. Perhaps that handsome young guy with the moustache, she thought, training her pistol on him. She squeezed the trigger and he fell backward, a bullet in his brain.

"There, he's dead, just like Romeo," she said aloud, waving the revolver.

Leslie threw back her shoulders and

primped her hair. "The show must go on," she proclaimed.

Then lowering her voice to a deep stage intonation, she recited:

"Pitiful sight! Here lies the county slain,
And Juliet bleeding, warm and newly dead."

At the nurse's station of Ward H in the psychiatric hospital, the black and white Sony portable was tuned to the Phil Donahue Show. Suddenly, a bulletin flashed across the tiny screen. From a local television newsroom, a woman reporter spoke directly into the camera.

"We interrupt our regular programming to bring you this special bulletin. We have just learned that a young woman has gone berserk in Grand Central Station, killing three people and injuring several others before fatally turning a gun on herself. The young woman has been identified as an off-Broadway actress named Leslie Bloch."

Nurse Abigail Tipton turned to her companion, Nurse Mary Kelly, and shook her head sadly. Mary pointed to the TV screen, which showed a publicity photograph of Leslie in her "Straw Hat" farmgirl makeup, freckle-faced and grinning foolishly.

"I don't believe it," Mary Kelly exclaimed. "I saw her in that play. She was wonderful."

Abigail frowned. "Isn't that the show where that actor went nuts? Killed a girl onstage?"

"My God!" said Mary. "You're right."

"Great," said Abigail, clucking her tongue.

"Bad enough we've got the junkies and the drug pushers—now we've got to watch out for the *actors!*"

The nurse's light flashed. In response, Mary got up and went down the corridor toward the doctors' offices. On either side of her stretched maximum security cells, whose heavy metal doors afforded no view inside save for small, rectangular, reinforced glass windows at eye level.

Passing by cell 5-H, the nurse saw no reason to look in on its occupant, who would have been very interested to hear the recent bulletin.

As Nurse Kelly's heels clicked off down the hallway, the patient in 5-H continued to stare in disoriented shock at his hands which were wrapped tightly in a pair of rosary beads.

Father James Hamilton, Society of Jesus, sat on his cot, his face haunted, his eyes filled with remorse.

Even in his stupefied state, Jimmy knew this much: he was alone. The Church would not be coming to his aid. The Church would deny any knowledge of his actions.

But if he prayed, maybe the dream would go away . . .

EPILOGUE

"FLIGHT 307 for Los Angeles, last call for boarding."

The gate attendants were preparing to take standby tickets when the last of the first class passengers strode serenely into the departure lounge.

"Well, you were worth waiting for," cracked the bearded young flight attendant at the counter.

The Woman handed him her airline ticket and flashed a dazzling smile.

"New York's loss is L.A.'s gain," the attendant said with a grin, pausing to admire her extraordinary beauty, before tearing off the decal on his seating chart. "Any chance you'll be coming back to the Big Apple?" he asked hopefully.

"You never can tell," she replied softly.

Half a mile away, as The Woman's plane took off for Los Angeles, another passenger sat in the JFK international departure lounge. He waited patiently until, at last, the public address system rang out with the announcement.

"Flight 73 for Rome, now boarding."

The passenger got to his feet. Looking grave but determined, Cardinal Madori walked toward the gate.